MW00945340

Neal Maresty was an only child originally from the Midwest. He had been born in either Indiana or Illinois, he could never remember. At the age of three, his mother had left his father and had taken Neal with her. Based on her account as told to Neal she had gotten tired of the beatings and the whoring. She told Neal that she had feared for her safety and for the safety of her baby boy so she moved sight unseen to Texas. Coming from her it all sounded very noble. Based on the way she treated the string of husbands and boyfriends that Neal had witnessed since that day 23 years ago, he realized his real dad might have been provoked. Either way, he had never seen or heard from his real father since.

GOHORSE

the debut novel by

Bryan Baese

Kelly

Thanks for your
help with Lester's-

Hopefully more deals
to come.

December
2018

Copyright © 2015 Bryan Baese
All rights reserved.
ISBN: 1508772231
ISBN-13: 978-1508772231

Great-Great-Grandsons of Heironymus Donsbach
Kingsbury, Texas
December 2013

GOHORSE

BRYAN BAESE

CHAPTER ONE

The first sign of trouble was when the gold fish bowl exploded. Heironymus Donsbach was nearest the fish bowl when the bullet passed through it but seemed to be the least startled of the three men seated at the table. The Mexicans, of course, found the entire sequence of events incredibly funny. There seemed to be something about the two fish flopping and the way their tails slapped the wet surface of the table that they found particularly amusing.

The day before, Heironymus, Bruno Bartoskewitz, and Karl Achterberg had made their way from Seguin, Texas to Del Rio by horseback and train with the hope of consummating a cattle transaction. The deal had been in the works for three months now, and having finally received confirmation from the owner of the cattle that the livestock had been successfully delivered to the stockyards in Del Rio, the trio had arrived to take possession of their cattle and make arrangements for their transport back to Guadalupe County. The inevitable delays in the business transaction - like those common to virtually all business transactions of significance for the thousands of years leading up to this day in the early 20th century in West Texas – manifested themselves and allowed for an afternoon in Old Mexico – a country neither of the three men had ever visited before. And so the three Germans found themselves seated at a rickety wooden table in a cantina in Acuña, Mexico. The establishment was dank, third-rate and populated mostly by lowlifes.

The Germans had they themselves laughed at the fish bowl when they'd taken their seats a few minutes earlier while the fish bowl was still intact. In their language they called it a *Fischglas*. It seemed funny to them because it was so inconsistent with the surroundings. But after the shot was fired, and the blood began to flow once again to Heironymus' brain, the idea occurred to him that there was a reason for the fish bowl's presence and that it had fulfilled the purpose for which it had been placed there. He realized that the fish bowl had not been shot because it was there; but rather had been placed there to be shot. The smoke from the antique revolver began to clear and the Mexicans made it clear through gesturing and body language that the revolver's discharge was not meant as a threat but as a joke, and the Germans were being invited to laugh along with the shadowy, smelly denizens of the cantina. Catching on, the Germans managed a strained collective chuckle.

****

Charlie Manor caught a glimpse of the figure that was approaching him from his left. The figure was still 50 feet off, but through instincts honed to a fine point in a way that only hard time in prison can hone them, Charlie could tell that the man was approaching him specifically. And he could tell that the man was Mexican Mafia. At ten feet Charlie stood to meet the man. He was careful to strike that perfect balance between confronting the Mexican and submitting to him. The Mexican was strong in his demeanor – they always were – and came close to Charlie, but not so close that Charlie felt that danger was imminent. He felt threatened but he was not fearful. Charlie looked him in the eye.

"What do you want?" Charlie asked the man.

"We know about gohorse," the Mexican replied in heavily accented English. Members of the Mexican Mafia here at the

Texas State Penitentiary in Huntsville did not like to speak English. They considered the language beneath them. When forced to speak it they exaggerated their accent so as to bring more clearly into focus the concept that they were a different people.

"Gohorse?" Charlie paused. "What the hell is gohorse?"

Charlie continued to stare at the man who had approached him, searching his eyes for some clue as to the nature of the statement. The Mexican glared back. His eyes were narrow and piercing but didn't reveal anything. Charlie had the feeling that the Mexican was also searching for something.

"If we're done here I'm going back about my business," Charlie said finally. He looked at the Mexican for a few more seconds then turned and walked away at an angle that allowed him to keep an eye on his adversary by peripheral vision.

The Mexican stood for a while and watched Charlie walk off then went back to the area of the yard where he belonged. He said to the man that was his superior, "Sabe nada."

Charlie Manor would never know the meaning of the word or how it would lead to his demise.

****

Jimmy Dale Klein was unmarried and childless. What he was *not* was gainfully employed. He lacked the motivation to hold down a regular job. It wasn't that he lacked the ability; he was, in fact, able-bodied and had a keen intellect. It's just that it wasn't in him. There was something in his genetic structure that prevented him from taking orders from the same guy day after day and week after week. The other problem was that he was prone to fits of laziness - the money being fast and easy it's a characteristic common to most drug dealers. He felt some inner shame at taking the easy way out by dealing drugs and it would occasionally bubble to the surface. When it did, he would drive around the construction sites and ask for a place on the crew. He was known around town as a competent worker and could generally land a job in a day or so. His prospective employer would usually be aware of Jimmy Dale's checkered past and knew that he would probably quit within six or eight weeks but it didn't matter. As long as he showed up for work in the interim he was seen as an asset. And since most of the guys on the job site had issues anyway, hiring Jimmy Dale wasn't seen as a negative.

Jimmy Dale was good at keeping his expenses low. He lived in a single wide trailer on three acres outside Seguin. The property had been left to him by his grandpa when he passed away six years ago and the trailer was purchased with money he borrowed from his mama. He'd paid that loan off a year ago after several extensions. And his eight year old GMC single cab pickup was running fine. He changed the oil regularly. His grandpa had always told him that if you don't do anything else at all in terms of vehicular maintenance, if you at least do that one thing, you're 75% there. So he did that one thing. And he kept wax on it. A couple of weeks ago he had entertained the thought of trading it in for a newer model. The car lot he'd visited had a King Ranch Edition F-150 that was tempting. And the salesman was convincing but the payments were outrageous so in the end, Jimmy Dale had declined. So the vehicular status quo had survived a trip to the car lot and at 31 years of age Jimmy Dale was living debt free. His standard of living wasn't much but he took solace in the fact that most of his contemporaries age-wise were up to their eyeballs in debt. He couldn't say that he slept at night, but at least it wasn't the money that kept him up.

Jimmy Dale had a clear mind and was able to take in facts and figures and absorb salient points which were mostly invisible to the population around him. He was smart. And he found the History Channel pleasant to pack by. It hit that happy median between mindless drivel and serious intellectual discourse. As he packed, Jimmy Dale kept the volume on the TV low. Not that it mattered - the single wide didn't provide much of an opportunity to get out of ear shot anyway so Jimmy Dale's ears perked up when he heard the narrator,

"…it is better to die on your feet than to live on your knees."

Jimmy Dale's interest in the program upgraded from the sub-conscious to the conscious and his tube socks went unfolded for the time being. He pondered the words for a moment and noted the muted, background uneasiness that frequently accompanies such moments of introspection. Jimmy Dale reflected on the times in his life when he had cowered. He decided he wasn't going to do it anymore.

****

The day before the Germans crossed over into Old Mexico, while riding on the train to Del Rio, Heironymus' mind had drifted and he contemplated the vast differences between the Texas landscape and that of his native Germany. It was hotter here…much hotter. And this, his first trip into the Chihuahuan desert of West Texas, only accentuated the chasm. It brought to mind the harshness of the Texas terrain when his family had first set foot on the soil of their new homeland all those years ago and how it had seemed so unwelcoming. The ground seemed to well up with heat and humidity. The vegetation, it turned out, which had looked so green and inviting from the boat, was guilty of false advertising. The prevalent mesquite was a cross between a tree and bush and lacked the majesty of the pines back home. The cactus poked. And the brush crawled with ants and a type of snake his family had never seen before - a strange serpent with a rattle on its tail. Lacking a specific word, Heironymus and the rest of the German immigrants took to calling it Die Klapperschlange - the clapping snake. They didn't know it at the time but it was the beginning of a new dialect - Texas German.

Heironymus' mind came back to the present and he thought to himself that the scene outside the train window is what Africa must look like. Heironymus was pondering the solitude of a scrawny heifer clinging to her meager existence some distance from the tracks when Bruno broke the silence.

"I'd like to cross the river into Mexico and drink a beer while we're here. I'd like to see what Mexico is like," he said in German.

The next day, as the three men approached the terminus of the bridge anchored on Texas soil, Heironymus took note of the writing on the sign - *INTERNATIONAL BRIDGE.* He noticed how the term was regal and formal, yet the span itself seemed to possess neither quality. The structure appeared functional

6 Bryan Baese

certainly, but the wooden components were mismatched, some older and some newer. It gave the impression that it had been repaired recently and Heironymus was unsure if this was good or bad. The men paused and watched a wagon laden with railroad ties and drawn by four mules make its way across. It wasn't that Heironymus and his business partners thought that the bridge would collapse beneath them, but the beasts' were struggling mightily and this testified to the magnitude of the load; so the men decided it was best to watch the wagon and its cargo and listen to the creaks and groans of the bridge before they committed to the crossing. The bridge, despite its lack of dignity, proved to be structurally sound.

Once across, the three men were immediately identified as auslanders and descended upon by the local children and widows. The men were surprised by the boldness of the beggars, many of whom would put their hands directly into the Germans' pockets. Attempting to put some distance between themselves and the swarm, they picked up their pace and arrived at the town square in a just a couple of minutes. There didn't seem to be a shortage of drinking establishments so they walked off the square to the east and picked a cantina about halfway down the block, mostly because it didn't appear to be any worse than any of the others.

It was dark inside the cantina but the Germans managed to make their way to the bar in the low light and ordered three beers. Like every drinking man the world has ever known, they knew how to order a drink in the language of the country that they were standing in. They could, in fact, speak some Spanish above and beyond bar speak…but not much. Although it was not something that had ever been discussed in any way, the best way to describe the range of their linguistic capabilities was to say that the men's German was to their English as their English was to their Spanish as their Spanish was to their Japanese. Their eyes now fully adjusted to the low light, the interior of the bar was in focus and Heironymus and his two friends could see that almost every table in the establishment was taken. One table though, toward the back with four chairs and inexplicably topped with a fish bowl containing three live gold fish, was unattended. Moving through the crowd of Mexicans the men commented on the table's décor.

They laughed at the weirdness of it all as they took their seats to enjoy the beer.

From their vantage point at the back of the bar the Germans took in the scene. Most of the Mexican contingency was raucous. But two men, seated in the corner of the cantina seemed to conduct themselves with an air of authority. They seemed to be in charge. One of the two was beefy. He was not tall compared to the Germans but seemed taller than most of the Mexicans hanging around the bar. He had a prominent moustache and an ammunition belt slung over his right shoulder that hung down across the front of his body. He wore a lightly colored hat that was stained with sweat where the inside of the hat came into contact with his head. The hat was round and modestly sized.

The second man of authority was a smaller man with a moustache that was even more prominent than the moustache on the first man. Where the first man was fierce, the second man seemed distinguished. The one inconsistency though, the one incongruous element of the mustachioed Mexican, was the outsized sombrero. From the German's perspective it was clownish and detracted from the authoritative air of the man.

The shot that obliterated the fischglas jolted the Germans, taking them on a roller coaster of emotions in a short span of time: surprise, fear, dread, relief, exhilaration, and whatever else a man feels after an unexpected close encounter with a bullet. It takes a while to recover from such an encounter and as their blood pressure was returning to normal, the Germans were approached by one of the distinguished men from the corner of the cantina. It was the larger man with the smaller moustache, smaller hat, and the ammo belt across his chest.

"¿Como estan?" the Mexican asked. He stood over the table and waited for the Germans to respond.

"Bien," Heironymus answered. He knew that the Mexican was asking how they were and he knew how to impart wellness in his response. He also knew that he was pretty much at his limit in terms of speaking Spanish to the man. Based on appearance he deduced that there was little chance of the Mexican speaking English or German.

Bryan Baese

Coming to the same realization - that there was no common language - the Mexican grabbed the back of the empty chair, and adjusting its position to suit him, sat with a thud. The Germans could see the dust puff from his clothes. The Mexican smiled broadly, and looking his three newfound drinking buddies in the eye each in turn, raised his glass in a mute toast. The Germans liked him and responded in kind. The four glasses met over the center of the table with a klink, precisely above the wet spot where three fish lay in a declining state, their gills now barely moving. The Mexican nodded his approval. First glancing and then pointing at the fish, he laughed out loud again before greedily consuming half the beer in one long draw. The Germans laughed too and each of them drank down their beer by half. They didn't realize it but they were following this man's lead. They did it without thinking because the Mexican was a natural leader.

The Mexican made no attempt at communication and sat staring into space for the next couple of minutes. Finally, content that he had made the appropriate impression on the visitors from Texas, he brought the glass to his mouth, consumed the second half of his beer, and then returned the glass to the table in one fluid motion. He nodded at the Germans to formalize his departure and returned to his seat in the corner of the cantina with his smaller, more distinguished, larger mustachioed, bigger hatted associate.

CHAPTER 2

"Few things are as inaccurate as an emotional woman practicing amateur psychology," explained Billy Sorenson to his co-worker Stephen Gorman, otherwise known as Cupcake, as they surveyed the front lot of Kuykendall Used Cars.

Billy was 33 years old and clinging desperately to the lower rung of a middle class existence. He had a wife and two kids and a nemesis in the form of a $1,200 mortgage payment that plagued him almost every minute of every day. His philosophical forays, especially with Cupcake, who although lazy at least had the brain power to keep up with an abstract concept even when the presenter skipped a step or two, helped him to forget his financial predicament and provided his mind a much needed respite. Billy thought a lot about how he perceived his mortgage – as the enemy really. It struck him how he viewed his financial obligations – like many of the challenges in his life – in military terms. He wondered why that was. It wasn't as if he came from a military background or anything. As close as he had come to military service were the stories his grandfather used to tell him about Billy's great-grandfather who had served with General Black Jack Pershing. But

25 years after hearing the stories, Billy really couldn't remember anything beyond the name.

Their vantage point inside the showroom - if indeed you can call it a showroom at all because it really wasn't a showroom as much as it was a room big enough to park cars in, and besides, weren't showrooms for new cars anyway, except for older classic cars which the used cars at Kuykendall were most certainly not – and behind the large pane of glass that was perhaps ten feet high and thirty feet across, allowing them a nearly complete 180 degree view of everyone and everything that occupied the 30% of the lot that stretched from the front of the building to the highway. The remaining 70% of the lot, the sides and the back, were outside their field of vision. But most of the activity occurred on this front portion, and so like the grizzly bears in that documentary on the Discovery Channel where the grizzlies congregate at the rapids and catch the salmon in their jaws as the fish attempt to hurdle the low but very swiftly moving cascade of downward rushing water, so did the salesmen at Kuykendall Used Cars congregate at the front window. That's where the fish were.

Cupcake was staring at the cars speeding past the lot on the highway as he listened to Billy's explanation as to why Cupcake was unable to reason with his girlfriend concerning some matter in which both Cupcake and his girlfriend were emotionally involved; the details of which aren't important, probably not even to Cupcake. Upon hearing Billy's explanation of emotional women, Cupcake turned in his chair and faced Billy, contemplating the wisdom of the hypothesis. At that moment Billy turned to survey the lot. A man in his 30's and of Mexican descent, of average height and weight and sporting a goatee had wandered in from the southeast. Billy had not noticed the man drive in; he had simply appeared as prospects on the lot are wont to do.

"You think about that Cupcake. I'm going to go and talk to this guy." Billy moved toward the door, covering the distance in six or eight steps, and once outside moved down the gentle slope of the lot to greet the prospect.

"How do? I'm Billy Sorenson." Billy shot his right hand out in greeting.

"Juan Antonio." The offer of the handshake was returned and the two men shook without the exaggeration that some of the salesmen on the car lot preferred. The shake was firm but understated. And as innocuously as that, began the most calamitous enterprise that Billy would ever involve himself. Months later, as he pondered this moment from his bunk in Huntsville, he would wonder to himself what might have happened if only he had let Cupcake take the prospect.

A test drive ensued and Juan Antonio was back in Billy's office in short order. Billy tested the waters regarding Juan Antonio's interest in purchasing the vehicle and the conversation turned to financing as it typically does.

"How's your credit?" Billy asked, "Would you say it's good or ok or how would you describe it?"

"I have a few hiccups but it's probably ok," Juan Antonio said. That statement, of course, meant that Juan Antonio's credit was in the toilet. Billy knew from years of asking this question that people with good credit would generally tell you straight out that their credit was good with no qualifications. People with terrible credit would generally rank their credit as ok and proceed to tell you why it's not as good as it could be. And it was that explanation, as opposed to the self-assigned ranking, that was the telltale sign that something was rotten in Denmark. It was an extremely rare person that would admit flat out that their credit was bad. It took strength to admit shortcomings. And since most people were weak they were generally unable to face personal demons like bad credit. It was easier just to lie and they did so without even realizing they were doing it. So Billy knew he was facing an uphill battle but was determined to struggle on. He gave Juan Antonio the application for financing along with a pen to complete the form. Billy asked his prospect to fill out the application to the best of his ability and then excused himself for some coffee. He was ready for a cup anyway but mostly he just wanted to be out of this man's presence. He returned ten minutes later to find the application mostly complete. All he really needed was the social security number anyway. The rest of the information may or may not be useful but it was usually best to go ahead and get it. The act of writing it down strengthened the idea in the mind of the prospect that he would be buying a car. Billy took the application to the sales desk and the sales manager typed in the name, address, birth date, and social security number. The results were back within a few seconds.

Name:	Juan Antonio Gonzales
Age:	42
Fico:	422
Transunion:	401
Experion:	406

"Doesn't look like we're buying a car today," Mike Josper, the sales manager on duty that day, said as he handed the information back to Billy. Billy didn't like Mike much and suspected that Mike felt similarly about him, but the two men tolerated each other nevertheless. Cupcake didn't like Mike very much either. He usually referred to Mike as a bonehead.

Billy glanced over the paper that had been handed to him. Repos…write offs…you name it. He commented on the first line - a credit card. "Ol' Juan Antonio here, it looks like someone actually took a chance on him last year, a credit card with a $500 limit. He maxed it out in one month and never made a single payment."

"You gotta respect that," Mike said smiling up at Billy from his seat behind the sales desk.

Billy took the single page of information back to his office. He was now entering the danger zone, the moment where the buyer felt compelled to offer a more complete explanation for his less than perfect financial situation. Why people cared what a complete stranger thought about their credit was beyond him. Billy had never figured it out. All he knew was that once a prospect found out that he was not going to be approved, the excuses began in earnest. The goal here was to get the prospect out of the office and move on to the next prospect. But Billy knew that in order to move on he must first endure the story of how some burger wasn't being flipped at some burger joint somewhere because of some manager that held an unreasonable grudge against the prospect's spouse. And since the spouse was fired they had gotten behind on their car payments and despite their best efforts the car had been repo'd. Oh, and besides that, the manager at the burger joint wasn't even qualified to be a manager since he had only gotten the job because his uncle owned the place. Or something like that.

As Billy took a seat across the desk from Juan Antonio he steeled himself against the expected onslaught of excuses. He also noticed that Juan Antonio appeared to be quite a bit younger than 42 years of age.

"I don't think we're going to be able to get this thing done. Not unless you have a substantial down payment," Billy said. Billy knew that this was almost never the case and thought of this statement as the beginning of the end of the interview.

"How much would I need?"

"I don't think it's worth even trying unless you have eight to ten thousand."

Juan Antonio pulled out an envelope that appeared to be full of money. He held the envelope in his left hand horizontal to the floor and perpendicular to his body, thumbing the bills with his right hand. Billy could see that Juan Antonio had an envelope full of hundreds.

"I'll have to think about it," Juan Antonio said. "But thanks for helping me out. This is for you." Juan Antonio took another envelope from a pocket in his jacket and placed it on the desk. "Don't tell anyone where that came from."

He rose and offered Billy his hand. The two men shook and Billy walked Juan Antonio to the door. Billy stood on the front patio of the dealership until Juan Antonio's vehicle was out of sight, then returned to his desk and picked up the envelope. In the envelope on Billy's desk was a $50 bill. A note was included:

*We pay $50 for a ss # w name, birth date, and address
If you could use $500 per day in cash Call JA.*

Billy pulled out Juan Antonio's application. There was a space provided for a home phone number where Juan Antonio had written something down. There was also an alternate number. Billy was intrigued but he fought back the urge to call right then. He went so far as to pick up the phone and dial three digits but decided against it and hung up. Caller ID might invite a return phone call if the party at the other end didn't pick up. The problem was that incoming phone calls to the dealership were recorded. According to Mike and the other sales managers, they recorded incoming calls in order to critique the manner in which the sales calls were handled. That was the reason they gave anyway. Billy suspected that the real reason the calls were recorded was so they could snoop in on personal conversations. So Billy decided that it was just as well if the management at the dealership was not privy to what he was going to talk about to Juan Antonio.

****

Charlie Manor didn't have much of a chance. And like most kids without much of a chance he also didn't have much of a father. His dad was present in the household when Charlie was growing up but most of the time he was sitting in his recliner with a drink in his hand. Years later, in Huntsville, with plenty of time on his hands for introspection, Charlie thought a lot about the day his dad had played basketball with him on the goal out front in the driveway. Charlie was nine or ten at the time and was in awe at his dad's ability and power. It was only an illusion of course as any grown man will seem overwhelming to a boy that age when posting up against him. But perception is reality and even years later Charlie could remember the feeling of being tossed and moved around like a doll as his dad made a move toward the basket. Like most people, Charlie remembered what he wanted to remember so when someone asked him about his father he had the basketball story at the ready. What Charlie didn't remember was how that was the only time his dad had ever played a sport with him.

Charlie had an older brother that really took the biggest hit in terms of paternal neglect. Raymond Manor was ten months older than Charlie and spent his entire adolescence preparing himself and his little brother for a life behind bars. Smoking dope and skipping school at 12, profanity laced tirades levied against a history teacher at 13, and shoplifting charges at 14, he was respected by the thugs and feared by the decent kids at school. Little brother Charlie looked up to him.

Esther Manor was Charlie's mother and had struggled mightily against the negative forces at work within her family. She went to church and dragged the boys along with her. She volunteered to help at the school Christmas programs and other functions. She put the boys in cub scouts and signed up as a den mother. She sent them away to church camp in summer only to drive back out at mid-week because Raymond was caught smoking or doing something else that pretty much guaranteed expulsion. She was so embarrassed at her older son's behavior that she would usually pull Charlie out too so as to not suffer the embarrassment of seeing the camp staff a second time at week's end.

Charlie was better looking than his older brother. Raymond had an edginess to his face. He was square-jawed with large puffy lips. He had blond greasy hair and eyes that were so blue that they seemed artificial. Charlie had some of the same features but brown hair with brown eyes and although you could tell they were brothers because the overall shape of the face was the same, Charlie's features were softer and much easier to look at. The big difference between the brothers though was their minds. Raymond was a predator. He didn't care what people thought about him and he didn't care about the consequences of his actions. Charlie, although capable of cruelty like his brother, also carried with him some compassion. And he cared – at least a little bit – about how people viewed him. He had at the very least a modicum of a conscience. This subtle difference between the brothers yielded a slightly different social network for the boys. Raymond's friends were exclusively punks but Charlie had friends in both worlds. One of Charlie's buddies was even in the school band and played the clarinet. The big difference though was the girlfriends. Raymond's girlfriends were all skinny skanks with foul mouths and weak chins. But somehow and someway – much to the consternation of the other boys in Charlie's class at school and to the unbounded satisfaction of Charlie's mother – Charlie always managed to lure in the really nice looking girls. Not only were Charlie's girlfriends pretty, they were also, in contrast to Raymond's girlfriends…clean. Clean might seem like a backhanded way of describing a pretty girl in her mid-teens, but if you were to look at the brothers' girlfriends side by side, it really was the best adjective available to an objective observer.

Esther was the person that had taken the picture of the boys and their girlfriends that would hang on the wall of the Manor household for many years. In the picture, the four kids were seated on the couch with Esther's sons bookending the girls. Raymond was on the left, Charlie on the right, and the girls in the middle. Long after the boys had been sent away to prison, Esther would look at the picture longingly. But she wasn't looking at her sons; she was comparing the girls. In her mind it represented what could have been. Raymond's girlfriend was trashy with stringy blond hair and something off color emblazed on the tank top that hung loosely on her scrawny body. Charlie's girlfriend was a pretty brunette with a nice figure and normal clothes. Esther knew even then that Raymond was a lost cause and that Charlie offered a glimmer of hope, and that's what the girls represented.

In the end Esther Manor's efforts at holding the family together were ill fated. Mr. Manor died from a self-inflicted gunshot wound to the head when Charlie was 17. And that was the end of the line for Charlie. It was at that point in his life that Charlie stopped listening to that little voice in his head that told him he was going down the wrong path, he stopped listening to his mother, and he stopped listening to his girlfriend. Charlie's affinity for and similarity to his older brother won out and he rode Raymond's coattails from delinquency to convicted felon.

****

The sun was peeking over the horizon as Jimmy Dale turned the GMC out of the gravel drive and pointed it toward San Antonio. Thirty minutes later he was downtown and since it was a Saturday he passed through without a holdup. He was a good ways west of town when he stopped for breakfast and by the time he did, the sun was pretty far up in the sky. Being mid-April, it imparted some warmth but lacked the brutality of July or August. He knew the chorizo sausage was not good for him but he liked the taste of it and he never planned on living long enough to die of a heart attack anyway so that's what he ordered. Leaving the convenience store, he grabbed a 44 ounce Big Red and settled in for the balance of the drive to Del Rio. Two hours later he was there.

For reasons unknown to him, Jimmy Dale preferred bars on the windows of the establishments that he frequented and Humberto's Ice House fit the bill. It was a simple cinder block structure painted a dull yellow with a cracked sign on a pole that angled a few degrees right of perpendicular. He refilled his drink, Big Red again, because he liked the sugar and the caffeine even though it didn't mix well with the chorizo he was in the process of digesting. The concoction in his stomach was acidic but somehow brought a strange psychological comfort. To Jimmy Dale it seemed the natural order of things that white trash should mix carbonated soft drinks with greasy Mexican food. Jimmy Dale paid the man behind the counter, a heavy set Mexican man in his mid 50's with a moustache but no beard other than a three-day growth. Humberto – Jimmy Dale made the assumption - handed him the change from the ten. Humberto's directions to the international bridge were free of charge. A few blocks further west Jimmy Dale realized that the directions were unnecessary. MEXICO. The letters on the sign were in all caps and seemed quite a bit larger than those on the sign he had passed twenty minutes earlier directing those so inclined toward Eagle Pass. There was a general commotion here at the international bridge and Jimmy Dale could feel the buzz of human activity.

Jimmy Dale nodded to the Border Patrol agent stationed between the incoming and outgoing traffic on the bridge. The brim of his cowboy hat leveraged the motion, making the almost imperceptible movement of Jimmy Dale's head just slightly more pronounced. The window was down, his left arm resting on the door and his left index finger lifted simultaneously with the head nod. The Border Patrol agent was white. If he had been Mexican, the digital greeting would not have been offered. The traffic heading over the river was light and within a couple of minutes Jimmy Dale was in Mexico. He made his way through the skinny streets, avoiding the shoppers and the vendors and the beggars as best he could. He was struck by the busyness of the place. He wondered to himself what an acceptable distance was for a person on foot to keep in relation to a moving vehicle and decided on eight to ten feet. This was, of course, what was acceptable to him and those like him back home in Seguin. The unspoken rules governing the interaction between vehicular and pedestrian traffic seemed to relax here in Mexico and it unnerved him that people got so close to him while he was driving at a speed that would yield a school zone speeding ticket in Guadalupe County.

After happening upon the town square, he decided that he had found a reasonable base of operations for his first afternoon in Mexico. He settled on a parking spot two blocks off the square and made the short walk back. On the far side of the square was a café. In actuality, there were maybe ten cafes within his field of vision, but something about the Café de los Toros struck him and he made his way across the street, through the grove of giant pecan trees that populated the open park space in the middle of the square, across the street on the far side and then inside the café. The Café de los Toros had a large window that faced the street and, being mid-day, was very bright. Jimmy Dale chose a table in the middle of the restaurant over the booths that were available along the walls and was approached by a waiter with a tie and a dish towel over his arm. The waiter placed the fried tortilla chips and the green salsa on the table.

"¿A tomar?" the waiter asked.

"¿Que clase de cerveza tienes?" Jimmy Dale asked.

Jimmy Dale's Spanish was decent but not great. He could understand it well enough to understand a speaker if that speaker wanted him to understand. But he couldn't speak it well enough to understand a speaker if that speaker wanted him to not understand. Jimmy Dale had always wondered how to respond when he was asked if he spoke Spanish or not. He wondered about it because although the query had the simple structure of a yes or no question, the response was anything but simple. It could be either yes or no or anything in between. The way he thought of it was that if anyone asked if he spoke Chinese the answer would also be no, so was it accurate to respond in the negative when asked about his Spanish? He wasn't anywhere close to fluent in either language yet there was a huge chasm between his ability to communicate in Spanish and his ability to communicate in Chinese. He had finally settled on telling anyone that looked like they spoke Spanish that he did not speak Spanish. If it was someone that did not appear to have knowledge of the language he told them that he was borderline.

"Pacifico, Modelo, Carta Blanca…" the waiter answered.

"Pacifico," Jimmy Dale interrupted and the waiter returned shortly with the beer.

Jimmy Dale inquired about the chicken salad. The waiter reaffirmed Jimmy Dale's initial instinct concerning his lunch suggesting to Jimmy Dale that the chicken salad was an excellent choice and he should proceed with the order. The chicken salad, too, was delivered in short order and Jimmy Dale enjoyed the light meal and the beer as he gazed out the window toward the park. He watched the people of Acuña as they went about their business and wondered which one among them would be his contact. He needed a supplier. Jimmy Dale had been a small town drug dealer in Seguin for some time and had never been caught. He attributed his avoidance of the law partly to good fortune but mostly to his own acumen. He could sense risk where it existed and was proficient in assessing it. Risk was a part of life of everyone and everything on the planet and Jimmy Dale had learned, very well in fact, to embrace it. He had worked out his philosophy on risk years before. The value lay, he was convinced, in one's ability to analyze it. Every action, whether taken or untaken, was a choice and every choice involved risk. The risk associated with crossing the street was being struck by a car, or perhaps turning an ankle in a pothole. Eating a piece of fried chicken could lead to choking on a chicken bone and should be considered when determining what to eat for supper. And if the desired course of action was establishing a contact for drug transport across the border into the United States and then delivering those drugs to a supplier in a major U.S. city, then being killed or imprisoned was the chance that one took. Was it worth it? Jimmy Dale had decided that it was.

Jimmy Dale ordered two more beers but drank them slowly and continued to try to get a feel for his new environment. After he had finished his third beer he left the café leaving a tip commensurate with the time spent occupying the table rather than the money spent on the meal and the beer. He moved out into the square and grabbed another beer from a vendor pushing a refrigerated cart. The logo on the cart was that of Modelo Negro and the contents of the cart were true to the advertising. He picked up a newspaper on his way to a bench and leafed through it casually after he sat down. He did this mostly as a way to remain inconspicuous but he wasn't sure if he was pulling it off. He continued to soak up the sunshine and the surroundings. Something would come to him. Something would happen. It always did.

CHAPTER 3

Two or three years before he started work at Kuykendall Motors, and before the moniker Cupcake had been assigned to him, Stephen Gorman had been a pretty good high school football player. Not good enough for Texas or Oklahoma, but still pretty good and had gotten a fair amount of interest from second tier schools about playing football at the collegiate level.

The head football coach at Stephen F. Austin University was a bit of a quirk. He had an undergraduate degree in chemistry and subscribed to The Atlantic. He was also a member of Mensa. So it was easy to strike up a rapport with the coach when Cupcake made his official visit to the campus as a football recruit. Cupcake liked the coach's eclectic interests and viewpoints. An old photograph that hung behind the coach's desk on the wall was especially intriguing. The coach noticed that Cupcake seemed distracted by the picture. Pleased, because that was the second of the two reasons the coach had placed the picture there – as a talking point for recruits and other visitors to his office. The first reason was that the coach himself was intensely interested in the subject of the photo.

"Do you know who Pancho Villa is, Stephen?" the coach asked.

"I know he was some Mexican guy. Wasn't he a bandit or something?" Cupcake answered almost giggling at the thought of riding around in the desert on a horse with ammo strapped across his chest and shooting pistols straight up into the air and, of course, yipping in a heavy Spanish accent to one's heart's content.

"Yeah you could say he was a bandit but he was also a talented military tactician and skilled politician. He was nearly illiterate but had an incredible grasp of human behavior. He had a natural ability to understand people and to lead men. No formal schooling to speak of and yet he rose to the rank of general and was Governor of the Mexican state of Chihuahua for a time."

"Who's his friend with the hat?" Cupcake asked still staring at the picture. "That's the second biggest sombrero I've seen today." Cupcake was in his element here with the eccentric football coach and felt comfortable letting his dry sense of humor encroach on the conversation.

The coach grinned at the comment. He liked the young man in front of him. Stephen reminded him of himself.

"That's Emiliano Zapata - the great general of the Mexican Liberation Army of the South," the coach replied.

Cupcake looked at the coach and smiled. At that moment the coach decided to offer Cupcake a full ride football scholarship. Three days later at a staff meeting, the coach's recruiting coordinator for San Antonio asked what compelled the coach to make the offer on the spot that day while he was visiting with the recruit.

"I took him for the entertainment value," the coach replied.

Three weeks later Cupcake was arrested for arson and the scholarship offer was rescinded.

****

Jimmy Dale spent his first afternoon in Del Rio in the town square studying the place and the people that populated it. Most noticeable of all the people in the square that day was the vocalist. The vocalist had a gray, untrimmed beard, a large sombrero, and was generally unkempt. No one article of clothing matched another and the overall impression of the man was that he was loony. His dark sunglasses gave the impression that his eyes were transfixed on some point in the distance but Jimmy Dale wondered if the glasses were only a cover that allowed the vocalist's eyes to roam without arising suspicion in the subject of his gaze. The vocalist stood facing the sun and Jimmy Dale wondered if he himself was being sized up. The vocalist seemed to know only one song. Each repetition of the song began softly building slowly to a crescendo that he punctuated by thrusting his open fist into the air and closing it tightly on the final note and then holding that note for emphasis. Jimmy Dale did not know the song but found he was singing along quietly to himself by the seventh repetition.

The well-bred Latina sat alone on a bench opposite Jimmy Dale. She brought to the square in the visual what the vocalist brought in the audible. She was striking with a form-fitting blue dress and high heels. Her legs were crossed and she leaned forward supporting her body weight with her arms – palms face down on the bench with her elbows locked and her wrists facing forward. Her black hair was long and straight and she wore dark glasses. Jimmy Dale thought that her position might be uncomfortable but if it were she didn't give any indication; she seemed perfectly at ease. Her foot rocked in time with the vocalist's song and she looked from side to side pretty much every time the vocalist changed verses. The balance of those passing by could be grouped mostly into five or six categories: Adolescents in groups of twos or threes, older senoras in frocks and sandals, older men dressed similarly to the vocalist, and vaqueros with cowboy hats whose belts and boots always seemed to be made of the skin from the same beast.

Twilight was coming on and Jimmy Dale decided to get going. He was glad to find the GMC unmolested at the spot where he had left it but walked past it a couple of blocks looking for a place to spend the night. He came upon a couple of prospects but passed them by either because of the odor or the number of loose dogs and chickens. The fifth posada was to his liking so he went inside and inquired. There was a fenced parking area – a selling point – and Jimmy Dale negotiated down to twenty American what he would have paid thirty for had the innkeeper held his ground. The room at the El Vaquero Posada was spartan but clean and Jimmy Dale collapsed on the bed. He wasn't sleepy as much as he was simply exhausted. He had traveled a fair distance, crossed over to an unfamiliar land and had taken the first steps toward putting a profitable, if criminal, enterprise into place. He laid on his back with his clothes on and stared at the ceiling waiting for the excitement in his blood to calm down. When he finally settled down he slept like a slab of granite.

****

The day that Billy Sorenson's respect for Terry Amman went mesospheric, Mike Josper was conducting training for all sales associates. Billy hated these training sessions with every fiber of his being. Mike gave his two favorite salesmen a pass from attending the meeting ostensibly to cover the floor in case a customer showed up. The erasable white board stood at the ready in the corner. Written on the white board in fancy script were the words, *The Greeting.* A sense of dread filled Billy's stomach as he settled into a seat at the back of the room.

Mike was fashionably late by three minutes and started the meeting with a hearty, "Good Morning!"

The response from the assembled sales team was feeble as Billy knew it would be and Mike responded just as Billy knew he would, "Oh come on, you can do better than that! GOOD MORNING!"

This method of addressing the sales team – meant to bring energy to the group - was straight from Sales Manager 101. It was overused and ineffective…a massive cliché. The meeting was barely underway, yet already it screamed for relief.

"GOOD MORNING," the salesmen collectively responded with false enthusiasm. Billy's stomach turned. He thought about how he was glad that he wasn't armed.

"Today we're going to work on the greeting," Mike began. "Studies show that 85% of all car deals are made or not made based on the greeting. It's very important to take control of the situation from the moment that you approach a prospect. You do that with words and with mannerisms. Who knows what you are

supposed to say when you first approach someone out on the lot?"
Billy looked around the room.

The rookies were looking wide-eyed at Mike and waiting
for their chance to impress him with their willingness to worship at
the altar of the esteemed *Used Car Sales God*. The salesmen that had
been there a few months hadn't yet reached the burned out stage
and were tolerating the propaganda. The long timers – like Billy –
simply went along. There was really no reason to fight it. When
asked a question, they towed the company line. When asked to
demonstrate a particular sales technique, they demonstrated it
flawlessly. None of these techniques were ever actually put into
action in a real life situation on the lot, of course. This was pretend
world. This was the time that Mike reasserted his control over the
group. His power was so vast that he could actually get a group of
grown men in a room and make them yield to his will. Exercising
that power made him feel good.

"Billy, maybe you could help us out here. When you're
out on the lot, what is it that you say when you approach an *up*?"

"You say, 'Good morning, my name is Billy and you are?'
They will always give you their name and it gets them used to
following directions. That's why you say it that way."

"Billy is exactly right. And the other component of the
greeting is the handshake. The handshake is an excellent tool at
your disposal that will allow you to establish dominance over the
prospect. What I need everybody to do is to line up single file in
the middle of the room. I'm going to go outside this door, make
an entrance and then I want all of you to greet me. We'll go one by
one until we get it right."

Billy looked around the room again. The newbies were
lining up but looked a bit sheepish. The middle of the roaders
looked disgusted and the long-timers took it all in stride. To them
it was just part of the job, something to be endured and moved
past. Time after time Mike entered, and time after time a salesman
would grasp his hand hoping the grip and the duration were to
Mike's liking. Each salesman would hope against hope that the
greeting was delivered on cadence and with the proper tone. Of
course they never were. Billy took note of one middle-of-the-
roader in particular. His name was Terry and he had been on the

lot for about five months. During the initial weeks of his employment, he had acted on par with most of the other newbies. But with the realization that compensation had been overstated by twice and the stress level understated by half, his enthusiasm had predictably waned. Gazing upon Terry that day during the training session, Billy sensed a straw; a straw about to placed upon the proverbial dromedarian back. It remained to be seen if this particular straw was THE straw.

Terry was the fifth salesmen to greet Mike in this thespianic exercise. "Good morning and welcome to our dealership. My name is Terry. And you are?"

Terry's hand went out and the two men jousted for the superior negotiating position. The exchange lasted perhaps thirty seconds. Terry was attempting to avoid being trapped, which was of course, impossible. And Mike was attempting to put his superiority on display by simply allowing Terry to talk and then criticizing whatever it was that he said, all the time quoting studies that have never taken place and psychological theories that have no basis in reality whatsoever. It reminded Billy of the children's fable: The Emperor's New Clothes. It was disheartening to watch.

"Terry, I thought overall you did a pretty good job, but I think you might be little flat on your delivery. Try adding a little bit of excitement to your speech. We're trying to get people excited here about buying a car."

"A little bit of excitement then," Terry deadpanned.

"Yes. A little more upbeat and I think you may have held on to my hand a little too long. That might put people off."

"I don't know how to shake a man's hand? Is that what you're saying?"

Billy thought to himself, *Go ahead Terry, take a swing at him. If you do I'll tell the cops it was self defense.*

"I know you know how to shake a man's hand. I'm just saying maybe you need to not hang on quite so long." Mike answered.

Mike's strength was that his self-esteem was so incredibly low - so low that it relieved him of the responsibility to answer legitimate questions, no matter how direct or pertinent to the situation. And once that takes place, once you remove your obligation to treat another person with respect by answering a direct question, you are free to talk and act in pretty much any manner you care to talk and act. The person you are addressing - the person on the other end of the conversation - is really irrelevant. If you're a thinking man, it's a painful exchange to watch, especially this one. Billy hated watching Mike dress down the sales guys. Terry was a grown man and yet Mike actually felt as if he had the right to criticize his hand shake. What arrogance. But the worst of it was that Mike actually appeared to believe the drivel he was spewing forth. He was the emperor from that fable about the new clothes that didn't exist. As Terry turned to get away from this idiot whose annual earnings were five times his own, he let off a little steam.

"Asshole," he muttered under his breath.

Mike pretended not to notice.

The psychological breakdown thinly disguised as a training session went on for about another 30 minutes. The salesmen were then implored to go out and make disciples of other salesmen and preach the gospel of the proper greeting. The whole thing was just so stupid. Mike made the rounds for the rest of the morning. He visited the office of every salesman and went through their records, making sure every lead was being followed up with properly. He eventually made his way around to Terry's desk and was sifting through Terry's prospect file. Salesmen are asked to keep a log that lists every prospect and notes on what action is being taken on that prospect. It's usually one or two pages. Terry had made sure earlier in the morning that his action log was in his prospect folder and that every piece of information was alphabetized by the last name of the prospect. On this particular morning, Mike zeroed in on the action log.

"Terry, the thing we need to keep in mind is that the Kuykendall Company provides tools that make our jobs easier. We need to make sure that we're using these tools. If we neglect to use these tools our production will fall. It's a proven fact."

Terry stared disdainfully into Mike's eyes.

"I noticed that your action log is a little sloppy. You don't seem to be putting much effort into penmanship and you're skipping lines when you write notes."

"That's the reason I'm not selling more cars then.   I'm skipping lines when I write notes about a customer.   That's what you're telling me?"

"What I'm telling you is that there is a tried and true system to selling cars and when we deviate from that system, our production will fall."   The non-answer rolled from Mike's lips like he was ordering cream with his coffee.   It was effortless.   He didn't seem to even have to think about it.

"So does it matter that I skip lines when I'm taking notes or not?"

"Terry, I'm getting the impression you're not interested in being a success here at Kuykendall."

"Maybe not.   But here's what I am interested in doing.   I'm interested in getting as far the hell away from idiots like you as I can."

Billy had the cube across from Terry and watched as the interaction between the immovable object and the unstoppable force unfolded.   He thought about the straw again.   Mike was positioned between Terry and the entrance to the glass cube.   He was, in effect, blocking Terry's exit.   He stared at Terry and maintained his position.   He also maintained his composure.   Always…always…always in character.   Never…ever…ever give the slightest indication that there could be another way other than his way – the Kuykendall way.   Terry stood to leave but Mike held his ground, blocking Terry's exit from the cube.

"Do you think your actions here today are somewhat unprofessional?"   Mike asked.

Ah yes.   The *unprofessional* card.   Always lurking out there ready to be played when things don't go the way they are supposed to.   As Mike said the word *are* he allowed the angle of his gaze to lower ever so slightly.   It went from a level stare directly into Terry's eyes to one that appeared to be fixed on the top button of Terry's shirt.   As he said the word *unprofessional* his eyes returned to meet Terry's.   Terry had a hard time consciously coming to grips with it, but he felt as if he had been put in his place.   He felt himself teetering.   Despite his abhorrence of Mike's style, indeed his abhorrence of Mike himself, he had to hand it to him.   Mike knew his way around the inside of a man's brain.   But Terry snapped out of it.

"Get the hell out of my way you whore," Terry said snapping free of Mike's attempt at hypnosis.

One cube away Billy was chuckling to himself. He watched Mike step aside as Terry slid past him. Terry hesitated as he passed in front of Billy's cube and Billy nodded in approval. Then Terry walked out like John Wayne into the sunset. Billy thought to himself, *You gotta respect that.*

****

When Jimmy Dale's eyes opened he decided to go ahead and get up even though it was still dark. There were only a few souls about as he walked past the bench where he had spent the previous afternoon and then on into the Café de los Toros. The waiter himself was a different man although the demeanor, attire and physical appearance – even the facial hair – were very similar. Huevos Mexicanos with refried beans and corn tortillas appeared to be the standard fare among the patrons so Jimmy Dale followed suit. He took his time eating, as he did the day before, and left the café about an hour after arriving.

He thought to himself that maybe he was a bit too nonchalant. Perhaps a more concerted effort was in order. Things had come easily to him in Seguin. But this was not Seguin. It was a bit early to hit the bars so he wandered about familiarizing himself with all the drinking establishments within a 10 or 15 block area and then returned to his domicile to wait for a more appropriate hour. He passed the time dozing and moved several times between a light sleep and a state of semi-consciousness. Around 10:00 he ventured out again, not really rested but eager, and as he passed through the square a wiry man approached him and offered directions. Jimmy Dale was tempted to ignore him but the man spoke good English and that made him all the more difficult to shrug off. Jimmy Dale told the man that directions were not necessary and continued eastbound through the pecan trees. But the man was persistent and matched Jimmy Dale's quick stride despite his pointy toed boots with high heels. Jimmy Dale gave him a second sideways glance. The man was dressed in black. The silver belt buckle was the only deviation from the uniformity.

His t-shirt was tight with sleeves rolled up twice above his biceps. The right sleeve contained a pack of cigarettes 50's style. The black felt cowboy hat completed the look and was pushed back in a casual fashion. After 30 or 40 strides and several unsuccessful attempts at conversation the man peeled off at an angle and made a final offering, "Let me know if I can help you."

Jimmy Dale responded with a sideways nod and escaped his pursuer heading east off the square. Four doors down he ducked into a cantina and stood awkwardly in the doorway waiting for his pupils to dilate. He could make out the forms of some men at the bar and perhaps a few of the tables but nothing specific. He felt like a side show freak on display, being watched but not able to watch back. He did not like feeling awkward so he moved to take a seat but surprised himself and everyone else in the bar when he came into sudden contact with a metal folding chair that materialized from thin air. The chair scraped and clanged against the table and the other chairs. If Jimmy Dale had been self-conscious before, then he was doubly so now. Jimmy Dale had never been given to feelings of futility but that very sentiment washed over him as he sat down and took in the sight of his own reflection in the mirror behind the bar. He was not immediately approached and he was fine with a few moments to himself. He wallowed but took solace in the knowledge that things were seldom as good or as bad as they seemed. His self-pity was but an emotion and would pass soon enough. He noticed the Wild Turkey in among the other bottles of liquor on the shelf immediately in front of the mirror. He caught the eye of the bartender and placed his order.

"Un Modelo y Wild Turkey sin hielo."

The bartender filled the order and returned to his station without asking for any money. Jimmy Dale sipped the whiskey from a glass and took pleasure in the slow burn. The beer was served in a bottle with a chilled glass, salt and lime, and was very refreshing. From the jukebox a Spanish ballad filled the room. The beauty of the language struck him once again as it had done many times before. The feelings of inadequacy and self-doubt began to melt away as the alcohol began to take a grip, and over the next half-hour his emotion shifted from self-consciousness to not really self-confidence, but something close. He considered his investment of five dollars American for two beers and two shots money well spent. His attempt at eye contact with some of the patrons was mostly unsuccessful. The time or two he succeeded resulted in blank stares that held no invitation. He decided to move along. He hit two more cantinas through the mid-day hours and two more that afternoon after a siesta. The result was similar in that he was largely ignored and treated as a gringo without connections should be treated. There were more moments of self-doubt but they also passed and Jimmy Dale stayed the course despite the lack of immediate success. After supper in an open-air café two blocks off the square, he retired at sunset to his room.

CHAPTER 4

Neal Maresty was an only child originally from the Midwest. He had been born in either Indiana or Illinois, he could never remember. At the age of three, his mother had left his father and had taken Neal with her. Based on her account as told to Neal she had gotten tired of the beatings and the whoring. She told Neal that she had feared for her safety and for the safety of her baby boy so she moved sight unseen to Texas. Coming from her it all sounded very noble. Based on the way she treated the string of husbands and boyfriends that Neal had witnessed since that day 23 years ago, he realized his real dad might have been provoked. Either way, he had never seen or heard from his real father since. Neal had dropped out of high school at 16 and worked with a small time HVAC company for a year. He bounced around waiting tables for a couple of years after that before getting his GED and then hooked up with a bail bondsman. He liked the bail bonds business because it put him into contact with people that were at or below his own station in life, which made him feel better about himself. Plus he got to play detective. Every now and then Joe, the owner of AAAA Bail Bonds, would go out and try to locate some deviant that had skipped and sometimes he'd ask Neal to go along. You never knew when you might need a second man to drive around the block or walk through the projects or stand on a corner and keep an eye out for something and sometimes Neal got to be that guy. So Neal had been pretty disappointed the day he drove up to the office and the door to AAAA Bail Bonds was padlocked. He had tried calling but the office phone and Joe's mobile were both disconnected. For whatever reason the fax line still worked, but without a fax machine to pick up, the call was destined for Purgatory. Even Joe's assistant, Gloria, had disappeared. Neal had taken a couple of days off but couldn't afford to hang around waiting for his boss to reappear so he wandered into the Wild Snail Pawn Shop on a Tuesday and asked for a job. Frank, Neal's future boss and current owner of the Wild Snail, called back on Thursday and Neal started work on Saturday morning.

Neal liked the pawn business for the same reason he liked the bail bonds business. He also liked it because it started at 10:00 and involved firearms. He'd been at the Wild Snail for three years now and had risen to the rank of assistant manager which allowed him to write the schedule and take off at 3:00 on Saturdays. And the endless supply of interesting items passing through the front door kept Neal's mind alert and working sharply. In the pawn business, you have to know what things are worth and you have to know if they are real. You have to know the right questions to ask to make sure you're not making a mistake. During Neal's second week of employment at the Wild Snail, Neal had taken in an A-Bolt Browning .270 deer rifle. The book said $1,200. The scope added $100 so he offered the man $1,300. Two days later Frank was checking the inventory and discovered that the gun had been made in Japan instead of Holland. That cut the price to $600. And sure enough, when Neal went to check the gun there it was, MADE IN JAPAN, right there on the barrel. How would anyone even know to look? Apparently the best way to learn is to make a $600 mistake and very nearly lose your job. But after that expensive learning experience, Neal settled into being a reliable, profitable employee. Despite the nature of the pawn business and the other guys at the Wild Snail, whom Neal liked quite a bit, he still missed the bail bonds trade. He had approached some other bail bondsmen around town, but most of the businesses were family owned and leery of outsiders. And Neal hadn't especially liked any of them anyway. He had a high tolerance for sleazy people but some of these guys were real dirtbags. At the last bail bonds establishment he had entered it struck him that it was not entirely clear which of the office's occupants were the bondsman and which were the bonded. That was pretty much when Neal decided to just give up looking for work in the bail bonds trade and stick with the pawn business.

Neal lived in an efficiency apartment on the second floor of the Adobe Palms, a small apartment complex in San Antonio consisting of three buildings and 30 individual units. He had a sleeper couch but it was too much trouble to pull the bed out each night so he normally just pulled the cushions off and dropped a sheet over them and bedded down right there on the floor. The other advantage to this arrangement was that he could change the channel on the TV without a remote control since it was within arm's reach. He especially liked 'COPS' and those real life prison shows where they interviewed actual prisoners in their cells and they talked about what it was like in the yard and everything. He liked ramen noodles and ranch style beans and baloney sandwiches. He lived cheap. This was his world. Not because he wanted to, but because he had to. He tolerated his state of near poverty but was never comfortable with it. He didn't despise his lifestyle, but did have a background uneasiness concerning it. He felt as if he should be able to do better. He understood all the statistics about people with degrees and how they earned something like $1 million more than those without degrees over the course of their careers. He understood the stats but dismissed them. As far as he was concerned it was just a bunch of bullshit. He was just as good as any of those guys with MBAs.

****

Billy took a late lunch around 3:00 deciding on the Burger King a half-mile down the highway from the dealership. He remembered that this particular Burger King had a pay phone in the parking lot and that was mostly why he chose to eat there. His curiosity over

Juan Antonio's note pretty much consumed him and he made the pay phone his first stop. He dropped a quarter in the slot and dialed the home number for Juan Antonio. An elderly woman picked up. She had never heard of Juan Antonio. Strike one. He dropped a second quarter and dialed the alternate number. The voice on the greeting - that of a man that sounded like Juan Antonio's – blandly invited him to leave a message. So Billy left one. Identifying himself simply as a friend and leaving the number of the pay phone. He waited about five minutes but the phone didn't ring so he went inside and ordered an upsized #2 combo. He ate on the patio as opposed to the indoor dining area because it was directly across the parking lot from the pay phone and he could hear the phone if Juan Antonio called back. Halfway through his meal the phone did indeed ring and Billy jumped the railing, dodging the drive-through traffic to catch the phone on the fourth jingle.

"Hello," Billy answered.

"Yeah I'm a friend of Juan Antonio's. You were trying to call him?" The voice sounded like the man Billy had visited with earlier in the day and yet he was identifying himself as a friend. It wasn't adding up. But then again, it was probable that someone might be cautious if they were engaged in an endeavor like this and would likely make an attempt to conceal their identity.

"Yeah I talked to him earlier today and I wanted to talk to him about a business arrangement." Billy paused. The other end was silent. "Juan Antonio? Is that you?"

"What kind of business arrangement?"

"Who is this?" Billy asked, needing a little reassurance.

"My name is Raul. Who is this?"

"My name is Billy. Where is Juan Antonio?"

"Just a minute."

Billy held the line for about 30 seconds.

"Hello." Another man answered. Billy noticed that the voice had a familiar tone but he was unable to immediately place it.

"Hello, my name is Billy. Is this is Juan Antonio?"

"Hey Billy this is Terry Amman. You remember me from the lot a few months back?"

Recognition flooded over Billy's brain. "Yeah. Hey Terry. How you doin'?
Are you?...uh…"

"Hey Billy," Terry interrupted. "I know that we haven't spoken in a while and I know that I'm kinda hittin' you cold here. You're probably struggling to get a grip on this conversation. Let me just give you an explanation. I have another line of work now. It's quite a bit more profitable than selling cars. The guy you upped today, his name's not Juan Antonio. It's Raul. He gave you a fake identity when you ran his credit. He's my business associate and I told him to cruise the lot and wait for you to up him. Looks like it worked out."

"You know I suspected that Juan Antonio was a fake. I called the home phone number and they had never heard of him. I'm guessing the address is probably a fake too."

"It is." Terry paused and then asked, "Hey is Mike still running the sales desk down there?"

"He is. I'm afraid we're still suffering under his tyranny."

"So my note got your attention did it? Did you enjoy the money?"

"Yeah I did. And thank you. Hey Terry, what are we talking about here?" Billy was going through the motions. He liked what he was hearing from Terry but was a little uncomfortable with the direction of the conversation. Billy knew Terry would soon be suggesting something to him that was certainly unethical and more than likely illegal. Billy remembered from the car lot that Terry was a man that was willing to cut corners. Billy wished he had a little bit more time to ease into the conversation. A little more time to get used to the idea of whatever it was that Terry was about to suggest to him. But it didn't look as if there would be any time for that. Terry moved on.

"The conversation we're having is this: You have access to data that I need for my business. If you can give me a name, a social security number, a birth date, and address then I will pay you $50 for that information. Does that sound like something you might be interested in?"

"I'm still listening." Billy paused hoping that Terry would take the hint and offer some information without having to ask specifically for it. The tactic didn't work and Billy continued,

"How does it all work? What do I have to do, when do I have to do it and how and when do I get paid?"

"How you get the information is up to you. You know the layout of the dealership and the best way to get what we need. As far as payment goes, I pay in increments of ten. $500 per delivery. When you have ten identities call me at this number. I will arrange for you to meet with my associate Raul. You provide him with the information and he will pay you. The first transaction I will hold back $250. The second transaction you will get the balance owed to you from the first transaction plus full payment for the second transaction. After that, it will be $500 per delivery. I bet that if you apply yourself, you could get ten names a day. What do you think?"

"I don't know. Maybe."

"Hey Billy, like I said, I know I'm hitting you cold with a pretty weighty topic. Why don't you just think it over…give it a day. We can talk tomorrow. You can call me at this number."

"I think that's a good idea. I'll call you tomorrow if that's ok."

****

When Jimmy Dale woke up to start his third day in Mexico he left his room and returned to the Café de los Toros. He had a salad and some lemonade and realized he was beginning to feel quite at home. To stay semi-permanently was, of course, out of the question. He had left Seguin with $1,800 in cash and had burned through about $300 so far, but he day-dreamed about the possibility anyway. If he paid a month in advance, he was certain he could negotiate the rate on his room down to a couple hundred a month. Twenty a day for food and incidentals – if he lived cheaply – and it suddenly seemed possible. But then the jolt to reality came as it always did. He was not here to get by and live stress free. He was here to make some money.

The Café de los Toros was busy so Jimmy Dale decided to sit at one of the tables on the sidewalk. He considered his situation. Perhaps he should make himself available to more people. Perhaps there was a connection between his failure to make a contact and the number of people he was coming into contact with. He greeted eight or ten of his fellow patrons, again to no avail. So he gave up and walked back to the posada. The GMC looked lonely and Jimmy Dale was too, so he started her up and decided to see where she might lead him. Maybe she was in tune with something he was not.

It was a Sunday evening and the bustle of the weekend was fading quickly. Matamoros Street was designed for faster transport than the other city byways so he headed southeast at 45 MPH. After a few minutes and three or four red lights he felt satisfied that he had entered a different barrio altogether so made quick right onto a side street to try his luck. But as the afternoon had yielded cantinas of a feather, so did the evening yield barrios. Jimmy Dale visited four. They were miles apart in geography but in terms of what they were – the essence of them, i.e. the interchangeable parts – they existed in parallel universes. Jimmy Dale picked up a quart of Pacifico and began to decipher the labyrinth of Acuña. It took him 90 minutes to find his way back the straight line distance of four miles that he had traveled over the evening. The day in Mexico was drawing to a close and, after reaching his room, he pondered his options while studying the pit marks and imperfections on the ceiling. He was in a semi-hypnotic state when the door shook on its hinges. The rap on the door was that of a man. It was not timid, but not so aggressive as to insult either. Jimmy Dale wondered about answering it but in the end decided to go to the door. Was there any reason not to?

"Hello my friend." Jimmy Dale recognized his visitor as his protagonist from the day before, the one dressed in black with the pointy toed boots and the fifties style t-shirt. "I came to see if there is anything I can do for you."

"¿Como Estas?" Jimmy Dale answered in Spanish but did it more from reflex than anything else. He didn't expect to carry on a conversation with this man in the Mexican's native tongue. Jimmy Dale lingered in the doorway with the door at a 45 degree angle. Not inviting the man in but still allowing access. It was a concessionary move yet still allowed for a cushion between the two men. Jimmy Dale was making up his mind.

"I saw you yesterday in the square. I wanted to see how you were doing."

"I'm gettin' along ok." Jimmy Dale felt awkward.

"Do you need anything?"

"Nope."

"Do you have any beer?"

"I just drank my last one," Jimmy Dale answered.

"I will get some beer and we will drink. I know a place nearby. I will be back in a very short time." The man in black punctuated his statements with both hands up and open palms that were facing Jimmy Dale. The man was leaning forward a bit at the waist.

"I will be right back." And with that the man turned and jingled down the hall.

Jimmy Dale waited for a few seconds at the open door and then shut the door incompletely leaving just a small opening such that an outsider could peer in from the hall using one eye. He sat on the bed leaving the metal folding chair available to his visitor when he got back. The man returned in less than three minutes and entered the room not bothering to knock. He took the cue and sat in the folding chair opposite Jimmy Dale. He set the six pack of Modelo on the ground between them with a clank, then pulled a can from the ring and motioned for Jimmy Dale to do the same. Jimmy Dale took the can on the opposite corner of the six pack. He opened the beer, took a drink, and then leaned forward to examine his adversary. A black and white snapshot taking them both in profile at this moment would have given the impression of weighty conversation. The age, ethnicity, and formality of dress required latitude, but other than these minor details it could have been Kruschev and Kennedy engaged in a test of wills. The moment lingered and then collapsed into that dimension where moments like these go. When it did indeed collapse, it was the Mexican who chose to speak first.

"What are you doing here my friend?"

"I'm enjoying a trip to Mexico."

"You have been here before to Acuña?"

"No."

The Mexican took his first drink from the beer can, leaning his head back but keeping one eye on Jimmy Dale as the can eclipsed the other eye. He returned the can to the ground and probed further.

"What are you looking for? A guero like you does not make this journey alone to a barrio such as this in a far place only to lie about and drink Modelo. You have a desired outcome. This thing that you seek, will you share it with me now?"

Jimmy Dale was unsure and decided to allow a small portion of his plan to be made plain to the Mexican. "I am looking to establish a business enterprise. I am hoping to make contacts on this side of the river that will help me out."

"¿Que clase de contactos?" The question in Spanish could be taken as a subtle nod to Jimmy Dale's linguistic skills. The Mexican thought that Jimmy Dale would take it that way – as a compliment. But the man also had hidden agenda. He knew where this conversation was heading and a better understanding of Jimmy Dale's ability to understand Spanish would be helpful.

"There's a certain kind of contact that I need," Jimmy Dale answered in English choosing to keep his cards close to the vest. "What is your name?" Jimmy Dale asked, changing course.

"My name is Chavo. And what is your name my friend?"

"Jimmy Dale Klein."

"OK Jimmy, let us drink to our good fortunes."

"OK." Jimmy Dale raised his can in a mirror image to Chavo and drank.

"Tell me Jimmy, what sort of work do you do?"

"I'm in construction mostly."

"What sort of construction do you do? Do you build buildings?"

"You could say that…yeah… I build buildings."

"Is there anything else that you do? Besides building buildings?"

"I'm a salesman I guess." Jimmy Dale felt as if the tide was coming in on him and he decided to go ahead and let his guard down. There was a certain inevitability to it. The two men stared into each other's eyes and Jimmy Dale waited for the question he knew would come next.

"What is that you sell Jimmy?"

"X, cocaine, things like that. Things that can make you some money."

"So this is the kind of contact that you are looking for - a contact that can supply you with drugs. Is that right?"

"You could say that." Jimmy Dale was in a mangy hotel room in Acuña with a man he did not know and he felt compelled to hold back.

"I have contacts here in Acuña. Would you be interested in meeting with them?" Chavo was really sizing him up now. He was beginning to get a feel for his new acquaintance and could sense that his initial instincts were proving true to the mark.

"Yeah. I think I would," Jimmy Dale responded, trying to be more assertive.

"Perhaps you could come with me tomorrow and we could visit a man that I know. We could talk about your business."

"Is it far?" Jimmy Dale was willing to take a risk but he was uncomfortable about driving into the desert. He was sure the desert outside of Acuña was littered with corpses of men seeking illicit business deals. In the split second it took to answer the question, Jimmy Dale decided he could just as easily be killed in some hotel room just like the one he was staying in now and decided that for the most part, it really didn't matter. Why would anyone want to kill him anyway? At least not now. He didn't have any money. He didn't have anything that anyone else would want.

"It's close by. I'll show you tomorrow. I will be here at 2:00 and I'll drive you. I like you Jimmy. I will take care of you." And with that Chavo once again raised his can. Jimmy Dale had no idea as to how the meeting with Chavo's contacts would play out, but was in agreement with Chavo's optimism. He raised his can to meet Chavo's.

CHAPTER 5

Neal kept a close eye on the patrons at the Wild Snail. His few years in the bail bonds business had left him with some intuition about people and their shadowy pasts. His original intent was to monitor the store for felons that might have skipped bail. He was looking for someone that he might be able to turn in freelance style to their bondsman and make some quick cash. But after a couple of months nothing had turned up. The number of felons frequenting the Wild Snail was considerable, but those of the *on the lam* variety was simply insufficient to support the plan. So out of necessity, Neal's extracurricular business enterprise officially shifted from freelance bounty hunting to blackmail. The basic premise was that everybody had something to hide. And he was already prepared to leverage his knowledge of someone's past indiscretions. So why not broaden the field of potential targets? In Neal's mind it really wasn't all that different than bounty hunting.

The plan was fundamentally a simple one. It would begin with an intelligence phase where Neal would uncover something in the background of his victim. This could occur by chance or by direct effort applied by Neal to uncover a skeleton in the closet.

Most likely it would be a combination of the two. The next phase would be to make contact with his victim anonymously and make the demand. Pay or be exposed. The communication media of choice was email. He set up an email address so he'd be ready to go when the opportunity arose – gohorse314@gmail.com.

Neal had picked up the phrase gohorse when he was a kid. One of the kids that lived on the same block with Neal had a dad who was into horses. Neal had been invited once to ride along with them to pick up a horse. The three of them had driven six hours to a small town west of Ft. Worth to purchase a quarter horse stallion. On the way back they stopped in San Marcos to give the horse some time out of the trailer. Turns out that had been a bad idea. The horse was excitable and jumpy. He tried to rear as his new owner attempted to back him down the ramp from the trailer, hitting the roof of the trailer with such force that the truck and the trailer both rocked from the impact. Billy and his friend both jumped back five steps. Then, once on firm ground, the horse broke away. Neal remembered being in awe of the horse's speed and power as he bolted down the median between the access road and the main lanes of I-35.

"He's a gohorse," Billy's friend's dad had said.

****

Later that evening after having talked with Terry Amman on the phone earlier in the day, Billy wrestled with the option put before him. He and his wife, Denise, had struggled almost every day since they had been married seven years ago. They had been within a week of foreclosure on their 1,600 square foot home on three separate occasions. Once, a last second car deal had saved them. Twice, Billy had been forced to call Denise's parents and ask for money. Those were hard phone calls to make. And although his father-in-law had been gracious, the scars from the calls remained with Billy. He had tried to put the emotion behind him but despite his efforts the bitter taste was still there. The resentment bubbled up and resurfaced in him now. What kind of man was unable to provide a reasonable living for his family? He thought about his two daughters, ages eight and five, and what several thousand dollars would do for them. He thought about maybe making a trip down to the coast and staying in a hotel and eating out at a decent restaurant instead of sleeping in a tent and cooking on the grill. And a new car for Denise. She had been driving the '03 Maxima for several years. It had 242,000 miles on it now and it had been a good car. But the fabric on the roof was sagging, the brakes squealed, and the air conditioner burdened the engine to the point where it over heated if the outside temperature was above 90 degrees. So if you needed the A/C, you couldn't use it. But if it was a cool day and you didn't need the A/C, it was available. Such was Billy and Denise's existence.

Last week, Billy's oldest daughter, Janie, had her final soccer game of the season. Billy knew from earlier matches that the charge at the gate was $2. To avoid the admission fee he dressed as a jogger and told the gatekeeper he was not going to watch the game and that he merely wanted to use the track. Billy had a suspicion that the gatekeeper had a suspicion. Billy cared, but not enough to pay the $2. So he swallowed his pride, did a couple of laps, and settled in at the far end of the bleachers to watch the game. The way Billy looked at it, the arrangement paid him $1 per lap. And then last month, Billy crossed a line. It wasn't a real big line, but it was a line nevertheless. He was two days away from pay day without two nickels to rub together. The gas tank was on fumes and he needed to make two trips back and forth from work. He waited until the sales desk was slow and approached nonchalantly. He grabbed the gas key – the one the salesmen used to fill up the tanks of the cars that they sold - without breaking stride then walked across the showroom floor and out the back. His truck was parked along the back fence where no one would notice a quick in and out. He took the truck out the back gate and one block down the back street to the private gas pump they shared with the Toyota dealership next door. He punched in the code and filled the tank. 22 gallons. He got back in the truck, retraced his steps and hung the gas key where he had found it behind the sales desk. No one was the wiser. When he got home Denise asked him what he had done about gas. She was keenly aware of these problems that just a few extra dollars would solve. Billy didn't answer so she asked again, this time specifically if he had filled up at work.

"I did what I had to do." Billy once again felt the shame of not being able to provide.

But now Billy had an option. An option that could lift him and his family from the day to day struggles that creep into one's life when there just isn't enough money. How wonderful it would feel to attend Janie's soccer match without having to fabricate an alter ego. Or purchase a beer at the convenience store without scrounging the parking lot for change like a beggar. Or fill the gas tank without having to balance the bank account first. Billy decided that he had to take Terry up on his offer. He'd sleep on it tonight, but he knew which way he was headed. He also decided that he would not tell Denise.

The next day Billy took his lunch at the Burger King. Billy ordered the #2 combo. Billy always ordered the #2 regardless of the restaurant. It was a way to stay out of the monotony. Billy considered the irony of the situation. He thought about how always ordering the #2 in order to break from monotony, was in fact, in and of itself, monotonous. He knew what he was getting when he ordered the #2 at Burger King. Some weeks he had it three or four times. But a rule was a rule and if the excitement of the #2 at an eatery off the beaten path in some town he had never been to before was to be maintained, then the monotony of the #2 at Burger King for the third time this week had to be endured.

"What can I get for you today?" the young lady behind the counter asked.

"I'll have the #2 with the supersize."

"That'll be $6.02."

Billy handed her his credit card and prayed it would go through. It did and she handed him the receipt with a #47 printed on it. While he was waiting for his meal, Billy went outside and placed the call. Raul picked up again just like the day before.

"Yeah this is Billy. I talked with Terry yesterday. Is he around?" Billy could hear Raul speaking to Terry. He heard him tell Terry who was on the line. Raul used Billy's name and spoke of him like they knew him and were sitting around waiting for the call.

"Hello Billy. Good to hear from you. What can I do for you?" Terry asked.

"It's probably more like what I can do for you, isn't it?"

"I suppose. Are we ready to get started?"

"Tell me again exactly what it is that you want me to do."

"You aren't recording this are you?"

Billy thought about the question and realized it was a reasonable one. "No," he answered.

Terry hesitated a few seconds then replied, "You realize of course that I am kidding around here, but if I was serious I would need you to use your access to the information that comes into your dealership. I would need the names, addresses, birthdates, and social security numbers of anyone that you can make available. I would need you to write them down and deliver them to me. I would pay $50 per name. Remember that I want them in increments of ten. As soon as you have ten names for me, give me a call, and we'll get together. It's that easy. If we weren't kidding around, how long do you think it would take for the first batch to come through?"

"Is a couple of days ok with you?"

"That's fine. I'll hear from you in a couple of days."

"We'll talk to you later then." Billy hung up the phone, returned to the dealership and sat in his office. The walls of the offices around the dealership were glass so everybody could see everything. If he stood up he could see maybe twenty applications sitting loosely on the desks near him. Like an open cash drawer on the other side of the counter at the bank. So close.

That evening Billy worked the late shift. The dealership stayed open until 9:00. After 7:30 or so the activity level really slowed down and it was mostly just a skeleton crew anyway. At 8:20, Billy walked from his corner sales office in the front of the building to the restrooms in the back corner which took him through the sales floor at a diagonal. Coming from the back the entire showroom was in front of him and anyone on the floor would generally be facing toward the front of the building. He walked past his buddy Julian's desk and grabbed the brown, accordion style folder that most of the salesmen used to keep the documents from car deals that were in progress. He took the folder to the copy machine and made copies of 13 loan applications. It took 90 seconds and no one gave him a second look. He put the applications back in the folder as he had found them and dropped the whole thing back on Julian's desk.

The drive home took about 20 minutes and Billy was home by 9:30. He took the copies of the loan applications and entered ten names, address, birthdates, and social security numbers into a Word document on the computer then printed a single copy. After printing he added beside each ID the name *Julian* and the date *April 12*. He saved the document to a flash drive. He was careful to leave nothing on the hard drive. He put the printed copy in a manila envelope and wrote *Terry* on the outside.

On the drive in to work that next morning, Billy picked out a pay phone that was free of vagrants and pulled over to make the call.

"Hello." It was Raul again.

"Raul, it's Billy. I need to speak with Terry."

"Terry's not here."

"I told him I would have that first package in a couple of days. So I got it and I'm ready to schedule a drop off."

"Meet us at the Jim's café at 410 and Blanco at 1:30. We'll be at the counter."

"Whoa…whoa...wait a minute. What's going on? I thought I was supposed to meet with Terry."

"Terry will be there. I will be there too. And we'll make the exchange."

"Are we clear on the agreement? I just want to make sure that…"

Raul interrupted, "Billy, we're clear. OK? Quit worrying about it and we'll see you at 1:30." Raul hung up the phone.

Billy hung up the phone and then stood with his hand still on the receiver for 60 seconds or so. The whole process seemed to be moving so quickly. That's good, Billy thought to himself. Right?

Three hours later Billy walked into the café with his manila envelope. There were six people total sitting at the counter. Three of them were elderly men all sitting by themselves and then there was one elderly woman. Terry and Raul were sitting at the far end drinking lemonade. Billy approached them and offered his hand.

"How you doin'? It's good to see you again," Billy said to Terry.

"I'm ok." Terry stood in response to Billy's greeting and grasped his hand. "I think you know my associate." Terry turned to his left and extended an open palm toward Raul, who also stood. Both men were dressed in slacks and wearing golf shirts. Billy wasn't sure what it was that he expected them to be wearing but found he was a bit impressed by their appearance. There was a certain professionalism about them.

"Hello Raul."

"Billy, how you doin'?"

They all sat and Billy slid the manila envelope toward Terry. Terry took the paper from the envelope and gave it a quick scan.

"This looks good. Here's your payment." Terry said and handed Billy an envelope with five bills. Billy slid the envelope into his back pocket.

"If you guys don't mind, I may go ahead and get back to work. I'm kind of pushing my lunch hour a little bit."

"Go ahead and do what you gotta do. We don't want to get you in any trouble," Terry answered. Terry and Raul were both well mannered and stood again prior to shaking hands and Billy leaving.

Billy now had $252 in his pocket and the feeling was electrifying. It was absolutely empowering. When he got back to the dealership he upped the first person he saw and sold a car. He negotiated like he didn't care – because he didn't - and two hours later the car rolled off the lot. Billy had just earned a $700 commission, due to be paid next Friday. He was off at 6:00 that night and treated himself to a Dos Equis big boy on the way home.

The very next day after delivering the initial batch of identities to Terry and Raul, Billy collected 37 IDs. The retrieval and delivery of this second batch had an easier feel to it. Billy was past the initial psychological barrier and he was now just following through with the plan. He took the first 10 names with him to the counter at the same café. He met with Raul only this time but the transaction went as planned and he was handed an envelope with $750 – the $250 that was held back from the initial batch and the $500 for the current batch. He preset the next appointment for exactly 48 hours in the future and told Raul that the next batch of IDs would be available then.

****

Chavo's mother did not love him. But she did provide him with one glimmer of hope - one small gift that Chavo would cling to for the rest of his life. There was a picture that hung above the hearth in the house that Chavo grew up in. It is an iconic picture that has taken on special meaning to the Mexican people. The picture, taken December 7, 1914 in the midst of the Mexican Revolution, is of Pancho Villa and other revolutionaries at the presidential palace in Mexico City. In the picture Villa is actually seated on the presidential throne. To Villa's left is the revered leader of the Ejercito Libertador del Sur – the Liberation Army of the South - Emiliano Zapata. There are maybe twenty other men in the picture gathered around the famed leaders of the rebellion. There is a young boy in the picture, still too young to fully peer over the shoulders of the seated men, who managed to situate himself to the right of Pancho Villa and immortalize himself in the process. Chavo's mother's gift was that she had told Chavo that his father was that young boy in the picture. She told Chavo that years ago, that very boy, grown to late middle age, had stopped in their town and had fallen in love with her. Chavo's mother had gone on to say that the two had planned to be married but that shortly before the wedding he had been called off to fight in some unknown skirmish, never to return or be heard from again. It was, of course, a fabulous lie, but one that the young Chavo eagerly embraced. Through the nights without supper and the beatings from the other kids in their pueblo, Chavo would cling to the fact that revolutionary blood coursed through his veins. In his mind he was an heir to the struggle against persecution and this combined with his inferior social standing, provided the basis for a very large and prominent chip on his left shoulder.

In reality, Chavo's father hadn't been a revolutionary at all. He'd been a drifter, smelly and shiftless, who had traded a strong drink for favors with Chavo's mother. He'd had his way with her and was gone before sunup. Perhaps it was the circumstance surrounding his conception that caused his mother's resentment of Chavo, or maybe it was the fact that he was a criminally inclined hellion that was cruel to the town dogs and the other children who were younger and weaker than he was. But despite her lack of feeling for her youngest son, Chavo's mother did at least provide to him the lie about his lineage that he would carry with him the rest of his life. Chavo left the pueblo at age 11 to live on the streets of Monterrey. At 16 he killed a man for the first time.

CHAPTER 6

"I'll shoot it," Heironymus stated matter-of-factly. And given his situation, his statement of intention was understandable.

The Germans were passing the afternoon in the cantina playing *Shoot The Moon* and Heironymus was holding the double six, the six-five, the six-trey, the six-deuce, the six-ace, the double four, and the four-trey. It was a strong hand. Practically a lay-down really and the sequence of plays required to win the hand was so simple that Heironymus didn't have to think about it. In contrast to their friend, Bruno and Karl were formulating a strategy to set him and were completely absorbed in that act.

As Heironymus played his final trump, the six-ace, he noticed that the Mexican leaders seated in the corner also had a domino game going. Bruno and Karl were thinking about their next move. Bruno had the next play and sat in contemplation with his left forearm across his chest, his right elbow resting on his left wrist and the palm of his closed fist supporting his black and gray whiskered chin. Karl sat with his arms folded across his chest and, if it's even possible, appeared to be in a more serious mood than Bruno. Heironymus could see that the Mexicans were playing straight dominoes. He had noticed this many times over the years back in Seguin and pondered the fact that he had never, in fact, seen a Mexican play *Moon*. He also noticed how the Mexicans held their dominoes. It was the Mexican preference to place their dominoes on end so they stood upright like a monument or something. Heironymus didn't understand why anyone would place dominoes on a table in such a way while playing a game. It seemed to him that the placement was less stable and more prone to have a domino tump over - especially given the substandard craftsmanship of the tables in the cantina. It just didn't make any sense to him.

Bruno finally looked up from his hand making eye contact with Heironymus. He moved only his eyes keeping his head immobile. He was in a predicament and it was his way of saying that he was about to make a decision. Bruno returned his gaze to the dominoes in front of him and in one swift motion broke his statuesque thinking man's pose to play the double five. Heironymus smiled at the play and shook his head subtly letting his friend know that his decision had been incorrect. The Mexicans in the corner reacted with laughter and pomp at a misplayed domino in their own game at almost the same moment.

****

The morning of Jimmy Dale's fourth day in Mexico he slept late and wiled away the morning hours. Chavo showed up at 1:50 that afternoon. He was dressed the same as he had been in previous encounters except this time the t-shirt was plain white with a pocket over the left breast. Jimmy Dale was a little nervous when he answered the door but he managed it well.

"Good day my friend. Are you ready to keep our appointment?"

"I'm ready if you are," Jimmy Dale answered.

"Come with me. I will take you." Chavo spun on his heel and made his way down the hall. His gait was distinctive. With every left foot fall he dipped his right shoulder and twisted his torso a little bit. Jimmy Dale took note of this quirk and wondered if there might be another quirk peculiar to Chavo – maybe an unpleasant one - that would prevent white boys in Chavo's presence from coming back alive from a meeting in the desert. Chavo broke into the sunshine of the courtyard where Jimmy Dale's GMC kept company with several other vehicles in various states of disrepair. Chavo approached a muted green El Camino circa 1970 and terminated his 40 strides as gracefully as he had begun them by sliding behind the wheel. Jimmy Dale took possession of the passenger seat.

The El Camino was well maintained. As an older vehicle, one would be inclined to assume it was a junker but there was, in fact, very little junkiness to it. The paint job was nondescript but rust free. The interior was without noticeable blemishes and was fairly comfortable. Chavo turned the ignition and the fly wheel whined twice before the engine took hold. Jimmy Dale was impressed with the sound of it. It had a low grumble that was felt as much as it was heard. Chavo allowed the engine to idle while he fumbled in his sleeve for a smoke. He put the cigarette to his mouth but did not light it allowing it to hang loosely from his lips Jimmy Dean style. Perhaps he felt as if it made him look cool and anybody gazing upon him at that moment would have agreed that he pulled it off. The sole of his pointed left boot slapped the clutch and he worked the column mounted shifter into reverse and then into first as they moved into traffic. The unlikely duo headed west and after several blocks Chavo decided it was time to light up and start talking.

"Did you sleep well Jimmy?"

"Good 'nuff. I haven't really slept well since I left the house," Jimmy Dale lied. He didn't know why he felt compelled to lie about such an unimportant event but he did it anyway.

"Where is that you are from?" Chavo kept his eyes on the road as he talked. His left hand gripped the steering wheel at 12:00 and his right hand remained on the shifter.

"I'm from Seguin, Texas. It's just east of San Antonio."

"I have been to Seguin. It is a nice town."

Jimmy Dale wondered why Chavo would have been to Seguin but decided not to ask. He didn't want to know. He also questioned Chavo's judgment regarding the attractiveness of urban areas. *He thinks Seguin is nice?* Jimmy Dale thought to himself.

"It's ok." Jimmy Dale answered.

"It is better than Acuña." Chavo lifted his hand from the shifter and swept it back and forth palm down as if to encompass the entire city. For the first time since leaving the posada, Chavo looked at Jimmy Dale and threw in a smile.

"Prah'ly so," Jimmy Dale answered and returned the grin.

They drove several more minutes and seemed to be on the edge of town when Chavo allowed the car to slow down naturally without applying the brake. Jimmy Dale could see that the house coming up on the right had security cameras mounted haphazardly to a mimosa tree in the front and guessed that this specific domicile was probably their destination. The house was painted green and purple and seemed out of place when compared to the surrounding hovels, but to Jimmy Dale everything seemed out of place in Acuña and by that standard was perhaps not out of place at all. There were two stone and concrete pillars that marked the entrance where incoming vehicles were to enter the property. There wasn't a driveway – just a path where the dirt and the rock were a little bit more worn down than the rest of the yard. The pillars were about four feet high and made from concrete and a type of stone that looked like it was indigenous to the area. They were in fact, Jimmy Dale thought, probably indigenous to the back yard. A section of fencing from a cattle pen hung on rusty hinges with the free end tied to the other pillar with baling wire.

Chavo tapped the horn twice and a boy in his late teens came out and half walked half ran to the gate. He unhooked the wire and dragged the makeshift gate to something a bit shy of 90 degrees. It was just enough to allow the El Camino to get through. Chavo said something to the boy as he passed by but Jimmy Dale wasn't able to understand him. There were two pit bulls chained to metal spikes in the front yard. Each dog had worn a circular patch of ground around the stakes. As near as Jimmy Dale could tell, the dogs disliked immensely every animate object within their field of vision. The lot was small and Chavo followed the barely perceptible two track path to a spot on the side of the house and parked the car.

"My friend, are you ready for our appointment?" Chavo said to Jimmy Dale as he shut down the engine.

They climbed the few steps to the porch and went inside. The interior of the dwelling was on par with the appearance of the exterior. It was adequately lit but just barely. A thread-bare couch hugged the left hand wall. A similarly worn area rug dominated the middle of the room with a TV, propane furnace, and recliner forming a rough ring around the perimeter of the room. A folding card table with four folding metal chairs stood in the center of the room awaiting their occupants-to-be. It occurred to Jimmy Dale that there was probably a custom cherry wood table with leather chairs doing the exact same thing in some boardroom on Wall Street. Why he made that particular connection he had no idea. The recliner was unreclined and occupied by a semi-intimidating man in his mid 40s. The doorway at the opposite end of the room was bookended by a couple of hombres that gave the impression they did not care what anyone thought of them. Bodyguards was the best term that Jimmy Dale could apply to them although sans body, it was difficult to say exactly what they were guarding. Jimmy Dale and Chavo entered and stood facing the three men. It was not a stand-off. It was more like limbo – or purgatory maybe. Jimmy Dale sensed no awkwardness in the sense that one might sense awkwardness in the presence of people that one is not familiar with. It was actually rather calm with all players unconsciously accepting the circumstances for what they were. Chavo had nodded to the man in the recliner when they had walked into the room. They appeared to know one another but Jimmy Dale had no way of knowing whether it was true or not. A Mexican novella played on the TV in the background and provided background noise.

After three or four minutes a man of some breeding entered the room through a hallway at the far corner from where Jimmy Dale and Chavo stood. The man reminded Jimmy Dale of Vito Corleone. There was an air of authority about him. The Patrón stood for a moment to allow everyone to get used to the idea that he was in the room and in charge. He then moved to the card table in the middle of the room and motioned with his hand for Jimmy Dale and Chavo to sit. Chavo sat first with Jimmy Dale taking the next seat to Chavo's right. The Patrón waited for his visitors to sit and then took the chair to Jimmy Dale's right and across from Chavo. The Patrón made eye contact with Chavo.

Jimmy Dale felt as if he were a gringo in a foreign land, which of course, he was. For now he was a non-entity.

"Mi amigo…Chavo…¿Que quiere?" the Patrón said to Chavo.

Jimmy Dale struggled to follow the conversation that commenced between the two Mexicans. They did not speak rapidly. In fact, it was quite the opposite: they spoke slowly, but the tones were hushed. Chavo motioned toward Jimmy Dale a number of times but the Patrón maintained a posture of ambivalence toward him. After three or four minutes the conversation ceased and the two men looked at each other. Another minute elapsed and the Patrón turned toward Jimmy Dale.

"This business is peligroso. You agree with me?" the Patrón asked Jimmy Dale.

Jimmy Dale had the feeling the Patrón's eyes were fixed on a point somewhere on the back of Jimmy Dale's skull and as such, his thoughts were available to the Patrón for viewing.

"It is dangerous," Jimmy Dale replied.

"You have the money with you?" The question seemed out of place to Jimmy Dale and he was not sure where to go with it.

"What money?"

"Chavo told me you have the money with you."

Jimmy Dale wished he had made a greater effort to follow the conversation that had just taken place between the Mexicans. He was in a position now that needed to be handled properly. He fell back on instinct.

"I don't have the money," he said.

"It's not wise to come here without money," the Patrón said.

Jimmy Dale was unsure if this statement was meant as advice or threat.

"Please leave. To the rear," the Patrón ordered as he stood and disappeared down the same hallway at the far corner of the room. Chavo followed the Patrón. One of the toughs in the room motioned for Jimmy Dale to stand up and for the first time he knew he was in trouble. His apprehension notwithstanding, he did as he was instructed. The same bodyguard that had motioned to Jimmy Dale to get up pushed him toward the hallway. The hallway was dark and Jimmy Dale felt as if he was walking into a buzzsaw.

The pain shot through his skull almost instantly as the blow was delivered. Weeks later, Jimmy Dale would wonder if he had heard the crack through his ears or if the blow had vibrated his ear drum directly. He was berated in Spanish as he lay face down in a state of semi-consciousness. He absorbed multiple blows to the rib cage but he felt very little after the initial shot to the head. Sometime later he was aware that he was being dragged and sensed the sunlight, then felt the vibration of the vehicle.

****

Raul Barrientos had been dealing drugs and stealing since he was 13. He showed up for a while at John Jay High School on the south side but it was ill-fated. His grandmother was raising him and was fighting the good fight but eventually Raul went down the path that he was destined to go down. He dropped out officially during the fall semester of his sophomore year. Although he always had something going on the side, Raul didn't immediately give himself over to a life of crime. He worked for a concrete company in dispatch for a couple of years and then found a job driving a bobcat rig delivering for a local lumber company. But the old neighborhood always had a hold of him. Small time drug deals and the occasional heist when he got tipped off that someone was going to be out of town. That was the other reason he liked the delivery job. He was always in contact with home owners and business owners that liked to talk. Raul never went out of his way to engage them, in fact he made it a point not to. He never wanted to be remembered as a guy who asked questions. He just let them talk. And one person out of 10 or 20 would drop something about going out of town for a while. Raul figured that if they were telling him about going out of town, then they were probably telling all the other delivery guys the same thing. He made a note of the surroundings while he was still in the house: dogs, alarms, cameras, etc. And then he showed up two or three weeks later in the middle of the night. His average take was about three or four grand and after fencing it with some of the guys from the neighborhood, he usually put about half of that into his pocket. It was a lot of extra money for a guy that was on payroll for $30,000 a year.

But he ended up getting caught. On one of Raul's heists there was a camera that he had failed to identify and it showed his face clear enough that the business owner recognized him. And when the prosecutor started digging and found out that Raul had delivered to that facility two weeks before the break-in, the writing was on the wall. With his juvenile record, Raul was facing three to five so he pled it out and agreed to serve 12 months. It was at the state facility in Huntsville that Raul went from small time hood to polished criminal. There were a number of inmates at Huntsville who were incarcerated for smuggling illegal immigrants into the U.S. In the vernacular, these smugglers were referred to as coyotes; the term presumably derived from their ability to slink through the brush undetected. Raul was surprised to find out that as part of their service, the coyotes would also provide identification to the illegals that would allow them to work in the U.S. In essence, the coyotes were bundling their services, not unlike the cable company.

So just through casual contact with the coyotes, Raul discovered a need. One coyote in particular, El Milagro, seemed especially interested in cultivating a contact within the U.S. that could provide a steady supply of I.D.s for their human smuggling ring. This information got back to Raul indirectly through the usual prison channels. Raul had never spoken to El Milagro, nor was he inclined to do so. El Milagro was a person of status within the prison walls and Raul knew that to approach him without an invitation would be a breach of protocol that could have negative repercussions. And beyond the difference in rank, the fact that Raul was a Chicano, a person of Mexican descent but U.S. citizenship, and El Milagro was a Paisa, a Mexican from Mexico, furthered the chasm.

But Raul was friendly with one of the Paisas that was regarded as a man of reason by both the Chicanos and the Paisas alike. So Raul asked his Paisa friend about how a Chicano like himself might go to work for a man like El Milagro.

"Why would you want to get involved with a man like that? He is very dangerous."

"Because I think I can make some money," Raul answered.

"Doing what? Running through the brush like an animal?"

"I heard that the coyotes need U.S. IDs that they can provide to the immigrants so they can get work. I think I might be able to do that." Raul responded.

"It's true that they need IDs that are valid. I will ask El Milagro to speak with you."

CHAPTER 7

The moment that would define Charlie's status in the prison came three weeks and two days into his 15 year sentence. Out in the yard Charlie noticed that the Mexicans were looking at him. Three or four of them seemed to be particularly piercing in their gaze, choosing to not avert their eyes if Charlie happened to glance their way. They were very good at intimidation. Charlie knew that he was being targeted and something was coming. He was scared but he knew the day that he walked through the prison gate that it was likely to happen so he was at least prepared for it and he glared back. Charlie, through body posture and expression, responded to his Mexican adversaries and their malevolent scrutiny, letting them know that while he might appear innocuous, he would not succumb. He would fight back.

After yard time Charlie was returning to his cell when the Mexicans got him. Yanked back from the main hallway into a laundry closet, three or four of the Mexican Mafia – Charlie never really knew – began to beat Charlie unmercifully. They whipped his neck and back with a chain, drawing blood. But the restricted confines of the closet worked to Charlie's advantage. His main protagonist, the one working him over with the chain, was never able to reach full extension and that took the edge off the blows. They were still brutal, but perhaps not quite as severe as they would have been had there been more room to swing the chain. It also kept the Mexicans from keeping a safe distance from Charlie and he landed maybe four or five blows with good impact. The Mexicans knew by the forcefulness of the blows and the persistent way that Charlie met the onslaught that Charlie was not going to give in. It didn't stop the beating that day in the laundry closet but it did instill a level of respect that quite probably forestalled any future run-ins with the Mexicans. He wasn't considered a badass, but he was known from that day forward as not being a bitch. And that was all he needed. All Charlie had to do from that point forward was avoid the Mexicans. And until the day he met El Milagro that's exactly what he did.

****

Jimmy Dale woke up the day after his beating in his room at the posada. Someone – presumably Chavo – had brought him home to the room and left two unopened bottles of Ozarka beside the bed. Jimmy Dale was thirsty and he wanted to gulp them but was just too sore so he nursed them instead. He took stock of his situation. He was hurt but not so badly that he couldn't move about. His head was especially sore. His ribs were sore too but not broken. Jimmy Dale knew that if they had really wanted to hurt him then they would have hurt him. Instead what he had experienced was a warning. His newfound associates wanted him to be scared and to understand his place in the hierarchy. He understood his place in the hierarchy – the bottom. He wasn't so sure that he was scared though.

That next morning Chavo knocked at the door. Jimmy Dale knew the strength of the knock and knew it was Chavo but he didn't say anything. Chavo entered anyway and placed a peace offering on the table. The barbacoa wrapped in tin foil and recently purchased from a street vendor smelled delicious.

"Our friends are dangerous. They are wary of outsiders." There was a long pause while Chavo attempted to get a feel for how Jimmy Dale would respond. "Would you like to eat?" Chavo asked glancing at the food. "I am sure that you are hungry. No?"

What Chavo really wanted to know was whether Jimmy Dale would hold a grudge for leading him into the ambush at the Patrón's house. Chavo had been aware of Jimmy Dale's fate before they had ever set foot on the property. And Jimmy Dale knew that Chavo had known. And it wasn't that Jimmy Dale didn't care – he did - but he accepted the reality of the situation. Allegiances were as they should be. The barbacoa was an olive branch and Jimmy Dale accepted it. It was good.

****

Terry Amman met Raul Barrientos through a mutual friend named Oscar, the owner of Rod Dog's Bar. Rod Dog's was near Kuykendall Motors where Terry had worked for a time and he had gotten in the habit of stopping by for a beer after work. That habit continued even after he had quit the car lot.

Oscar worked the bar himself as much as he could. Employees would steal and if Oscar wasn't there to keep an eye on things the profitability of the business would drop. So Oscar was there pretty much every time Terry stopped by for a drink. The two men weren't really friends but more like acquaintances with a mutual respect. Terry always had the sense that there was more to Oscar than just being a bartender. Oscar had told Terry once that he had been in Vietnam. The topic had come up within the normal course of conversation and Terry knew that Oscar would have never mentioned it except that it was central to the conversation. Terry also knew that Oscar had worked as a policeman in a small town somewhere in South Texas for several years.

One afternoon a young man dressed very neatly in casual business attire came into the bar. He gave Oscar a casual nod and took a table in the middle of the establishment. Oscar nodded back and joined the man at the table. Terry was seated at the bar so that the two men were behind him and to his right and from that position it was difficult to observe them without being obvious about it. But after a few minutes Terry's curiosity got the better of him and he turned to look at them. Oscar was already looking at Terry…or at least he was looking in Terry's direction. But his gaze seemed to be fixed on some point directly behind Terry. There was a heaviness to Oscar's stare. Oscar's line of sight seem to bore right through the back of Terry's skull and come to rest on some object 1,000 yards distant. The neatly dressed young man visited with Oscar for another ten minutes or so, then left and Oscar returned to his duties behind the bar. Terry wanted to ask Oscar about the nature of the visit but knew that he didn't know bartender well enough to do so.

Some weeks later, Terry stopped by Rod Dog's as usual before heading home. It was a Tuesday and the joint wasn't busy. Terry took a seat at the bar where he always sat and ordered a beer. He sat for a few moments like always taking in the atmosphere. Midway through his second beer Terry was approached by Oscar.

"Terry, you seem to be an intelligent young man." In keeping with Oscar's style, his delivery of the statement was low and without emotion. It was not meant to flatter but merely the opening statement of fact leading to the purpose of the conversation. "And my impression of you is that you have some ambition. That you are open to opportunities that might improve your station in life."

Terry was not expecting this line of conversation but took it in stride and nodded in agreement.

"I have someone that I would like for you to meet," Oscar said.

"Ok," Terry said wondering where the conversation was going.

"My nephew, Raul, has a business opportunity that could be fairly lucrative but he needs a partner. He needs someone with expertise in auto financing." Oscar knew that Raul had recently been released from prison and that the business opportunity was of questionable legality, but he didn't feel it was worth mentioning to Terry at the time.

"I don't have expertise in auto financing," Terry responded.

"You work at a car lot don't you?"

"I used to work at a car lot." Terry put the emphasis on the words *used to*. "But I sold cars. I never worked in financing."

"But you have an idea about how the world of finance works don't you? I mean you know what it takes to get a loan."

"I suppose I know something about it.   But I'm no expert."

"Would you be willing to talk to my nephew?"

"I suppose."

"I'll have him come by the bar tomorrow at 6:00 and we can talk."

The next day Terry was at the bar at 5:55 and recognized the young man on the bar stool talking to Oscar as the same young man that had come by and talked with Oscar three or four weeks before.

"Hello Terry." Oscar extended his hand over the bar and when they had finished shaking he invited Terry to sit in the stool occupied by the well dressed young man.

"This is my nephew, Raul. Raul, this is Terry. He's the guy I was telling you about."

"Hello Terry.   My name is Raul."   Raul stood and extended his hand.

"Terry Amman. Good to meet you." Terry stood while they shook hands and then took the seat offered by Oscar.

"Terry, I have a business opportunity that has presented itself and I need some help. I've told my uncle about it and he seems to think that you might be able to help me."

"What did you have in mind?"

"My opportunity is somewhat sensitive. If word got out that I was involved in what I'm involved in it might be unpleasant for me. My uncle tells me that you can be discrete. Can I trust that what we talk about today will not be repeated?"

"Sure."

"I have contacts in Mexico that help people cross over the border into the U.S. to work." Raul paused and looked into Terry's eyes. Tio Oscar had vouched for Terry and Raul knew that his uncle had good judgment but he wanted to get a feel for Terry and whether he could be trusted. He searched Terry's eyes for some clue as to what kind of a man he was dealing with.

Terry looked back at him.

"My contacts also provide their clients with identities so that they can work legally in the U.S."

"So it appears that they are working legally." Terry confirmed.

"Yes. So it appears that they are legal." Raul repeated the statement to make it plain to Terry that he understood the difference between working legally and simply appearing to work legally.

"And they need to get these identities from somewhere. They will pay a good price for the IDs, but I don't know anything about it. I've tried a couple of different ways to go about getting IDs but they've failed and I feel like this thing is slipping through my fingers."

"What have you tried?"

"One thing I tried was to get in with waiters at restaurants. I figured that they had access to credit card numbers and IDs and they might be able to help me out."

"That won't work, they don't have access to social security numbers," Terry said.

"I figured that out. That's when I realized that I need somebody that works in finance. I mean a guy that works with loans and stuff would have access to all that kind of information. Right?"

"Yeah"

"And you worked at a car dealership where they financed car loans right?"

"Yes, but like I told your uncle, I never worked in the finance department."

"Does it matter?"

"Probably not."

"Then will you help me?"

"What does it pay?" Terry inquired.

"My contact charges his clients $500 for a valid social security number, name, and birth date. He'll give us $250 per. He has other guys that work for him so he'll buy as many as we can provide."

"I think I can help you. We split the profits down the middle?"

"Sure." Raul agreed.

"I have an idea about how to go about it. You gonna be around here tomorrow evening?" Terry asked.

"Yeah. I'll be here."

"See you tomorrow night then," Terry confirmed.

Terry left to go home to his wife and kids. He waved at Oscar as he rose from his place at the bar and Oscar waved back. On the drive home he contemplated the opportunity that had been placed before him.

****

By the time Jimmy Dale was two days removed from the beating at the hands of the Mexican thugs he began to feel much better. He was still sore but the rawness of the injuries had eased and breakfast at the Café de los Toros cheered him up a little bit. He was late for breakfast by Mexican standards and when he left at 9:30 Chavo was making the rounds in the square, identifying marks. Jimmy Dale made eye contact with his partner and motioned him toward where he was sitting. Chavo freed himself of whatever entanglement he was currently entangled with and joined him.

"Good morning my friend. You are looking much better."

"What do we do now Chavo?"

"You must get the money. Our friend is not a bank. He wants $10,000."

"$10,000? If I had $10,000 I wouldn't need to come to Mexico and get my ass kicked." Jimmy Dale got up implying that he was abandoning the deal and would be seeking out another source.

"Perhaps we could work out a more attractive price for you," Chavo hollered before Jimmy Dale got too far.

Jimmy Dale turned and looked at Chavo. "Perhaps."

"What is it that you would like to pay?"

Jimmy Dale returned to the bench and reengaged in the conversation. "We're talking about a kilo here right?"

"Yes. One kilo of cocaine."

"Uncut."

"Yes. Uncut. The highest quality."

"I will pay $2,000 and you deliver. And I will not go back to your place of business. Not with two grand in my pocket. I'm not interested in talking with those goons anymore."

"I will inquire on your behalf." Chavo promised.

"Don't inquire. Just make it happen. I'll see you tomorrow."

Chavo left and Jimmy Dale was overcome with the feeling that he he'd had enough of this godforsaken city and decided he needed to get back to America already. He gathered his things from the room and was just nice enough to the innkeeper to maintain his welcome when he returned. At the terminus of the bridge on the U.S. side, Jimmy Dale took note of customs and the border patrol agents that manned it. The German Shepherds were active, ceaselessly sniffing and searching nearly every inbound vehicle. The GMC too was unceremoniously sniffed in turn and Jimmy Dale proceeded through traffic toward US 90 and the Motel 6 he had seen on his way in.

He checked in and paid for a single bed for one night. It felt good to hear the English language again. He was assigned room 214 and hit the shower first thing. He blasted his bruised body into oblivion with the hot water and emerged twenty minutes later much refreshed. Feeling some spark he attacked the buffet at the Pizza Hut across the street and pretty much handled an entire extra large sausage and mushroom pie by himself. He flirted with the waitress who brought him his drink but got nowhere. Her name tag said Clarice and she was too young for him anyway so he left. It was only 4:00 so he searched out a Dollar General and picked up a copy of *The Last of the Breed* by Louis L'Amour. He read the first four chapters and crashed.

****

Neal Maresty and Terry Amman had been friends since grade school. Terry was probably Neal's closest friend but it was not clear whether Neal was Terry's closest friend or not. And that was indicative of the way that they had always related to each other. Neal had always operated in Terry's shadow. Terry was better looking, a better athlete, and had better luck with girls. As adults the divide had continued; Terry was more successful than Neal - which is to say that he was not a complete failure.

"Damn this guacamole dip is good," Terry said between hits on the beer can. Terry was having a few friends over for his son's birthday party. Terry had three sons and his youngest, Jack, was turning two. Terry and Neal and the four or five other guys were hanging around on the back deck drinking Pearl beer and keeping an eye on the grill. The women were chatting in the kitchen. The kids were everywhere. The guys around the grill took it all in. The sizzling. The aroma. The smoke. No element of the cookout was overly represented. The visual, the audible, and the aromatic were in perfect balance. Terry stressed the word *damn* strongly. He was starting to get motivated in his partying and was beginning to sprinkle his speech with some color.

"Hey Terry, are you going to the coast this year?" Bobby asked.

Bobby was another friend of Terry's and Neal's from high school. In between Terry and Neal in height, Bobby had an athletic build but was not athletic and wore his blond hair in a flat-top 50s style.

"I'd like to," Terry said as he turned the brats. "I'm just not sure if I can squeeze it in."

"I'm thinking about putting something together for two weeks out if anyone is interested," Bobby said.

"I might be able to do that." Terry nodded, his eyes locked on the flames the grease from the brats created on the charcoal as they cooked.

The conversation was not able to hold Neal's attention and he began to admire Terry's backyard. Terry didn't have a whole lot to work with. The physical space was small and irregularly shaped but it was well landscaped. The grass was green with no bald spots. The planting areas had fresh mulch with a variety of plants that Neal had seen before but didn't know the names. No weeds. He found he wasn't even listening to the guys anymore and drifted into the house without really thinking. He wandered down the hall to the restroom but the door was locked. Terry's office was across the hall from the restroom. Neal stood with one foot in the office and one in the hall with his back against the door jam, facing back down the hallway waiting for the restroom to open up. He took in the layout of the office. It was picked up neat and the built-in book shelves were pretty well stocked. The desk had a monitor and a key board, a phone, a printer, a framed picture, and a manila folder full of papers. The folder seemed to grab Neal's attention. He was on auto pilot at this point and his mind was seeking something to latch on to. Neal stood in the doorway for a few more seconds and then wandered over to the folder and opened it. Neal scanned the top page. Names, social security numbers, birthdates, addresses, etc. There appeared to be six or eight entries. Neal thumbed the pile and found the other 30 or 40 pages to be laid out in an identical manner and filled with sensitive information. Stapled to the inside of the folder in the upper left hand corner was a business card. *Billy Sorenson. Kuykendall Autoplex.* The door to the restroom opened and out walked Terry's wife, Barbara.

"Oh hey Neal, how you doing?" Barbara asked.

"Oh hey Barbara. You know this really is a nice picture of you and the boys." Neal was holding the framed picture and admiring it. The manila folder was closed on the desk.

CHAPTER 8

Rosalie Chambliss was 29 years old, 5' 7" tall and 130 pounds. Her hair was light brown and reached the bottom of her shoulder blades when she chose to wear it down, which she usually did. She had excellent fashion sense and preferred dresses that complimented her figure but still fell within the boundaries of good taste – although just barely. She was very pretty. She had always been pretty. As a little girl she had noticed that the little boys always seemed to like her. Even the adult men treated her differently from the other little girls. She had always seemed to be favored. And that popularity had continued through adolescence and into adulthood. She had that best kind of charisma, the kind that is muted and understated, yet somehow very powerful. Without even realizing it, people around Rosalie were drawn to her. It was like gravity.

Out of financial necessity, Rosalie and her son Zack lived with her mother, Linda, in a small frame house east of Seguin. There was no child support. At least none received, although she was accruing a sizable amount due should Zack's father, Charlie Manor, ever find a decent job and hold it down for more than a month. And as remote as that possibility might seem on the surface, it was made even more remote by the fact that Charlie was serving 15 years in Huntsville for armed robbery.

After graduating high school Rosalie had tried taking a few classes at the community college but ended up dropping most of them and finally resigned herself to the fact that she just wasn't cut out for school. So she waitressed for a while before landing a job with a local law firm six years ago. The Law Offices of Sage, Sage, and Blinn focused mostly on family law and had helped Rosalie out when she'd had trouble locating Zack's father prior to his arrest and incarceration. Since she was an employee in good standing they had performed all the work pro bono. That was a pretty big benefit for a single mother. And the attorneys understood if Zack was sick or if there was something else that required her to be away from the office. And to top it all off the work was mildly interesting.

Rosalie had been dating Jimmy Dale for a year and a half. She had known of Jimmy Dale in high school but had never been around him socially until one night at the downtown beer joint called The Oak. She came in after work that afternoon with a girlfriend and he was at the back table playing *Shoot The Moon* with his buddies. They weren't being obnoxious or anything but they were laughing and having a good time and Rosalie found herself being keenly aware of their presence. She rarely looked in their direction, but rather monitored them through a combination of senses consisting of the visual periphery, the audible, and women's intuition. So when Jimmy Dale got up from the domino game she coordinated her trip to the bar and greeted with him a smile. That smile did him in. He was hooked. Almost awestruck, he stammered an awkward *hello* and went back to his seat. But Jimmy Dale was quick to recover from a set back and after a successful shooting hand with sixes trump and a four off that was covered by the double, Jimmy Dale decided the time was right to approach Rosalie and her friends at their table.

"My name's Jimmy Dale."

"I remember you from school," Rosalie answered.

"This might seem like an unusual request. But my buddies dared me to come over and say something to you that I'm not

willing to say. It's a little off-color and disrespectful so I'm not
going to say it. But I was thinking that maybe you could slap me
and it might give the appearance to my white trash friends over
there that I followed through with the bet."

Jimmy Dale searched her eyes for a response and could see
that she was on the fence. He closed the deal by adding emphasis,
"It needs to be pretty hard to make it believable."

Jimmy Dale could see the corners of Rosalie's mouth start
to turn upward as she raised her open hand and swung. The slap
was forceful and it bit on Jimmy Dale's cheek but felt good at the
same time. It was a moment frozen in time. The bar went silent.
Jimmy Dale looked into Rosalie's eyes and fell completely and
totally in love. His plan to break the ice and pull her into his orbit
– or perhaps to get her to allow him to fall into orbit around her –
had worked to perfection. Rosalie smiled back at him, angelic and
glowing. Jimmy Dale's white trash friends snickered like second
grade school boys.

****

The next day in Mexico was the sixth day of Jimmy Dale's
excursion. He crossed the bridge back into Mexico, again taking
note of the procedures the border patrol agents were subject to. At
mid-morning he was back in the square and within 45 minutes
Chavo showed.

"Good morning Jimmy."

"Good morning Chavo. Did you take care of all those
things that you were going to take care of?"

"I have spoken with our associate and we are prepared to
proceed."

"So it's agreed that you deliver the product and make the
exchange for the money?" Jimmy Dale asked.

"It's agreed. But my associate must know in advance the
location for the exchange."

"That's the only thing he wants?" Jimmy Dale was making
sure there was no confusion.

"That's all."

"Can we schedule the exchange for two weeks from
today?"

"Yes. Two weeks."

"I need to be able to contact you by cell phone. Do you have a cell phone number?"

"A cell phone number is not necessary. I am always available."

"Chavo. I need a number. It's not too much to ask. I am not always around and I need a way to contact you. I'll only call if it's very important. I don't want to talk to you any more than you want to talk to me."

Chavo looked at Jimmy Dale for a few moments then pulled a beat-up business card from his wallet and handed it over. Jimmy Dale found it curious that a drug dealing con man would have a business card. Jimmy Dale looked at the number on the card and found the arrangement of the digits strange. It wasn't like an American phone number.

"I can call this number from here in Acuña. Is that right?"

"Yes." Chavo confirmed.

"'I'll call you in two weeks. If you want your portion of the money, be available," Jimmy Dale said

"I am always here. Vaya Con Dios."

"Igualmente." And with that exchange, they shook hands in the Mexican gangster style with each man grasping the meaty part of the hand and their forearms coming together to form an upside down V. Jimmy Dale departed and crossed the bridge heading east. He was glad to be heading home.

****

When Rosalie was 17 years old she had a baby. The daddy lived in the next town and was three years older. Rosalie found out she was pregnant the last day of her sophomore year of high school although she had suspected for at least two weeks before that. She didn't tell anybody for a couple of weeks because she was scared as any unwed teenager would be. She thought about telling her best friend Emily but didn't. She thought about telling her mother but was ashamed and couldn't bring herself to say the words. Finally she made an appointment at a pregnancy counseling clinic where a 50 year old woman that drove a new GMC Denali told her that the decision was hers and hers alone and that she needed to do what was right for her.

Rosalie was put off by the pretentious countenance of the counselor. She felt as if the counselor's words, despite advocating choice, were implying a certain course of action needed to be taken. But Rosalie didn't feel any better about anything. And so she walked out of the session an hour later feeling more confused than when she had entered. She felt as if the woman whose job it was to help her in this time of stress had ended the meeting by notching her own belt. As she walked to the car Rosalie envisioned the woman high fiving her co-workers and soliciting accolades for her role in furthering the cause of enlightenment. All Rosalie knew was that she was glad to be out of there. Rosalie didn't cry often but she cried that day. It started as she clicked her seat belt and continued as she drove to the park and then came again in another wave as she parked her car in the most remote parking space that she could find.

The pressure to have an abortion was intense. The arguments for having one were strong and compelling. She wasn't ready to care for a baby. The daddy was irresponsible and less able than she was. There would be no help from him and she knew it despite her fantasies to the contrary. *BUT SHE COULDN'T DO IT*. Despite her tender age, she intrinsically knew that an abortion was not the end of the problem but rather the beginning. It was permanent and could not be reversed. She had the foresight to know that there would never be a day that went by that she wouldn't think about the baby that would have been. She had overheard her mother once, talking with a friend in the kitchen. Her mother's friend had been talking about an abortion that she had gone through with several years earlier.

"My baby would be 15 years old now," the woman had said.

The two women had no idea that a 13 year old Rosalie was listening to them from around the corner and the impact that the statement would have on the adolescent girl. That statement and the remorse that Rosalie had heard in the voice of her mother's friend came back to Rosalie as she sat in her car in the park that day. She dialed her mother's number and when her mother answered the tears came out with their full force.

Sobbing into the phone Rosalie cried out, "Momma ..."

"What is it baby. Are you ok?... Rosalie?"

Rosalie broke down completely. "Momma…Momma… I'm so sorry!"

Eight months later Tyler Vernon Chambliss was born. He lived for six minutes. Rosalie had felt the glow of motherhood for only 10 or 15 seconds before she knew something was wrong. He wasn't crying and he wasn't breathing. The doctors and the nurses scrambled madly to correct the situation with the baby boy. Doctors ran in and out and pushed each other around. They reached over each other to get at the baby and prod him or insert whatever apparatus it was that they thought would save him. Nothing worked. The baby refused to respond. Rosalie's world imploded. They allowed her to hold the body of her baby boy. She wailed and rocked back and forth with the overwhelming grief. Finally the nurses pulled the body away from her and her mother rushed forward to take the baby's place in Rosalie's arms.

They buried Tyler next to Rosalie's great great grandfather three days later in the Kingsbury cemetery. Rosalie stared blankly at the fresh earth piled up around the grave site and spilling over on to the grave of Heironymus Donsbach. The old man's grave had a marker that designated it as the final resting place of a confederate veteran and Rosalie pondered the magnitude of time. How all these years later little Tyler was being placed here and how 100 years further on no one would even be alive that would remember Tyler.

Linda called Tyler's daddy the day Tyler had been born and died. He feigned grief but she knew he was relieved. She told Rosalie that she had called him and that he had expressed remorse which of course was true. But that was all she told her daughter. The douche bag didn't even show for the funeral.

****

It was 4:00 in the afternoon when Jimmy Dale pulled into his driveway. He found the trailer as he'd left it. He was always mildly surprised that his place was untampered with after a long absence. He felt his trip a success and, although a long, long way from consummation he felt like celebrating. If nothing else, he had gotten home alive. He cracked the Steel Reserve tall boy at 6:00 and at 6:45 he placed the call to Rosalie. She picked up the phone on the second ring.

"I'm cookin' beef ribs on the grill if you're interested," Jimmy Dale said.

"Do you have any margarita mix?" Rosalie asked.

"No but I could get some if it makes a difference."

"How 'bout tequila?"

"Just got back from Mexico. Got two big bottles."

"Any potatoes or garlic bread?" Rosalie inquired further.

"No. Just the ribs. Ain't that good 'nuff?" Jimmy Dale responded.

"We need some fixin's darlin'. I'll be there in a bit."

Rosalie showed up at the trailer about 30 minutes later. The sun was going down and the color of the sunset on the clouds matched the color of the coals in the pit as they neared perfection. She looked good in her red tank top, blue jean cut-off shorts and flip flops. Jimmy Dale was glad to be home.

"What happened in Mexico baby?" She pushed her body against Jimmy Dale's and held him tight around the waist with her left arm. Her right arm hung at her side with the bottle of margarita mix at the end of it.

"Just took care of bidness is all."

"Looks like it might a took care of you."

"I'll be alright." Jimmy Dale assured her.

He had avoided the subject and she allowed him so do so. He had told her a few days ago that he was going camping. And at the time she suspected that something was amiss but chose to keep quiet about it. So Rosalie hung around and drank while Jimmy Dale cooked. The beef ribs were pretty good and by 9:00 that evening it was pretty much a foregone conclusion that she would spend the night. At 10:00 she called her mama and asked if she would mind putting little Zack to bed. The request didn't seem to bother her mother too much.

At 10:05 they were on the couch. She sat with her legs crossed sipping her margarita. He had laid down on the couch face up with his head in her lap. The back of his head was tender and swollen so he eased into the reclining position slowly and moaned a little bit as he did it. She held her drink in her left hand and combed his hair with the fingers of her right hand being careful to miss the tender spots on his head. She didn't say anything. She just looked at him. He looked at the ceiling.

"I guess you're wondering what happened and why I went to Mexico."

"The thought had occurred to me." Rosalie responded.

He didn't say anything. He just kept looking at the ceiling.

"You're not in any kind of trouble are you? 'Cause if you are I'll help you." Rosalie was reassuring. She wanted to be an asset to him.

He didn't say anything. After two minutes he leaned his head forward just enough to keep from spilling his Steel and took a sip. She was still caressing his hair. The silence was palpable and he squirmed under the weight of it. Rosalie knew that he was uncomfortable with the silence. She didn't say anything.

"I'm trying to put a deal together."

"I thought that was it". There was a trace of disappointment in her voice but she wasn't angry.

After a minute or so he shifted his gaze so that his eyes met hers prompting her for further comment. She didn't give any so he decided to ask for one, "You're disappointed in me?"

"I think I'm worried more than I'm disappointed. What happened to your head?"

"Just got jumped is all. That always happens when you're around people like this for the first time. They take any excuse they can to get the upper hand on you. They want you scared."

"Are you?"

"No."

"Why not?" Rosalie asked further.

"I don't know." Jimmy Dale smiled at his response. He actually felt a little bit of pride. He'd never really thought about the fact that he didn't get scared much.

"Maybe you should be scared. Maybe you should quit."

"Sweetheart I can't do that." He tilted his head back a little bit again and looked at her. "This is my chance to have something."

He let his neck straighten out again and his eyes returned to the tiles on the ceiling of his mobile home. The one he was staring at was broken on one corner and the one to the right of the one he was staring at had a stain on it.

"Do you remember me telling you about that guy in Chicago that I got to know a little bit last summer when I was up there on that construction job?"

"I remember," Rosalie answered.

"Well I'm going to call him tomorrow and see if he's still interested in helping me out. He has connections up there so my plan is to get the product in Mexico and deliver it to Chicago and let them distribute it."

"Sounds a little overly simplistic. There are a few more details in there somewhere aren't there? You didn't say anything about how you were planning to get everything across. Don't they have guards that search everybody? Aren't there dogs sniffing around for this kind of stuff?" She was being a little sarcastic but she had a right to be and she knew it.

"I know. I have a plan for all that."

"You have a plan…you?" She emphasized the second *you* and put a questioning tone on it implying with continued sarcasm that it took Jimmy Dale, and not the cartels in Mexico, or any of the other millions of seasoned, creative drug runners to concoct a plan to get cocaine across the U.S./Mexican border. "It took you - Jimmy Dale Klein – to come up with a plan to thwart the United States Border patrol in their efforts to control the flow of drugs into the United States."

"I just think I know a way to do it is all. I'm not getting greedy. I'm not trying to move vast quantities or anything like that. I'm just moving enough to make some good money and take some of the pressure off you and me."

"So you're doing it for me, are you?"

"I said *you and me*. Not just you…and Zack," Jimmy Dale added after a pause.

"I just don't want you to get hurt is all. Or killed. You understand?"

"I understand. I'm being careful," Jimmy Dale assured her.

"I just don't think that being careful is enough. I think when you deal with people like this that people get killed. I don't want that."

"I know."

"Well are you going to tell me your plan?" Rosalie asked.

"It's actually pretty simple."

"Aren't they all?" Rosalie replied, stating the obvious.

CHAPTER 9

Throughout the month of May, Billy continued to steal identities and to stock pile cash. He was meeting with either Raul or Terry pretty much every other day and began to wonder where all this was heading. His involvement in Terry and Raul's ID ring wasn't becoming deeper but it was becoming more long-lived. Questions began to germinate within his mind concerning issues he never considered when he embarked on this life of crime. Exactly how long was this going to last? If he continued long enough, he would almost certainly be caught. Eventually somebody somewhere would connect all the dots and this house of cards would come crashing down - and probably in a most unpleasant fashion. If he accepted this prognostication as true, then wouldn't it be wise to stop? Perhaps he should stop now. He did not have enough money to retire, but it was enough to provide a few minor indulgences for him and his family and serve as a safety net for a long, long time. Never again would he need to call his father in-law for money. Probably not anyway. This line of thinking began to make sense to him. Yes. Why not? Why not stop now? Plenty of money buried around here and there. And no prison. No criminal record. It made sense to stop. The question then became how to go about quitting. Would Terry allow it? Did it matter? Would Terry threaten him with exposure? But wasn't Terry in a position of compromise at least equal to Billy's position? If Terry threatened to expose him couldn't he then in return threaten to expose Terry? Billy weighed his options and decided that up until now the risk had been worth it. But to continue…to continue to expose himself and his family to the possibility that he could be arrested and convicted of a felony…it wasn't worth it…not anymore.

Billy continued to provide identities to Terry for the next week or so as he formulated his exit strategy. Billy decided that the thing to do was to pick a likely candidate on the lot, a salesman with a checkered past, especially one that might lend itself to a criminal enterprise such as the one in which Billy had entangled himself. And then wait for that salesman to quit. As soon as he quit, Billy would discontinue his operations and it would give the appearance that Billy's target was the culprit. For the plan to work, of course, Billy had to whittle down the likely candidates to any salesman that was employed there at Kuykendall Motors when Billy had begun his walk on the wild side. Billy pulled out his work schedule for the next week. Every salesman was listed and among the 22 salesman on the list, there appeared to be 14 that had been employed at the dealership long enough to qualify as a scapegoat. Out of the 14, eight could be pretty much eliminated right away for various reasons, one was a former cop, three were in their fifties or older, married, and were regular Rocks of Gibraltar when it came to anything in the gray area. The other four were either too stupid or too scared to attempt anything as brazen as stealing identities. That left Billy with six candidates and he very quickly focused in on three.

Like the mob, most everyone on the car lot has a nickname. Nicholas Barnard's nickname was Slick Nick. Sometimes the guys just called him Nick and sometimes they called him Slick; the names were interchangeable. Slick was an excellent salesman. He was smooth, his product knowledge was the best outside of the service department, and he worked like a drudge. Slick was there every day when the dealership opened and he was there when the doors were shut. He called it working *ding to dong*. He came in on his day off and he even came in on Sunday when the dealership was closed just to hand out cards to anyone that might wander across the lot. It was tough to beat a guy that had that kind of dedication. Slick had been with the dealership since December. He had started December 12th and still very nearly won salesman of the month for that month. From January through April, Slick had been salesman of the month every time. In 2004, Slick had made a mistake. Billy was not completely aware of the details but he knew it had something to with Slick and his stepdaughter and he also knew that Slick was a convicted felon. He knew this because the only time Slick was away from the dealership was on Wednesdays after 5:00. A couple of months after Slick had started Billy had quizzed him about Wednesdays and Slick had shared with him that Wednesday evenings he had his weekly meetings with his parole officer. The rest of the details of Slick's misstep, sketchy though they were, had filtered down to Billy from the girls in the office. Despite his failings, Slick was very personable and fair. He was honest and Billy found that he could rely on Slick to help in any way. Slick took responsibility for his situation and was trying desperately to get life back on track. Billy liked him.

Sometimes a guy's nickname was his actual name. That was the case with Billy's second candidate, Leonard Gatewood. Gatewood's official nickname was Gatewood. Gatewood had begun working at the dealership that previous February and was a so-so salesman. Billy speculated that the reason Gatewood didn't sell more was the way he looked. Gatewood was huge and menacing and black as the inside of a cat. He reminded Billy of the prisoner character in the movie *The Green Mile* except that Gatewood was more sinister in appearance. His chest was deep and his back was wide. Gatewood was in his mid 40s and his close cropped hair was speckled with gray. His unofficial nickname – the one no one would ever use in his presence - was Silverback. The last thing about his appearance, and Billy had no idea why Gatewood would do such a thing, were his glasses. The rims, the arms, everything but the lenses themselves were gold plated. Against the backdrop of Gatewood's black face, they appeared even shinier than they actually were. And they were pretty shiny to begin with. Billy had driven by the dealership many times on test drives and had noticed Gatewood out on the front patio waiting for an up. Even from a hundred yards out speeding by on the highway the combination of Gatewood's size, blackness, and gold rimmed glasses made him extremely noticeable. Billy wondered if customers had seen him standing on the stoop and chosen not to enter the dealership for that reason alone.

In 1987, Gatewood had been a young man and was involved in inner city gangs. The details were sketchy, but apparently there had been some kind of conflict with a rival, and, as young men in inner city gangs are wont to do, an argument ensued. Gatewood had felt slighted and had killed his rival on the spot. Gatewood had been arrested two days later and was sentenced to 15 years for Murder 2. He was released eight years later a changed man. All this Gatewood had shared with Billy one night a couple of months ago when they were both working the night shift. Gatewood had told Billy that he knew there would be a background check when he was hired so he decided it was best to go ahead and let the girls in the office know about his past. And since they knew, he figured everybody else in the dealership would know soon enough, so he may as well not even try to keep it a secret. When Gatewood had shared all this with Billy, Billy had wanted to know more. He had wanted to ask Gatewood about the crime and about prison but he suddenly felt very white and very suburban. Billy had been around enough ex-cons to know that it was considered bad form to pry. Like Slick Nick, Gatewood's background was not a very good indicator of his demeanor, and he was actually very nice and personable. Billy would occasionally hear Gatewood open up about his past to someone else in the same manner that he had opened up to Billy. The recipient of the information would usually be surprised and it showed despite their best efforts to conceal it. Gatewood would usually follow up with some statement about how harmless he was. Billy liked him too.

The third candidate was Stephen Gorman. Stephen's nickname was Cupcake. Cupcake was in his mid 20's, six feet tall and about 300 pounds. He had played offensive tackle in high school and looked like he had probably been pretty good. He was heavy, yes, and he had some fat on him but he was not pudgy or pear-shaped. Cupcake was drifting aimlessly through life. He was very intelligent but lacked the drive to be successful at anything. During his first week on the lot he had backed a van into a customer's car doing a combined $1,500 worth of damage to both vehicles; lost control of the used Corvette the dealership had for sale after he had sneaked it out the back gate putting a sizable scratch on the passenger's side door when it ended up in the ditch; and had fallen asleep at his desk – a distinct no-no when the walls are see through. The sales manager Mike had joked that he hadn't hired Cupcake to sell but instead for the entertainment value.

Two years ago Cupcake had been picked up for arson. He and his buddies had been at a party and gotten into a bit of a scuffle with some other guys. The next thing you know the house was on fire. That was all Cupcake seemed able to remember. He was singled out as the culprit, arrested, and eventually convicted. The other guys walked. Cupcake was sentenced to time served, restitution, and 500 hours of community service. Billy had learned of Cupcake's community service while hanging out on the patio with the other salesmen one day waiting for an up. Billy noticed that Cupcake was nervous. Cupcake shared with the group that he had a court date later that afternoon and he was worried about going to jail. He'd had two years to perform the community service but hadn't completed even a single hour. So Cupcake had spent the morning - before heading to court later that afternoon - seeking legal advice from the sales staff. It didn't make much sense, but many things that Cupcake did failed to make sense. At 11:30 he drove off the lot and bets were made all around as to whether he would return later on. Billy's money was on Cupcake. When Cupcake returned at 3:45 he was all smiles. He had been given a reprieve. He'd been given another two years to complete his community service requirement. Billy collected his $20 from Gatewood and listened to Cupcake give the blow by blow of his court appearance. Apparently, according to Cupcake, the judge, who was female, had actually hit on him.

"Hey Cupcake," Gatewood asked from across the patio and loud enough for most of the people on the lot to hear, "What color is the sky in your world?"

Everyone laughed. Some were laughing with Cupcake and some were laughing at him. Billy laughed too but he wasn't sure which category he was in. Maybe both. Billy liked Cupcake. He actually liked him quite a bit. He liked him but he knew that Cupcake was his mark.

****

Rosalie woke up around 5:30 without the aid of an alarm. She got up and dressed quietly so she wouldn't disturb Jimmy Dale and was out the door in five minutes. She had about eight minutes of quiet introspection on the drive back to her mother's and her mind drifted. She already had one ex locked up in Huntsville and wasn't real keen about adding another to the list. She thought about the day of Charlie's trial. She remembered Charlie's explanation of the crime and how he had walked into a Stop N Go in Gonzales, Texas and stuck a .45 in the clerk's face. He had told the judge that he was beside himself with grief over an argument with Rosalie. Rosalie had noticed that the judge – a very average looking middle-aged man with a receding hair line – had glanced at her when Charlie made mention of her name. It seemed to her that the judge understood how Charlie could feel remorse at upsetting such a beautiful creature such as herself. And she sensed that the judge had been lenient on Charlie because of it. All this was conveyed to Rosalie in the space of one second of eye contact with the judge. It wasn't much time, but Rosalie didn't need much time. She had keen instincts and could tell what a man was thinking when he looked at her.

Surprisingly, the public defender assigned to Charlie's case hadn't been smitten with Rosalie at all. Rosalie remembered that he'd had bad breath and bad shoes. But his legal advice had seemed sound to Charlie so he took the counselor's recommendation that he accept the plea deal being offered. That choice broke a really long string of really bad decisions; the final result of which was that Charlie was now a convicted felon and in the process of serving seven years at the Huntsville Unit of the Texas State Correctional System.

And then her thoughts shifted to the current man in her life. Rosalie liked being with Jimmy Dale. There was hope for him and she could see that. He could work hard when he put his mind to it, treated her as well as his means allowed, although it wasn't much, and was a good father figure to Zack. Jimmy Dale took Zack fishing once a week or so and Jimmy Dale had even taken to throwing the football to him and teaching him how to catch. Rosalie had been especially encouraged when Jimmy Dale asked her to enroll Zack in the little league football program. She could see that he was taking an interest in the boy all on his own. She didn't even need to prod him. She hoped that he might ask her to get married sometime soon but she was willing to wait.

But now Jimmy Dale was taking a big step...one with serious consequences and she was worried that she wasn't worried. He was making the move from small time hood to full time dope dealer. If caught, he would go away for a long time just like Charlie. She didn't want that. She did want him to be happy and to be a good provider for her and Zack. And right now Jimmy Dale wasn't living up to that standard. So she reconciled herself to the fact that she wanted this for him as much as for her and she started to pray. She prayed to God that He would protect Jimmy Dale from the men that he was involved with and that no further harm would come to him. She prayed that despite the nature of his activities, that they would be prosperous. And she prayed for her family members and for her ex in prison. She worked her way down the line beginning with those closest to her and ending with her employers and Zack's day school teacher who she'd heard had been sick. By then she was in the drive way at her mother's and as she walked toward the door in the morning twilight she felt peace.

****

Jimmy Dale slept until 8:00. He occupied himself with tidying up the trailer until 9:30 and then decided to place the call. Like most people in the 21st century he didn't remember phone numbers – the phone did that – so he highlighted Larry's name and hit the *DIAL* button. The greeting on the voice mail was anonymous with a female voice repeating the number and inviting him to leave a message but he decided against it. Within a minute the phone rang back and Jimmy Dale could see it was someone at Larry's number calling him back.

"This is Jimmy Dale." He hoped that the person on the other end might recognize his voice or his name.

"Uh, yeah, I just received a call from this number." The words themselves did not fit the manner in which they were delivered. The speaker was unused to using proper English. The words were ill-fitting, like a suit on an adolescent boy at a funeral. Jimmy Dale looked past it. He had to. Dealing with morons was a fact of life.

"Hello, am I speaking with Larry?" Jimmy Dale asked.

"Whoozis?"

"Larry this is Jimmy Dale Klein. I rewired the lights in your building last summer." Jimmy Dale paused, searching for some hint of recognition, but none was forthcoming.

"You told me to call if I could ever use your services." Again Jimmy Dale paused waiting 20 seconds before he spoke again.

"It was about that thing…" This time Jimmy Dale waited for a response.

"My lights?" Larry asked not yet grasping the nature of the call.

"Yeah, the lights in your building. I did ya'll's unit and all the units on the 6th floor on up through the 12th floor. You remember? I was there around June time. I saw you and your buddies there in the courtyard a couple of times and we talked about stuff."

"Yeah…yeah…the lights…that's right…the white dude…from Texas. Yeah I remember you now. Yeah man what's up?"

"Well we talked about putting a deal together. You remember?"

"Yeah. I remember."

"Well I'm interested. I got somethin' cookin' down here and I thought I might head up your way in three or four weeks if that's cool with you."

"Yeah man, it's cool. How much we talkin' 'bout here?"

"Just one to start with. I want to make sure everybody can deliver on their promises."

"Yeah man I'll deliver. I always deliver." Larry laughed. He warmed up to Jimmy Dale considerably once he realized who he was. "I need good shit though man, y'know what I'm sayin'?"

"It's alright. I got my end under control. I just wanted to make sure the number still worked. You might've been in prison or something. Might've been out of business."

"Yeah man, I'm in business awright."

"Alright. I'll call you in three or four weeks. Remember who I am next time."

"Awright man, awright."

Jimmy Dale hung up the phone and felt good about things. No disasters thus far.

****

The letter showed up at the used car lot on Thursday afternoon. The receptionist held out the envelope for Billy without taking her ear off the phone. Billy was surprised. He'd never received a letter at the car lot before. He glanced quickly at the front taking note that it was indeed addressed to him and that it lacked a return address. He opened it immediately.

Billy,

I know that you are stealing IDs. I will not turn you in to the authorities if you pay me. Put $1,000 in a sealed envelope. At 12:00 on Friday, go to the Red Barn restaurant on Cimarron one mile west of the car lot. Walk up to the counter and order a drink to go. Do not stay for lunch. As you are walking out, by the door, there is a trash can on the right. Drop the envelope in the trash can and leave. I'll be watching you.

A Friend

Billy was scared now and remorse rushed over him. He wasn't cut out for criminal activity. He was a salesman who'd had trouble making ends meet. That was all. How he wished he could go back to simply being broke. At least he had a great wife and kids and his worries didn't extend beyond the financial. Billy cussed himself, then God, then his blackmailer. Then he cussed himself again. He couldn't work so he told the receptionist he was taking a long lunch. He drove to an abandoned warehouse several blocks away and sat in the truck under the shade of a pecan tree in the parking lot. He felt like crying but he couldn't do it.

CHAPTER 10

Nearly two weeks had elapsed since Jimmy Dale had last set foot on Mexican soil. He had spent this time getting equipment together and thinking. He'd buy something at the hardware store or off the internet and then he'd set it on the coffee table and look at it and think. He'd think about whether he could put it to good use. Sometimes he'd decide that he couldn't use it and he'd take it back or send it back. Sometimes he'd take what he'd bought and try it out in the back yard. He'd shoot it or wrap it or drop it or whatever it was that this particular thing was supposed to do. And he'd make a determination if he could actually use it or not. It was Friday afternoon and he needed to be in Mexico that next morning to complete his transaction with Chavo. He made his final preparations that evening and left at dawn just like the last trip. Since the last trip had been a success, he decided he would duplicate his stops. He stopped at the same convenience store west of San Antonio, and then again, once he got into Del Rio, at Humberto's. He stopped at the Motel 6, but 9:30 was too early to check in so he decided to take a drive down to the river.

Jimmy Dale took a left on Highway 277 heading south. He drove two or three miles until he came upon a lightly used track that seemed a like a good candidate and made a right. Within a couple hundred yards he found himself paralleling the river as it meandered south. Jimmy Dale drove past one of the specially equipped, white and green Yukons used by the Border Patrol. Jimmy Dale exchanged a wave with the agent that was more an acknowledgement of each other's existence than it was a greeting. Jimmy Dale drove on for another twenty minutes and passed one other Border Patrol agent in that stretch. At this point, Jimmy Dale felt as if he had a decent feel for the place and he was happy with it. He got out, walked down to the river and stood on a rocky beach. He looked across the river at the road and the shanties on the other side. The US side of the river at the point where he stood was genuinely rural. The Mexican side was a lightly populated barrio. Jimmy Dale sat on his haunches, his gaze fixed on the boulders, cinder block walls, and tall weeds on the Mexican side of the river. *Yes,* he thought to himself, *I think this will work.* His curiosity satisfied and his fears put to rest, Jimmy Dale got up and returned to the truck. He drove back up the road until he came upon the border patrol agent he had first seen. He got out and approached the agent.

"Is it ok to fish down here?" Jimmy Dale asked the agent.

"It's a free country," the agent responded.

"Is there ever anyone down here fishing? I didn't see anyone out here today."

"There's guys down here every now and then," The border agent answered.

"Alright then. I'll see you around."

Jimmy Dale got back in the GMC and drove back to the Motel 6. It was 11:00 and the proprietor said that there was a room that he could make available. Jimmy Dale checked in then headed to Mexico. The lines at the bridge were short and he was over quickly. Once in Acuña he took a left on Libramiento and more or less mirrored his drive down the river from when he was on the Texas side. After a few wrong turns, he came finally to the spot he had spied from across the river three hours earlier. Surveying the area from the Mexican perspective it began to dawn on Jimmy Dale that his plan might actually work. In his mind he dubbed the location Cape Canaveral.

By now Jimmy Dale was getting to know his way around Acuña and was able to make his way back to the square where he had spent so much time two weeks earlier. He parked a block off the square and walked to the Café de los Toros and then past it to a small curio shop two doors down. He bought a picture frame and a pair of baby shoes asking the clerk to put the items in a bag. The bag was feminine, with white and blue vertical stripes and sturdy looped handles on each side; it looked like something Rosalie might take to a baby shower. He took the bag and its contents to the men's restroom at the Café. He locked the door and pushed back the ceiling tile above the urinal. In the space between the ceiling and the roof he placed the picture frame, the baby shoes, and $4,000 cash. He folded the bag with the stripes and the sturdy loops and put it in his hip pocket. Then he walked across the street that formed the Eastern boundary to the square to a pay phone and made the call. He pulled the card from his wallet and pushed the buttons after dropping the coins in the slot.

"Bueno," Chavo's voice came back. The connection was slightly tinny. Not like the pay phones in the U.S.

"Hello Chavo. This is Jimmy Dale. How you been?"

"Hello my friend. I was hoping to hear from you today. Are we prepared to complete our transaction?" Chavo asked.

"Yeah. I think we are. I have the money if you have the product."

"The product is available. I can meet you any time that you like," Chavo answered.

"To be clear: I will give you $2,000 in cash and you will give me one kilo of cocaine. It will be you and you alone. That was the agreement." Jimmy Dale didn't trust the Mexican and tried his best to forestall any attempt by Chavo to change the agreement and then plead ignorance.

"I told you I would inquire for you Jimmy. That was what I agreed to."

"And when you made that inquiry what did he say? Jimmy Dale knew that Chavo had never agreed to the price. Not that it mattered. Even if he had a renegotiation would still have taken place.

"I can provide the product for $3,000."

"That's $1,000 more than I agreed to Chavo!" Jimmy Dale knew that three grand was a decent price and allowed plenty of room for him to make money. He actually had been prepared to go higher but he protested anyway to prevent Chavo from bargaining for more.

"I can pick you up in one hour if you like," Chavo said assuming that there would be no further argument.

"You're not picking me up anywhere. I'll meet you at the Café de los Toros on the square. There is an outdoor seating area. I'll be there in one hour. And come alone Chavo. Don't bring any of your friends. I really don't get along too good with those guys."

"I'll see you in an hour," Chavo said and hung up the phone.

****

Billy was worried. He had prepared himself for the fact that one day he would probably get caught. But that acceptance of the inevitable was based on the premise that it would be the authorities that would catch him. He had never considered the fact that another person might discover his activities and attempt to blackmail him. A blackmailer was much more difficult to deal with than law enforcement because a blackmailer had the dual advantages of anonymity and lawlessness. All this was tempered by the fact that a blackmailer had no legal authority and could not take any official action against him – like imprisonment. Still, a blackmailer was a very big problem. His knowledge of Billy's activities and his willingness to make that knowledge known to the authorities could determine whether Billy went to prison or not. Which brought to mind an entirely separate option - what if the authorities did find out? Would he go to prison? Was it for certain? Maybe not. This was, after all, his first offense. Billy's mind was racing. He tried repeatedly to calm himself by reasoning out the situation. Surely, given the facts as they are, one best course of action could be decided upon. And so Billy began the process again of working through his options. But one supposition led inevitably to a required action that in turn led to another required action that ultimately led to some required action that would invalidate the original supposition. And in this way, Billy's mind continued to churn; it was like an engine running wild at 5,000 RPMs.

On Friday, at 20 minutes before noon, Billy sat at this desk at the car lot with a blank piece of paper in front of him. He picked up the pen and allowed the words to flow out on to the paper:

> *You are blackmailing the wrong person. I am not involved in the ID theft ring. But I know who is. His name is Stephen Gorman.*

Billy put the paper in an envelope and drove to the Red Rooster. He parked and went inside. He ordered a sweet tea at the counter and then left. As he walked out the door he dropped the envelope with the note in the trash can.

****

After Jimmy Dale hung up the phone he moved quickly back across the street and walked calmly into the café. He placed the empty blue and white bag on the table, ordered lemonade from the waiter, and then sipped it casually while he waited. He wondered if he was being watched. It was unlikely, but it was possible that Chavo had been in the square when Jimmy Dale had placed the call and had him under surveillance since he entered the café. So with his sunglasses concealing the direction of his gaze, he scanned the square.

Nearly an hour later Chavo skipped across the square and gave Jimmy Dale an almost imperceptible nod as he crossed the street. He was wearing what he normally wore: black cowboy boots, jeans, a tight t-shirt and a black cowboy hat. He approached the table with a smile, grabbed Jimmy Dale and pulled him close when Jimmy Dale rose to greet him. Jimmy Dale was actually glad to see him. He didn't really know what it was that he liked about Chavo, but he knew that he had grown to like him at least a little bit.

"It is good to see you once again my friend."

"It's good to see you too," Jimmy Dale said smiling.

"It will be a good day for us today, no?"

"I believe it will be. You came alone. Right?" Jimmy Dale decided it was best to address the point directly with Chavo and be able to search his surroundings without trying to sneak glances. As he spoke to Chavo he overtly scanned the square again looking for a sign, a sign that something was not as it should be.

"I am alone as promised. And I have the product. You have the money. Is that right?"

"I do."

"It is here with you? Right now."

"It is."

"Then let me see it."

"Hand me the product. I will go to the bathroom to check the purity. There is no other way out of the building. You can go first to check it out if you like. And when I come back you will have the money. I'm sure you have people watching me now anyway. There's no way I could actually escape if I decided to run."

Chavo hesitated a moment and then said, "Aqui esta." He handed Jimmy Dale a package bundled tightly with tape and brown kraft paper

"A little obvious don't you think?" Jimmy Dale said to Chavo referring to the fact the package was sitting right there in the open. Jimmy Dale took the package and placed it in the blue and white bag with the sturdy handles that the clerk had given him at the curios shop and headed for the men's room. He cut open a tiny slit in the kraft paper and the plastic lining underneath, sticking his moist pinky in and withdrawing a small amount of the fine powder. He tasted it. It was pure. Jimmy Dale took a quick inventory of his possessions before leaving the men's room and returning to the table in the dining room.

"I got to hand it to you Chavo. The quality of this delivery is pretty good. Here's your money." Jimmy Dale said pushing an envelope across the table toward Chavo. "There are 30 $100 bills inside."

Chavo retrieved the envelope and thumbed the bills keeping everything below the level of the table top. Apparently satisfied, he put the envelope in his shirt pocket. Jimmy Dale was surprised that Chavo was so casual with the money.

"How are you planning on getting across the river and past the check point? It's a difficult task. You have a plan?" Chavo asked.

"Can I call you in a month or so and arrange another buy?" Jimmy Dale replied, ignoring the request for more information about how he was planning on getting the product across the river.

"I will be here."

"Hey Chavo, I got a question for you," Jimmy Dale said taking the stress level down about ten notches. "What's your last name?"

"My last name is Chavo."

"Ok. Then what is your first name?"

"My first name is Chavo."

Chavo smiled at Jimmy Dale. Jimmy Dale had dealt with enough scumbags in his life to know the nature of the smile. When the smile was received Jimmy Dale could see in a glance much of what he already knew about his business partner and adversary. Jimmy Dale could see that Chavo wasn't incredibly bright, but also that his mind was very finely sharpened in the ways of criminal manipulation. Jimmy Dale could see that Chavo had no honor – only motivation - motivation to gain the advantage on every person that he came into contact with. If a normal person were able to perform the Vulcan mind meld on Chavo, they would be surprised at the lack of some very basic qualities: qualities like conscience, sympathy, or mercy. An average person might wonder how anyone could be that unfeeling, that averse to the sufferings of others. The problem with asking a question like that is that it implies choice. It was true that Chavo possessed the capacity to choose. And that anytime over the last 20 years he could have made the choice to abandon his rapacious lifestyle and seek reputable employment. But a choice like that would have been so far outside his natural way, so counter to his genetic make-up that the effort required to make such a choice would've had to have been truly monumental. Chavo was genetically predisposed to predation and the forces that compelled him to make the choices that he did were, for the most part, simply out of his control.

Jimmy Dale accepted the smile from Chavo. A smile that said so much to someone that was able to read it. He returned the smile in kind.

****

Neal needed to take off on Friday from his job at the Wild Snail. Fridays were generally pretty busy and Frank wasn't real happy about it so they compromised and Neal agreed to work 4:00 to 7:00 during the busy time but would have off during the day. That was fine with Neal. All he needed was a few hours around mid-day. Thursday evening Neal had scoped out the Red Rooster pretty thoroughly. He needed a concealed place to observe the entrance of the restaurant without fear of being found out. There were two or three good options but he finally decided on the apartment complex parking lot about 150 yards to the northwest. There was a large vacant lot catty-corner to the Red Rooster and the apartments were adjacent to that vacant lot so that the parking lot at the apartments provided a clear view of the Red Rooster once you got past the eight foot shrubs that bounded the property. Neal parked his Grand Cherokee in the parking lot behind the shrubs and could barely make out the restaurant through the greenery. He took out the clippers and cut a four inch square hole that yielded a clean line of sight and noted with satisfaction that with the aid of the Bushnell 8x26 binoculars he could read the fine print on the OPEN sign that hung on the front door.

At 11:00 the next morning Neal returned to the apartment complex to take up his vigil. The spot he had prepared the night before was unoccupied so he pulled in and parked. The night before that side of the parking lot had been fairly deserted and it hadn't occurred to him that someone might park there during the night and occupy his point of surveillance. He realized it now, though, and felt lucky that it was unoccupied. Then he waited. Every ten minutes or so he pulled out the binoculars and refocused. He committed the hours on the OPEN sign and the warnings listed on the PARKING FOR CUSTOMERS OF THE RED ROOSTER CAFÉ sign to memory. At 11:55 Neal saw Billy pull in to the parking lot. Neal crouched down so that just his eyes and binoculars were above the dash of the Jeep Grand Cherokee, like a hippo or an alligator. He saw Billy walk inside and then exit the restaurant two minutes later with what appeared to be a sweet tea. On his way to the car, Billy dropped an envelope in the trash can and drove off.

Neal sat and watched the trash can. It was surreal. Every five minutes he would look up and down the street and check for anyone that might be watching him watch the trash can. Neal watched the trash can for two hours. Nothing. Finally, at 2:06, Neal decided to check it out. Should he drive the 150 yards to the restaurant or should he walk? It occurred to him that Billy could very well be watching the trash can right this minute. Neal hadn't thought about that. So he dialed the number to the dealership and asked for Billy. The receptionist mentioned off hand that she thought she had seen him come back from lunch and Neal felt some relief. He hung up when Billy picked up at the other end after a long hold. Neal started the Jeep, drove to the Red Rooster, parked and walked across the parking lot to the trash can. He lifted the lid and retrieved a plain white envelope sitting on top of a half eaten bacon and egg taco. As he walked back across the parking lot with the envelope Neal thought about how Billy could have someone else watching the trash can. He suddenly felt like a hack, which of course, he was. Neal headed off in no particular direction other than away and opened the envelope. Who in the hell is Stephen Gorman? Now what? The sense of amateurism crept up on him again.

CHAPTER 11

"Ok Chavo, I'll talk to you later," Jimmy Dale said laughing quietly to himself and rising from the chair.

"Bueno suerte," Chavo said.

The unlikely duo shook hands with each man headed in a different direction when they exited the café. Chavo crossed the street in front of the café and walked back into the square. Jimmy Dale headed around the corner and down a street that took him away from the square. He was walking quickly but not so quick as to draw attention to himself. Halfway down the block he heard shouts to his rear.

"Alto. Guero. Alto. Alto."

Jimmy Dale turned and saw three shabbily dressed policemen apparently engaged in a low speed, pedestrian pursuit. The cop that appeared to be in charge was wearing a khaki uniform with a hat and no tie. He was yelling at Jimmy Dale to stop. The other two were very skinny and had similar uniforms except that they were short sleeve. Neither of the two skinny cops were wearing a hat and one was wearing a black tie. They all had badges prominently affixed to their chests and they all had guns. Jimmy

Dale gave a fleeting thought to attempting an escape but decided against it. He stopped and waited for the policemen to catch up to him. The hatted one in the lead spoke to him in rapid Spanish as he came within normal speaking distance. Jimmy Dale was unable to follow the commands. The only thing that Jimmy Dale was able to discern with any certainty was that they were indeed commands.

"¿Mande?" Jimmy Dale responded, and asking in Spanish for the cop to repeat himself.

"¿Que tienes aca?" the lead cop asked.

"Do you mean the bag?" Jimmy Dale asked back.

"Si. ¿Que tienes?" The cop motioned toward the bag.

"It's just a bag," Jimmy Dale answered.

"Damelo," the cop said sticking his hand out palm upwards and curling his fingers back quickly and repeatedly. Jimmy Dale recognized the universal hand-signal for *give it to me a*nd handed him the bag. The cop opened it and saw the picture frame and baby shoes.

"Es para mi nino," Jimmy Dale explained.

The cop locked eyes with Jimmy Dale questioning him without saying it; he was wondering where the drugs were.

Jimmy Dale stared back. He fought back the urge to smile. The other two policemen flanked their leader. They were behind him and on either side. The cop on the left, the one with no hat and no tie, broke the stalemate.

"Arrest," he said. He had his hands in his pocket and was looking into the distance at something unknown, probably not even known to him.

Jimmy Dale looked at the hatless, tieless Mexican policeman that had just spoken and wondered what in the world was going on. Nobody said anything for 15 seconds and finally Jimmy Dale looked back to the cop in charge.

"Handcuffs," said the same Mexican cop that had spoken before. He had the feeling that the Mexican was unsure of himself and he wondered if the young man even knew the meaning of the words or if he was simply repeating sounds committed to memory.

"What are you talking about?" Jimmy Dale asked.

The cop that had spoken the one word command kept his eyes fixed on some point above the horizon looking over Jimmy Dale's left shoulder.

"¿Que me dices?" Jimmy Dale tried again thinking an attempt at Spanish might help.

Hearing the Spanish language, the cop's eyes darted to the left and met Jimmy Dale's eyes for just a moment only to move quickly back to that same far off point. Jimmy Dale had the feeling that the young policeman was embarrassed in some way.

"Arrest," the cop said again with the same monotone delivery. And again the awkward pause.

"Are you saying you are going to arrest me?" Jimmy Dale asked the group as a whole.

"Si," the lead cop replied and handed him back the bag.

The young policeman that specialized in one word sentences went mute but continued his vigil on that enigmatic point on the horizon.

"What's the charge? ¿Por Que?" Jimmy Dale inquired.

Jimmy Dale wondered if he was being subjected to a run-of-the-mill shakedown unrelated to the cocaine. It was difficult to know for sure. But regardless of their original intent, it appeared now that the trio was simply looking for a bribe. At least Jimmy Dale hoped that was the case.

"¿Que necesito hacer?" Jimmy Dale asked trying to get the policemen to verbalize what it was that they wanted him to do.

But nothing. They continued to stare at him. Jimmy Dale decided to take it a step further and prompt them.

He couldn't think of the Spanish word for *fine*. So he inquired in Spanglish, "¿Necesito a pagar un fine?"

"Si. Un Fine." Apparently the policeman in charge was familiar with this English word. He didn't seem to know how to say *hello*. But he did know the word *fine*.

"¿Cuantos?" Jimmy Dale inquired. He just wanted to get out of there.

"Cien dolares."

They were asking for a hundred dollars. Jimmy Dale took out his wallet and showed his tormentors the contents: three twenties and a ten. The lead policeman gave Jimmy Dale the gimme sign again with this hand and Jimmy Dale handed over the whole amount. The cops divided it amongst themselves with El Jefe receiving the lion's share. For the fifth or sixth time they all stood looking at each other wondering what was going to happen next. It went through Jimmy Dale's mind that they seemed somewhat inept at the process. Jimmy Dale waved both hands back and forth with palms facing outward to signify a close to this session of blackmail and then turned and walked away. He resisted the temptation to turn to see if he was being followed. But when he made a right turn at the next intersection he managed to sneak a sidelong glance. The recently compromised law enforcement officials were standing and discussing something among themselves. God only knows what they were talking about.

Jimmy Dale was one block away from the back entrance to the Café de los Toros and walked quickly in that direction passing the Café and entering a different restaurant that was just a little farther down. Like the Café de los Toros and most of the restaurants in Acuña, the Café Gomez had an outdoor patio area that was suitable for surveillance. He took a seat somewhat behind a supporting pillar and ordered a Modelo. He maintained a constant vigil on the street and on the back door to the Café de los Toros. No one was following him. Every five to ten minutes a busboy would open the back door and throw out a bucket of water or some trash. Finally, with no sign of the bungling Acuña police force, or of Chavo, Jimmy Dale took some of his remaining money, $10 from his right sock, and left it on the table. He crossed the street slowly and approached the back door of the Café de los Toros. He was 15 feet from the door when it began to open. He took a $50 bill from his left sock and approached the busboy.

"El baño…el baño…por favor…el baño. Es un emergencia." Jimmy Dale said to the busboy.

He showed the busboy the fifty and with hand signals and body language made it apparent to the young man that he needed to use the bathroom and that the boy would be paid handsomely for allowing him in. The busboy was astonished at his good fortune and ushered Jimmy Dale through the kitchen, through a swinging door, and across one corner of the dining room before entering the narrow hallway leading to the bathrooms. Jimmy Dale glanced out across the dining room and on to the patio. At his table, the very one where he had been seated with Chavo 45 minutes earlier, he saw Chavo sitting quite amicably with the three policemen.

I thought so, Jimmy Dale said to himself.

****

Chavo wasn't happy with his crime fighting buddies at all. He had watched from a distance their interaction with Jimmy Dale and had seen them bested by the American. Unable to recognize that in fact the opposite was true – that Chavo himself had indeed been bested – led to the amplification of the facts as they supported Chavo's position and a complete dismissal of any evidence that pointed toward Chavo's role in Jimmy Dale escaping the trap unscathed.

It was true that the three policemen were lazy and they just didn't seem to try very hard. They had given up pretty easily when confronting Jimmy Dale outside the cafe. But then again, they had applied for and been accepted into the Acuña Police Department. The majority of the men on the force sought the position out not because of an innate desire to help their fellow man by enforcing the laws and statutes of the Mexican nation, the state of Coahuila, or the city of Acuña, but rather because it offered the opportunity to collect a paycheck with very little effort besides observing the comings and goings of the denizens of Acuña. Not to mention the steady stream of Americans from which the occasional unlucky soul was plucked to be accused of some imaginary crime; the penalty for which was generally a fine to be paid on the spot in cash and which was ironically almost always equal to the exact amount the alleged offender had in his pocket.

No, Chavo wasn't pleased with his buddies at all. But he had to admit that Jimmy Dale was smart. To be that forward thinking, that insightful, that he managed to slither through the shakedown without repercussion was impressive. This American had more sense than Chavo had given him credit for. Chavo knew that Jimmy Dale was unlikely to consider his interaction with incompetent police mere coincidence, which created another problem in that Jimmy Dale had now been alerted to the fact that he was probably a target. A criminal was hesitant to write anything off as coincidence. And in the criminal mind, as the stakes climbed, the probability of a coincidence fell proportionally until they reached zero.

****

Jimmy Dale was only in the dining room for a second, maybe two, and was lucky enough to escape detection. The busboy that had let Jimmy Dale in through the back door under the pretense that he was experiencing a restroom emergency showed him directly to the nearest restroom. The sign on the door read *Las Damas*. Uh oh.

"Pero soy un hombre," Jimmy Dale said.

Jimmy Dale attempted to explain his unwillingness to use the lady's rest room even when beset by an emergency necessitating a bribe of $50. He realized the absurdity of his objection. The inconsistency was underscored when he handed the busboy the money.

"Esta occupado," the busboy said explaining that the men's room was occupied. The busboy's response was accompanied by a puzzled look. At just this time the door to the men's room opened and an older Mexican gentleman exited.

"Gracias," Jimmy Dale said to the busboy as he squeezed past him in the hallway, slipping into the men's room and locking the door behind him.

Jimmy Dale stood on the toilet and lifted the ceiling tile directly above him and from the opening retrieved the cocaine. He placed it in the bag and went out the way he had come in: through the hall and across that corner of the dining room and then through the kitchen. Jimmy Dale glanced once again in the direction of the table he had been seated at earlier. Chavo and the cops were talking but never looked in his direction. Jimmy Dale had needed to take a chance that one of his adversaries might spot him but it didn't happen. Once outside he jumped in the truck and set the coke on the seat next to him. It was in the bag and the bag was in plain sight. There really wasn't any use in hiding it. If he was stopped now, he was in trouble anyway.

Jimmy Dale drove down Libramiento to Cape Canaveral. As he passed the spot he slowed down and looked quickly across the river. He saw the border patrol sitting there. Jimmy Dale could make out the form of a large man with his hands to his face and elbows out as if he were holding binoculars. It looked as if he might actually be looking directly at Jimmy Dale, which he probably was. The scene across the river from the Texas side can be a little mundane and the appearance of an American in an American vehicle can draw the eye. Jimmy Dale was aware of this so he didn't stop, but instead drove past slowly and disappeared from view. Once obscured by houses and brush he rolled to a stop and surveyed his surroundings. He took the package of cocaine and placed it under the seat. The economic condition of the families in the area was such that children were tempted to steal almost anything they could get their hands on, no matter how cheap or worthless the item. He didn't want to tempt anyone. Out of sight, out of mind was the best policy.

As was the case with almost every city block in Acuña, an eating or drinking establishment was nearby with tables available outside on the sidewalk. Jimmy Dale sat and quickly took inventory. It seemed to be ideal. His truck with the merchandise was 20 feet away and from his vantage point behind the brush he could just see the top corner of the border patrol agent's vehicle. It'd be dark soon and when the agent moved along, Jimmy Dale would be free to make his move. He was hungry so he ordered a plate of puffy tacos and lemonade.

It was dark in an hour and an hour after that Jimmy Dale saw the lights of the vehicle across the river switch on. He moved across the street to get a better look, squatting among some low bushes. He saw the brake lights illuminate and then the white lights indicating that the SUV was being placed in reverse. The agent backed up about ten feet to the road then headed north along the river road toward Del Rio. Jimmy Dale watched him until he was out of sight then watched another five minutes more to be sure. When he was satisfied that all was quiet he walked back to the truck to get the cocaine and the air gun. The air gun and the other miscellaneous supplies were in a duffel bag and he added the cocaine to the contents of the duffel so he'd only have a single bag to carry. Duffel bag in hand, he returned to the spot where he had been squatting and then descended the embankment toward the river. He reached a spot near the water's edge that was still well hidden and took a seat. He scanned his surroundings. He was about ten feet from the river, maybe forty feet from the opposite river bank, and sixty to sixty-five feet from the brush on the Texas side.

He took the air gun from the duffel and attached the CO2 cartridge. He checked the gauge and found the cartridge to be fully pressurized. Based on his practice sessions back in Seguin, Jimmy Dale knew that he had probably 20-25 shots when starting with a full tank. He knew he wouldn't need anywhere near that many – maybe four or five. He then took the kilo of cocaine and began to subdivide it into smaller baggies of about a half pound each. He ended up with five smaller baggies and once they were sealed up, he wrapped them completely in duct tape to prevent them from tearing. He then wrapped each of them again in the remnants of an olive colored t-shirt and secured the cloth surrounding the baggie with string. The gun was intended to be used as a t-shirt launcher at sporting events and the rags allowed for easier loading and firing. They also served as camouflage once the product had landed in the brush on the Texas side. All systems were go.

There was a set of train tracks that ran behind the restaurant where Jimmy Dale had kept vigil. He had noticed that trains passed by about every 15 minutes so he decided to wait; a passing train would provide excellent background noise to muffle the sound of the air gun. When discharged, the air gun did not produce a report anywhere near as concussive as a regular firearm but there was a noticeable pop when the package exited the end of the barrel and the pressure from the gun was released. So he waited. The gun was loaded and Jimmy Dale was ready. After a couple of minutes a train rumbled by. He decided the time was right and blasted his first shipment of coke through the air and onto U.S. soil. Luckily the train was a pretty long one and its passing allowed enough time to load and fire all five parcels. Each package landed quietly and inconspicuously in the weeds pretty much right where he had planned. The practice sessions had paid off.

Jimmy Dale kept an eye on the opposite bank as he loaded up his limited inventory of equipment. He put the air gun in the duffle bag and the trash from his repacking of the cocaine, along with the gloves, in a separate bag. He threw the duffle bag in the bed of the truck and the trash bag in a storm drain. In a few minutes he found himself entering a very long line at the international bridge. Forty-five minutes later he found himself exiting that same line. He affirmed his U.S. citizenship to both the guard and the German Shepherd and then made his way to Humberto's Ice House. He was glad to see that Humberto carried live bait. It just made it easier – he didn't want to have to go to Walmart. He grabbed a 12 count of night crawlers, a taco, and a soda water and paid Humberto the $6.13 he owed him.

Jimmy Dale then drove to the point on the Texas side that was directly across from Cape Canaveral. He grabbed his fishing pole, tackle box, night crawlers, taco, and soda water and walked down to the river. Since he knew where to look and what to look for, he easily spotted the five parcels despite the darkness. He continued walking past the parcels without changing stride or looking in either direction. He took a seat on a rock on the bank, baited his hook, and dropped the line in the water. Then he picked up his tackle box and started walking back to the truck. Jimmy Dale pretended to gather stray grass hoppers for bait as he gathered the packages with the cocaine. He wasn't completely pretending. He actually caught two or three of the bugs and was happy to have them. If a border patrol agent came by for a visit it would help complete the illusion that he was fishing. He put his merchandise in a bucket in the back of the truck and covered it with the lid. Then he went back to the river to tend to his fishing pole. If there was someone watching, it might look suspicious if he left quickly and he didn't want to raise suspicion so he stayed about thirty minutes and fished. He had several nibbles but never hooked anything and he'd worked through an entire box of worms after thirty minutes anyway, so he left.

CHAPTER 12

The next morning Jimmy Dale went directly to the Aztec Tool Rental shop and rented an arc welder. He told the guy that wrote the ticket that he just needed to weld a hitch on the back of his truck and asked if it was ok if he just took care of it in the parking lot. The manager stepped up and gave him permission to weld on site but asked that he use the back storage lot. So Jimmy Dale pulled the truck around back and parked next to the welder they had pulled from their inventory. He laid the prefabricated metal tube on the ground behind the truck right next to the hitch that he would use as his cover in case anyone walked up. The tube was about a foot long and had a diameter of about three inches. One end had already been welded shut. The other end was open. Jimmy Dale placed the drugs in the tube and then an inch or two of fire resistant insulation between the drugs and the open end. He positioned the metal cap over the open end and then welded the tube shut. He left the arc welder where it sat and waved at the manager when he pulled out of the parking lot.

Back at the motel he got ready for the trip back to Seguin. He packed quickly and threw the metal tube with the drugs in the tackle box and checked out. He drove a mile or two east on Highway 90. On the right hand side of the highway just a little past Humberto's was the Kountry Kitchen Restaurant. It was a large establishment and had a modest crowd even in the middle of the afternoon. He took a booth on the western side of the room and sat facing north. From his seat he could see out the windows and keep an eye on the activity in the L shaped gravel parking lot that was adjacent to Highway 90 and along the western side of the building towards the back of the property. He placed his order with the waitress for the #2 dinner and began his vigil.

The #2 arrived and Jimmy Dale was pleasantly surprised – meatloaf with gravy and a couple of sides. He watched the parking lot while he ate. Every few minutes another vehicle would arrive but the demographic was never quite right. As he ate, Jimmy Dale thought about how he came to arrive at this particular place at this particular point in time and engaged in this particular activity. There had been so many choices available to him. What had led him to make the choices that he made? Were they even choices? Jimmy Dale wondered about how much of everything was predestination. Was his whole life laid out for him before he was even born and his body was merely the vehicle in which he was destined to move through these preordained events? This seemed unlikely. He believed in free will. Jimmy Dale had spent many hours pondering and he always came to the same inevitable conclusion. It's both. Events are preordained but there is also free will. Circumstances and genetic predisposition will always serve to channel one's activities. But even within these sometimes narrow constraints, free will does exist and allows one to make a choice to break free of the path most recently travelled and elect to proceed down a new path. This choice is both a blessing and a curse. Exercising this choice provides reward. Not exercising this choice, but merely being aware that it exists provides peace…the peace that comes with knowing that the reward is there and simply waiting to be claimed. The reward and the peace are the blessing. The curse is knowing that the blessing is there to be claimed, and then delaying the action. It's the same as being overweight for five years and always saying, *tomorrow I will go on a diet*. Well, tomorrow never comes. And right now Jimmy Dale was cursed. After this drug deal, when he had cash in his pocket, he would go on the straight and narrow. But not today.

It was 6:15 when a white F-350 pulled into the parking lot and parked six spots down from Jimmy Dale's GMC. Jimmy Dale first spied the F-350 eastbound on 90 a half block before it arrived at the Kountry Kitchen. With a fifth wheel camper goose necked to the bed of the truck, Jimmy Dale knew it was a good candidate. When he saw the blinker indicating a right hand turn his interest was piqued. A man in his 60s wearing a cowboy hat got out of the truck and accompanied his wife to the front door of the restaurant. They chose a booth on the opposite side of the restaurant from Jimmy Dale. Jimmy Dale was familiar with the undercarriage of the Ford trucks so he knew he had some time. He closed out his bill so he would be ready and then waited for the couple to order and receive their food. When they were halfway through their meal Jimmy Dale made his move.

Jimmy Dale left the restaurant and walked to his truck to gather the package together. He covered the 50-60 feet between his GMC and the F-350 in a few seconds and walked to the opposite side of the Ford so that the body of the truck was between him and the restaurant. He didn't look around. He used his peripheral vision only and when he was alongside the driver side back quarter panel he dropped to the ground and scooted on his back so that he was looking directly up at the C-channel frame of the vehicle. He placed the tube containing the drugs in the upward facing groove of the metal frame. The industrial magnets, purchased a few weeks before for $25 each, secured the metal tube to the frame. There was no way the tube was going anywhere unless manually removed. Next he attached the mobile GPS device next to the tube and crawfished back out from under the truck. There was a man walking nearby and he noticed Jimmy Dale crawling around on the ground but Jimmy Dale played it off. He nodded to the man and fumbled in his pocket for some unknown item in his possession, all the while staying close to the vehicle and giving the impression that he owned the vehicle. When the man had passed, Jimmy Dale returned to the GMC for a system test.

He powered up the hand-held GPS device and allowed the signal to lock. Within a few seconds the complicated jargon of the machine indicated that the remote device was located 57.3 feet

along a line that was three degrees west of due north. With
everything in place, Jimmy Dale walked to the convenience store
next door to use the restroom. He might be in for a long ride and
he wanted to be able to ride in comfort. He didn't want to use the
restroom back in the Kountry Kitchen because the couple might
see him and it might raise suspicion in their minds at some point in
the future should they happen to come into visual contact with
each other. Jimmy Dale waited in the convenience store for the
couple to finish eating. He watched as the man started his truck
and pulled the trailer out on to Highway 90 slowly building to
highway speed. Jimmy Dale was relieved to see the truck head
toward San Antonio and not back towards Del Rio. He had
guessed correctly. The couple were heading home, wherever that
was, after a stay on the border in their camper trailer. Jimmy Dale
stood and watched as the truck and trailer disappeared from view.
The range of the GPS unit was unlimited so he was in no danger of
losing his partners, and he wanted to stay out of visual contact, but
he also wanted to be a few cars back when they rolled through the
federal check point just west of Uvalde. Then when they stopped
on the other side of the check point, he wanted to be close enough
to close in quickly and take back his merchandise. He decided to
give them a ten minute head start.

****

Jack Johnson and his wife, Elsa, were returning from two weeks in
Del Rio. Jack was a retired electrician. He had sold his electrical
contracting business three years ago and now he and Elsa were
enjoying an active retirement. Jack had worked hard for 30 years,
built the business, and acquired some assets here and there: a
modest 401k of around $300,000, two small rent houses, a duplex,
and a small apartment complex off Northwest Military Highway in
San Antonio. They lived in a three bedroom, brick front house on
a cul-de-sac behind the apartment complex. Being an electrician,
Jack was handy and served as his own maintenance man at the
apartments.

Jack and Elsa enjoyed the border country and tried to
come for a couple of weeks three or four times each year. While

they were away, their oldest son, handled the repairs at the apartment complex. When visiting the border, they almost always took their 2004 Montana Keystone Fifth Wheel and they almost always stayed at the Lamplighter RV Park because a couple they were friendly with owned the campground. When returning to San Antonio they almost always stopped at the Kountry Kitchen Café on the outskirts of Del Rio and had the meatloaf. It was nearly 7:00 by the time they had finished their meal and Jack unconsciously scanned his rig as they crossed the parking lot. He had given the camper a pretty good going over before they left the Lamplighter and was comfortable with its road worthiness. After opening the truck door for his wife he climbed in the driver's seat and fired up the diesel engine to head home. The line at the border check station west of Uvalde was longer than usual and the wait added about 15 minutes to what is normally a 2.5 hour drive so they didn't pull into their driveway in San Antonio until nearly 10:00. Jack was ready for bed and left the trailer hitched to the truck. He'd decided to deal with it in the morning.

****

Neal was unsure about how to handle Billy's response to the blackmail attempt. Neal had expected his targets to just lie down. And now he had already hit a snag. Billy wasn't cooperating. The way Neal saw it there were two options: The first option was that Billy was telling the truth. It was possible that this Stephen Gorman person was stealing ID's at Kuykendall Motors. But even if he was, how likely was it that Billy would be aware of it? If Billy knew then either Billy and Stephen were friends and Stephen had confided in Billy, which in turn meant that Billy was still probably involved, which meant that Stephen would probably take Billy down with him or; if Billy and Stephen were not friends, then that meant that the rank and file were privileged to this information and the blackmail might not work because the criminal, whether it was Stephen Gorman or Billy or even somebody else, was about to get busted anyway. The second option was that Billy was lying. This seemed more plausible. It seemed to Neal that Billy's plan was to either confuse his blackmailer so that the blackmailer might simply give up, or, get the blackmailer to actually pursue the false target, in which case the false target would probably not pay. In fact the false target would almost certainly not pay and would, in all likelihood, go to the boss and let them know what was happening. Neal began to see what Billy was attempting to do and came up with what he thought was the correct counter move. He dialed the number for Kuykendall Motors and asked for Billy.

"This is Billy."

"Hello Billy." Neal paused for effect. "This is your friend. How you doing?"

"I'm ok." Billy wanted to take control of the conversation and give his friend the sense that it was useless to talk with him since the real culprit was Cupcake but Billy really didn't know how to do that.

"That was a nice try Billy..." Neal was overusing Billy's first name as a way of reaffirming his superior position in the negotiations. By repeating Billy's name in nearly every sentence Neal was sending a signal to Billy that he could be relaxed and casual in a situation that was anything but casual. "...but I really don't think that this Stephen Gorman fellow is the person down at Kuykendall lifting IDs."

Billy didn't say anything.

"Here's what I need you to do. I need an email address from you. You'll receive instructions from me in a little bit about how to transfer that $1,000 to me. And you're going to need to go ahead and get that done pretty quick Billy. I'm going to need that money within 24 hours or I'm going to let everybody know what's going on down there at Kuykendall Motors. You on board?"

"I'm listening," Billy answered.

"Send me an email to gohorse314@gmail.com. It's spelled just like it sounds. I'll send instructions back to you."

"Got it. Gohorse314@gmail.com. Got it."

Click.

Billy sat with the receiver to his ear for another few seconds then set it down gently. He didn't like what was going on. He was going to have to pay.

****

Jimmy Dale's optimism crept slightly higher when he saw the long line at the check station. This was the last major hurdle in getting the cocaine into the U.S. and the more cars in line, the less chance that the F-350 pulling the fifth wheel would be scrutinized. Not that there was much chance of that anyway. But you never know. There was just a bit of daylight left as Jimmy Dale took his place at the end of the line and he was glad to see that the truck carrying his cocaine as cargo was 10 or 12 vehicles ahead and had not yet passed through the check station. When the truck finally arrived at the front of the line, the border patrol agent appeared to keep the conversation brief and to the point. Jimmy Dale knew what they were being questioned about. He'd been through the drill. *Is everyone in the vehicle an American citizen? Where are ya'll headed to today? A*nd then finally, *Please pull through.*

The border agent on the passenger side was leading a German Shepherd past all the vehicles. The dog gave the truck and the fifth wheel the once over and then backed off about six feet. The dog sat down and looked down the line of waiting vehicles the same way a short order cook might take a break from the grill to glance at a lunchtime crowd coming through the door. The agent conducting the interviews took one step back and waved the Ford with the travel trailer through. Jimmy Dale noticed that he didn't feel relieved. To be relieved he would've had to have been worried in the first place and he wasn't. He had expected the operation to work and it had. Now all he had to do was follow the trailer on to its destination and retrieve his stash.

As he headed east, Jimmy Dale would pull over every 30 minutes or so to check the location of the camper trailer. An hour and a half after the interior border patrol station he stopped at a rest stop for a critical check. By now his quarry should be giving some indication of their final destination. A continued eastward trek along I-10 would indicate that they were probably going to Houston. A jog to the North up I-35 would be less conclusive; could be any number of towns along the I-35 corridor. Dallas being the biggest. But Dallas was also the farthest at about 280 miles and Jimmy Dale was hoping to get out of driving to Dallas tonight. The GPS receiver lit up and took about ten seconds to calibrate. North San Antonio. OK, Jimmy Dale thought to himself. Mr. Cowboy could be heading almost anywhere. Five minutes later Jimmy Dale took another reading and saw that the truck had come to a rest. Jimmy Dale hoped that the cowboy wasn't just stopping to take a break. But the reading on the GPS device seemed to indicate that he was stopped in a residential area so Jimmy Dale was hopeful. It was only eight miles away and Jimmy Dale headed that direction.

Fifteen minutes later Jimmy Dale pulled past the Adobe Palms apartments on Northwest Military. He drove slowly to survey the situation but not so slowly as to draw attention to himself. On the third pass he caught a glimpse of the rig behind building three and pulled into the parking lot. From the parking spot at the far end of the lot he could see the camper. Everything seemed quiet and the scene had the appearance of being settled for the night. Still, he waited 20 minutes to be sure. Then he skipped across the 20 yards of open lawn, onto the drive way, and slid under the truck. The metal tube containing the drugs was right where he left it. He retrieved the tube, rolled out from underneath the truck and started back the way he had come. He was halfway across the lawn when he heard the dog and knew that it would be close.

CHAPTER 13

Neal was reading before turning in for the evening when he heard the crunch of truck tires on the gravel drive way. Being poor, he tended to keep the a/c off and the windows open, especially during the fall and spring and was generally privy to the comings and goings of his neighbors. In this case, his neighbors were also his landlords, the Johnsons. He wasn't nosy so much as he was simply aware. He assumed without thinking about it that it was Jack Johnson and his mind never really detached from the article he was reading on global warming. When he heard the dog he leaned forward to look out the window. Neal had heard Jack Johnson call the dog Bullet and now he knew why. The dog was a fast runner and quickly exited the field of view that was available to Neal out his back window. Neal ran to the front door and stepped out onto the front elevated walkway to observe a person in a gray GMC pickup truck trying very hard to get off the premises. Neal was witness to the end of the contest with Bullet being denied in his quest to apprehend the interloper. It was apparent to Neal that the man in the truck was doing something that he was not supposed to be doing so he memorized the license plate. He went inside and wrote it down then walked back out the front door to see what he could see.

Bullet was still in a heightened state and patrolled the parking lot like he was waiting for his nemesis to return. Then, with his nose to the ground, traced back and forth several times the path the intruder had taken. Bullet paid special attention to a spot under the trailer. Neal watched the dog pace and then just listened to him pant and snort when he was behind the building. The dog returned to a spot near the parking lot and was scratching and gnawing at something. When Neal heard the dog crack an object in his jaws he decided to walk down and take a look. Neal was not friends with Bullet so he wasn't sure if his advances would be well received. When he got close the dog stood and faced him directly. The dog was sizing him up. He had a black object in his mouth. It was a box or something, made from plastic or metal and it had what looked like a small antennae attached.

"Hey Bullet. How you doin' boy?" Neal asked the dog rhetorically trying to get a feel for how the dog might respond to him.

At the sound of his name the dog sat down in the Sphinx position and wagged his tail. His ears were straight up at attention. Neal took this as a good sign. He still had the box in his mouth.

"Hey Bullet. What'cha got there?"

The dog wagged his tail again and lowered his head.

"Can I see what'cha got boy?" Neal moved toward the dog and patted him on the head with his right hand. He felt as if he had the dog's trust and pulled the box from the dog's mouth with his left hand. Bullet resisted a little but it was more like he was playing than being disagreeable.

"Thanks boy. You did a good job tonight." Neal gave the dog a good rub behind the ears.

The device had a crack in it and was covered in dog slobber but Neal recognized it as a GPS homing device. There was the occasional off brand from China, but most of the GPS units that were brought into the Wild Snail were pretty sturdy. Neal knew them to be fairly able to withstand physical abuse so he wasn't really even all that surprised when it powered up. Neal even recognized this particular model from his days working with

Joe at the AAAA Bail Bonds. He was able to pull up the most recent trips to see exactly where this unit had been. There was a screen on the unit itself and Neal was able to make out some rough locations but it was really designed to interact with a PC. Two minutes later he had it up and running on his laptop. Not that it did much good. There was only one trip loaded into memory. Apparently someone had driven to San Antonio from Del Rio. Neal didn't know what to do with that information so he didn't do anything. He got up and poured himself some cheap Canadian whiskey mixed with the sweet tea you make from the mix you buy at the grocery store – a poor man's half and half highball. His nerves were beginning to calm now from the recent activity and he sat back down at the computer and stared at the screen.

Every now and then Neal would come up with a good plan and this was one of those times. As the amber liquid greased the synapses of his delinquent mind, Neal realized that he could pretty easily reprogram the GPS unit with a second password that would allow him to access the information from that unit on-line. The perp that dropped it might not even know that the unit could be reprogrammed in such a way. And even if he did, he wouldn't have a reason to believe that a second code had been set up. So why would he look? And even if he did look, all he would see is a second code. He would have no way of tracing that code back to Neal.

The GPS tracking website prompted Neal through the process of setting up a second account. According to the warning message a total of five accounts came with the purchase of the unit. Neal could see on screen that only one account had been set up. JD123TX. So Neal set up the second account. He gave the account the innocuous pseudonym JD124TX. It seemed like the kind of account name that might go undetected by the unit's owner. The website prompted Neal for a password and gave simple instructions on how to enter the password into the unit after it had been set up on the website. Neal chose STARR as his password. He always used the name of a Texas county for his passwords. The website then generated an access code and informed the user that all three pieces of information would be needed to access the location of the unit from the internet: the account name, password, and access code. He made a quick check

on the website to confirm that he could see the location of the
GPS and then ran the unit back outside and put it down where he
thought the dog had probably picked it up. He worried a little that
Bullet might come back and pick it up but decided that it was
simply a chance that he had to take. Neal ran back upstairs to his
efficiency apartment and looked out the back window again. Jack
Johnson's porch light was on at the house like it usually was and he
could see Bullet lying there asleep. Then he logged back into the
website and checked the position of the unit. The website showed
that the unit had moved 56 yards North Northeast since the
second account had been set up.

****

It had started as a low rumble but then blossomed into a full-blown
growl as the dog reached full stride. Approximately a half
nanosecond later, Jimmy Dale was very purposefully striving to
reach the GMC before the dog was able to reach him. The thought
occurred to him, as he moved mercurially over the ground that
separated him from the truck, that he didn't know he could still run
so fast. He had the metal tube with the drugs in one hand and the
GPS in the other. Ten yards from the truck he fumbled the GPS
and dropped it. With the dog closing fast, the thought of stopping
to pick up the device never entered into Jimmy Dale's head. He
was so intent on getting to the safety of the truck that he never
even noticed that he was, in fact, no longer in possession of the
unit. He hit the door of his truck at nearly full speed and was
inside just as the dog closed the gap. The dog was light brown with
white markings and appeared to be a pit bull mix. And he was
angry. Slobbering…growling…and angry…very angry. He stood
on his hind legs with his forelegs up on the truck door. It wasn't
doing much for Jimmy Dale's paint job but at this point he really
didn't care. Jimmy Dale started the engine and pulled out as
quickly as he could without squealing tires. He could see the dog
in the rear view mirror giving chase and then abandoning the effort
as the truck pulled onto the main thoroughfare. As Jimmy Dale
made the turn and lost sight of him, the dog gave a few last gasp

whoofs and still had an angry bearing about him but seemed to be calming.

The prospect of being mauled has a tremendous capacity for focusing the mind. With that threat removed Jimmy Dale became aware of how elevated his breathing and heart rate were. Jimmy Dale spent the next ten miles calming down before he stopped at a convenience store for a big boy Steel Reserve.

"Shit that was close," he kept saying to himself.

And it was. He could've been found out. He could've been bitten or mauled. He could've been arrested! And if anyone had seen him that possibility was still on the table. But how in the hell could he have known there was a dog? Most people that have dogs kept them in fences or on chains. And right there in town! What kind of an idiot just lets his dog run loose like that?

Ten minutes later he was on the interstate and well on his way to Seguin when he accepted the fact that he could not blame the cowboy for having a dog. That's when he realized that he didn't have the GPS. *Shit!* Jimmy Dale thought to himself. He took the next exit and sat in the parking lot of an office building for five minutes deciding what to do. He couldn't just leave it. If the cowboy had seen him, then he might call the police and they might find the GPS. It was a long shot but they might be able to trace it back to him. But then again, why would they even try. Nobody knew what he was doing and why he was on the property. Trespassing? That's not very high on the priority list for the SAPD. So from the perspective of legal exposure, there really wasn't much of a reason to go back for the GPS. But he turned around anyway. The dadgum thing cost him $259 and he was going back for it. The dog be damned. When he got back to the Adobe Palms he made one drive by and all seemed quiet. He pulled back into the same spot and retraced his steps. There it was - right where he'd left it.

****

Neal had to be at work by 10:00 the next morning and he slept 'til 9:00. He fried an egg and toasted a piece of bread. He sat down with his plate and typed in the password to the GPS site between bites. Seguin? The GPS unit was in Seguin? Neal walked out the front door of his apartment making a left and skipped down to the rail at the end of the walkway. He leaned over the railing and looked down and to his left. It wasn't there. He turned and ran to the stairs and then down to the parking lot and around the side of the building. He paced back and forth like Bullet had done the night before but the unit was gone.

"I'll be dang!" Neal said to himself. "That s.o.b. must have come and picked it up already."

The pawn shop had an account with a company that provided unlimited background checks. Frank had even splurged and purchased the premium package that provided access to the license plate database for the state of Texas. So after he got to work but before the activity level picked up, Neal logged on and checked out his visitor from the night before. He typed in the license plate number first and the computer yielded a name and address:

James Dale Klein
2046 Polar Bear Drive
Seguin, Texas 78155

"Ok," Neal said to himself. Then he switched to the background check application and typed in James' name and address:

James Dale Klein

Criminal Mischief Under $500
Guadalupe County, Texas
August 2007

Possession of Marijuana under 2 Oz
Guadalupe County, Texas
November 2007

Possession of Marijuana under 2 Oz
Guadalupe County, Texas
July 2010

Neal stared at the printout. Seemed pretty normal. No outstanding warrants or anything. And from the looks of it James Dale Klein wasn't a big time criminal or anything, just a little misdemeanoring. So why was this James Dale guy messing around at the Adobe Palms and aggravating dogs at 11:00 at night? Neal didn't know but he was about to find out.

****

Neal checked the gohorse email account that evening. He wasn't dumb enough to use his personal laptop or anything at the Wild Snail. He drove to the Brookhollow Branch of the San Antonio Public Library and used their internet access over there. He had to hand the librarian his ID but there was no permanent record of his visit and if anyone ever came to ask about him Neal knew there was almost no way the librarian would remember anything.

Inbox (1)   culebra837@gmail.com

Neal opened the message.

Here I am. What do I need to do?

Neal hit reply and then typed:

Forget the Red Rooster. Dial this number (888) 676-8000. It's a customer service number for a prepaid credit card. Put $1,000 on this account. 7472-8203-5545-1191.

Gohorse

The next day Neal checked the account and could see that Billy had made the deposit.

******

Rosalie's mother, Linda, was a volcano. Sometimes she exploded and sometimes she only vented. When dormant there was always a background tension that something was coming because it always was. It made life difficult for those around her but Rosalie had learned over the years to deal with it. Rosalie's ability to live with her mother's condition began in an instant after arguing with Linda for the 10,000th time about God only knows what. For some reason: illumination, divine intervention, maybe it was just exhaustion, but for whatever reason Rosalie realized at that moment that her mother was simply unreachable. No argument was clear enough and no case could be made that was overwhelming enough that would allow her mother to grasp another person's point of view. The acceptance that her mother was unreachable had been the beginning of the metamorphosis within Rosalie. And then slowly – oh so incredibly slowly – Rosalie came to accept that Linda did not have the capacity to understand another person's perspective.

And Linda could not be blamed for it - at least not entirely. The wiring did not exist and those particular synapses were simply not firing. With the realization that her mother was more or less incapable of compassion, Rosalie found it easier to accept Linda's domineering behavior and live with it. Rosalie's father had never mastered this trick and Rosalie was convinced that the stress of living with her mother is what killed her father. The application of pressure over the years by Linda had taken a toll on the man. Finally, emasculated and unable to fight back any more, Rosalie's father had given in and relinquished control; all decision making and independent thought were gone. Rosalie didn't know when it happened exactly but remembered sensing as an adolescent girl that her father had ceased being a man. What was left was a shell.

He had died at 51 of a massive heart attack. Yes, there was some history of heart disease in the family and he drank, but he weighed what he was supposed to weigh and was active physically. And Rosalie realized the day after his death, when she was 13 that the situation that she had grown up in – mother in absolute control and the father playing a subordinate role – was not normal. She also realized on that day that it was the combination of her parent's faults that had caused the situation. Her father had not been blameless. Most notably he had abdicated his position as leader of the family and had allowed his subordinate position to become the norm. Her father's faults were now no longer an issue but her mother lived on. She lived on to torment Rosalie throughout her pregnancy and stillborn birth of her son at age 17 and she lived on now to torment her on her choice to be with Jimmy Dale.

"Rosalie, you do understand that Jimmy Dale might not be the best choice for you right?"

"Yes momma, I understand that."

"Then I don't understand why you're selling yourself short." Linda looked at Rosalie long and hard. "That's all I'm saying."

"I understand momma," Rosalie replied with the appearance of acquiescence.

CHAPTER 14

Heironymus always played the widow. When placing his bid he always counted on the domino in the middle – the one awarded to the high bidder – to better his hand. Sometimes he was right and sometimes he was wrong. But that afternoon in Acuña he was right more times than he was wrong. The standing bet in their game of *Shoot the Moon* was two bits per game and a dime a hickey. Heironymus was up on Bruno and Karl by two dollars.

Heironymus watched the Mexicans in the cantina as he played and came to the conclusion that they were the same people culturally as the Mexicans he knew back in Guadalupe County. Heironymus looked over at the regal Mexican with the ammo belt across his chest that had made the effort to sit and share a beer with the Germans earlier. The Mexican caught Heironymus' eye and raised his beer as a gesture. Heironymus responded in kind. He thought about how the Mexicans seemed quick to make friends. And how they laughed easily. Heironymus reflected on how he hadn't laughed since he'd arrived in Mexico earlier in the day. He had shared humor with Bruno and Karl, to be sure, but it was dry and lacked the show of emotion that seemed so prevalent with the Mexicans. It was the German way.

****

The origin of the salute was mostly lost to the recesses of the alcohol and drug dependant minds of the white salesmen at Kuykendall Motors.   Even Cupcake didn't know for sure. Although years later he would attempt to bring it to mind, he would not be able to remember that he had been engaging the sales force on the front stoop of the dealership when the thought first formed. Like many concepts that spring from the interaction with others, the progenitor of the idea is usually unable to pinpoint exactly when or how the idea originally occurred to him. Cupcake *was* able to remember when the idea was *not* present. And he was able to remember when he knew for sure that the idea was there and fully formed. That much he could do. But for the life of him he was not able to remember exactly when he had come up with it. Billy, on the other hand, remembered the day and the time that the concept of the salute had leapt fully formed from Cupcake's brain. Race relations, just like sex, politics, money, movies, religion, women in general, sports, food, automobiles, get rich quick schemes, alcohol, music, and any other topic that might be of interest to a group of guys of varying ages and cultural backgrounds would come up for discussion in due course. And on this particular day Gatewood broached that exact topic.   Being black, he was expounding on the difficulties of dealing with the parents of a Mexican girl that he had gotten pregnant some 30 years earlier. The exact course of the conversation was not nearly as important as the mere fact that the topic had come up.

Two new customers on the lot along with a couple of salesmen being beckoned to the finance office served to break up the impromptu discussion leaving only Cupcake and Billy to carry on. Cupcake decided to dig a little deeper into the topic.

"You know, maybe some of our Aryan ancestors were right about a thing or two," Cupcake opined still smiling broadly. Billy grinned, sensing that Cupcake was about to get on a roll, and not wanting to miss out on the opportunity to witness the young salesman's mind at work, allowed himself to be sucked in.

"You think so huh?" Billy said, goading him forward.

"Yeah, maybe so. I mean I know we're all created equal in the eyes of the Lord and everything, but the Lord made us different too…right?"

"I'm with you so far," Billy said going with the flow.

"So isn't possible that maybe black folks might be better at one particular thing and that white folks or Mexicans might be better at something else?" Cupcake paused waiting for Billy to join in.

"Isn't it possible?" Cupcake asked again after a few seconds realizing Billy was not going to jump in at that exact moment.

"Yeah I guess it's possible," Billy said finally.

"I mean those Chinese guys in high school kicked everybody's ass study wise. Right? Us white guys didn't have a chance. Right?" Cupcake continued.

"They're smart all right," Billy agreed.

"And you don't think that black guys are better basketball players?" Cupcake continued.

"They're pretty good," Billy answered, still in agreement.

"Then what are people arguing about? Why all this uproar about how everybody is so equal and everything? Can't we just say that every race, just like every person, has some gift from God and then just leave it at that?" Cupcake asked.

"Yeah I suppose we could say that."

And then Cupcake delivered the zinger, "But we really know we're better, don't we?" Cupcake said smiling broadly as he turned to move toward the door entering the showroom.

Billy had to laugh at the content and the delivery of Cupcake's viewpoint, not knowing Cupcake had one final thought to impart.

Cupcake turned back and said, "You know I think that's what Hitler was saying in code when he put the Heil Hitler salute into effect in Germany." Cupcake raised his right arm at the elbow so that it was parallel with the ground but with his hand up and palm facing outward. Billy, since he was privy to the nature of the conversation, knew what Cupcake's arm position represented, but to the casual observer, it might appear that Cupcake was motioning for Billy to stop.

"I think he was saying, 'Secretly we know we're better...don't you think?" Cupcake asked.

"I don't know Cupcake. I think he was of the opinion that the German race was superior. I'll agree with you on that," Billy replied, amazed at the machinations of the young man's mind. "But I'm not so sure that he was trying to be secret about it."

"Well secretly I know I'm a little bit better," Cupcake said making a joke of it. "And this is my sign to show that I know," Cupcake said mostly joking as he began to move through the giant showroom double doors swinging them wide open for emphasis.

Cupcake turned, and as the doors, slowed by the hydraulic devices attached overhead to prevent slamming, gradually came together, not unlike the curtains at a theatrical production, ever so subtly delivered the salute. This time Cupcake took the salute down another level so that his whole arm hung straight down with only his hand bent upward at the wrist, and instead of the whole palm facing out he simply extended his index and second finger out and up. He simultaneously gave Billy a slight nod of the head downward to give the salute an element of being a greeting also - a greeting between two white men that celebrated an unsavory historical reference. Billy couldn't help himself and shot the salute right back to his cherubic co-worker as the glass doors that connected the showroom to the north side of the car lot came to a close.

****

The week before Jimmy Dale left for Chicago, the one unaccounted for element in his plan fell into place. He couldn't simply put the stuff in a bag and the lack of a good transport container nagged at him. But an idea came to him like it always did and he went immediately to work on it. He had a 40 quart cooler that had been used for everything from cold drinks to harvested wild game to mixing concrete. It was replete with abrasions and perfect for the task in such a way that another abrasion would go unnoticed. He turned the cooler upside down and drilled a hole near the center. He was careful to puncture only the outside wall of the cooler and leave the interior wall untouched. He then positioned two 2x4s parallel to each other across the bottom of the cooler while it sat on the ground upside down. They were placed so that they ran perpendicular to the length of the cooler and were about ¼ inch apart. He took his jigsaw and placed the saw's shoe on the boards so that the blade was in position between the boards. The 2x4s acted as spacers and allowed the saw to sit sturdily and evenly a little bit above the level of the bottom of the cooler. Pulling the jigsaw back from its rest, he tapped the power button a few times to get a feel for the up and down motion of the blade. He then placed the saw on the spacer boards confirming that the blade would cut the outer wall only, never coming into contact with the inner wall of the cooler. In this fashion he then cut a square foot section from the bottom of the cooler. There was foam insulation between the inner lining and the outer wall so he removed it. The resulting space was about one inch deep. He divided the cocaine into smaller bags, double bagging every time and he put the bags in the space. To reattach the removed square foot section of the bottom of the cooler he cut two 1x4s, each a little longer than a foot. He slid the ends of the boards into the empty space on either side and secured the four loose ends with screws through the outer wall of the cooler and into the board. The previously removed section fit nicely back into its original position on top of the 1x4s. Screws held it in place and some epoxy filled the seam around the edge. Some paint and some mortar splashed on the bottom of the cooler camouflaged the modification and Jimmy Dale was good to go. The cooler was well over 100 pounds when loaded down with ice and drinks and snacks so the weight would further discourage law enforcement from messing with it. If they looked at it all it would be to examine the contents.

The day before Jimmy Dale left for Chicago he changed the oil in the GMC. He checked his hoses and belts and checked the pressure in the tires. Then he broke out the Atlas and divided the 1,200 mile one-way trip into two segments. Day one was Seguin to Dallas to Little Rock. Day two was Little Rock to Memphis to Chicago. Operating capital was beginning to dwindle and he contemplated his usual cash conservation method of sleeping in the truck at a road side park but quickly dismissed it. He'd had a couple of rude awakenings over the years and couldn't risk an interaction with someone of less than honorable intentions. Or worse yet, he might attract the attention of someone sworn to public service. The one night at a Motel 6 in Little Rock would only set him back about $35 and it was a small price to pay for the peace of mind.

He slept restlessly the night before he left and when he woke up for the fourth time at 4:00 am decided to go ahead and leave. He was on the road by 4:15 and was halfway to Dallas by 6:30 missing Austin traffic entirely. He kept the truck at 70 mph and at 65 through metro areas. He'd had a girlfriend once that had been pulled over for doing 55. The cop had told her that vehicles driven under 60 mph on the interstate by drivers under 40 years of age were targeted by law enforcement. The cop had told Jimmy Dale's girlfriend that it was uncommon behavior and they were generally believed to be involved in something unsavory. So Jimmy Dale made a point of not being conspicuous by driving just like everybody else - a little over the speed limit.

In Temple there was a Whataburger on the east side of the interstate. It was an easy off and on so Jimmy Dale decided to stop for a bite. He ordered two taquitos and took a plastic number 22 to a booth so the girl behind the counter would know where to deliver the breakfast. At a table in the center of the restaurant and more or less facing Jimmy Dale was a large Mexican man about 45 years old. His eyes were closed and his head was nodding forward resting on his double chin. Unshaven and 100 pounds overweight, he gave a slovenly impression. Jimmy Dale sat for minute watching him when the man jolted forward a bit spewing a vile concoction from his mouth that spilled down his chest. The man appeared to be completely unaware of what he was doing. Three more upheavals followed, but the man remained blissfully asleep. The wait staff didn't notice or made it a point not to notice. How many hours of binge drinking, Jimmy Dale wondered, would cause a man to pass out and throw up on himself in a Whataburger? How many years of indulging an addiction did it take before a man stooped to this level?

A girl on the tail end of a night shift delivered the taquitos and Jimmy Dale got up to leave. He paused over the man that had disgraced himself. The dawn was beginning to soften in the east and Jimmy Dale wondered if there was someone out there that cared for the man. Jimmy Dale felt empathy. He had his own demons and could relate to men that were bedeviled in such a way. He decided to talk to him.

"Hey man, are you ok?" Jimmy Dale asked.

No response.

"Hey…buddy…you can't do this…you need some help."

Still nothing. Jimmy Dale looked around the dining room but the man didn't seem to be raising any concern at all. There was a red phone in a holster on the man's belt. Jimmy Dale scanned the room once more, took the phone and hit the down arrow. He was searching for a woman's name. As near as he could figure, this man's buddies would probably leave him high and dry. He needed a wife or a mother or something. There were about 40 entries but only two of them were female. Esmerelda and Josefina. Jimmy Dale chose Esmerelda and hit the dial button.

"Bueno," a female voice answered. It sounded decent and caring.

"Hi there. My name is Jimmy Dale. I have a man in front of me that's about 45 and weighs about 300 pounds. Do you know him?"

"His name is Lorenzo. Is he ok?" Esmerelda asked. Jimmy Dale could hear the concern in her voice.

"He's alive. I couldn't say if he's ok or not. I can say that he's drunk and he needs to be taken care of. Are you his wife?"

"I'm his sister. Every wife he's ever had has left him. Where is he?"

"He's at the Whataburger here in Temple. I found him puking on himself. Can you come and take care of him. He'll be in jail soon if you don't."

"I can be there in five minutes. Will you stay with him?"

"I'll stay but you have to hurry. I don't want to run into anybody that I don't want to run into."

Seven minutes later a beat up Buick pulled into the parking lot. Esmerelda was in her late 30s and served as quite a contrast to her brother. She was slim and attractive in a practical sort of way. Jimmy Dale found himself wondering if it was possible that she was Lorenzo's half sister since there seemed to be a disconnect in the gene pool. She was accompanied by two young men - perhaps her sons – both well-mannered. The first one to the door held it open for his mother. She greeted Jimmy Dale and thanked him again for helping Lorenzo. Jimmy Dale could see that the family was struggling. It was evident by their car and their clothes. But despite their circumstances there was a quiet dignity about this family. Despite their meager means they held themselves with an understated pride. Jimmy Dale sensed neither apology nor bitterness for their station in life. Esmerelda spoke quietly to her brother and managed to bring him around. He rose unsteadily and walked slowly out the building with the two boys serving as wing men. Esmerelda thanked Jimmy Dale a third time and followed the men outside. She took the passenger seat alongside her younger son with Lorenzo and her older son in the back. They made the u-turn through the drive through and pulled away just as the Temple police department arrived.

The cop car pulled in quickly but without the blue lights. The Temple cop entered the Whataburger just as Jimmy Dale was leaving. Jimmy Dale was prepared to speak to him but the cop seemed pretty intent and was avoiding eye contact. Jimmy Dale glanced at the cooler in the back of the GMC as he climbed in. He made the u-turn around the restaurant just like Esmerelda had done with Lorenzo and her family and he could see the cop talking to the store manager. He wondered what would happen to Lorenzo. He thought about the billions of people on the planet; each person with his own problems and successes, joys and sorrows. How people's paths crossed each other's like ants going about their short lives. He thought about how his path had crossed with Lorenzo's and wondered if he would ever see him again. He wondered if what he did this morning would make a difference in Lorenzo's life. Probably not. Had he really helped Lorenzo or was he just trying to make himself feel better? Jimmy Dale realized he was in a downward mental spiral and was committed to pondering the universe until he tired of it but was thankful that he had something to occupy his mind for the next 30 minutes. When he finally came out of it he was nearly to Dallas.

Jimmy Dale got to Little Rock at about 4:30 and thought about pushing on to Memphis but the day was beginning to wear on him so he decided to stick to his plan and stop for the night. He checked in to the Howard Johnson off Chicot Road paying cash to the Indian man behind the counter who was kind enough to oblige Jimmy Dale's request for a room on the first floor. He dumped the water from the cooler and checked his secret compartment. He looked for evidence that it was becoming dislodged but was glad to see that everything was ok. The next morning at 5:00 he grabbed a stale tuna fish sandwich from the 7-11 next door for breakfast.

The Mississippi river was meandering beneath him when the sun started to peak over the horizon. The Memphis skyline lay before him and had the appearance of being devoid of human population. In the early morning light it was serene and seemed more like a mountain range – something more of divine creation than of man's. But like so many things the beauty evaporated as he came closer. He could see the people below him in their suits and heels and cars, with all those things that seem important to us now and Jimmy Dale realized that he was no different than anyone that he could see. The very people that he was figuratively and literally looking down on, were in fact, just moving through life in the best way they knew how. And wasn't that what he was doing? He was perhaps more free because he did not have to be at work at 8:00. On the other hand he carried the burden of potential imprisonment. Jimmy Dale thought about the ants again and wondered if they were free as he left Memphis behind and drove on to Chicago.

CHAPTER 15

Chicago is to Memphis what a Harley is to a Vespa. It's louder,
bigger, stronger and more menacing. There was a strength
and a hum to the city and Jimmy Dale could feel himself tapping
into that energy as the skyline rose from the horizon. He exited
95th Street off 94 on the south side. It had been a two-day day and
he wanted to be on his game when he met with Larry so he
stopped for an energy drink. He put the cooler in the front and
locked the passenger door. It was a minor detail to put the cooler
in the cab of the truck but it might draw attention later when he
got to Larry's and Jimmy Dale wanted to avoid that. Then he
drove the final three blocks to Larry's tenement. Jimmy Dale was a
little nervous. In Mexico, despite the language and the beating,
Jimmy Dale felt culturally only one degree removed. He was an
outsider, but at least he was familiar with the people and they were
familiar with him and his kind. He wasn't a Mexican but at least he
was used to being around them and knew how to act while in their
midst. He was comfortable with it. But here in the black
community of the south side he was self-conscious. He wasn't just
an innocuous visitor like he had been in Mexico. He felt more like

an interloper and he could sense it. The Texas license plate didn't help. He parked as close to building 3 as he could get, nonchalantly locking the door behind him. It was just a few steps across the yard and a few more up the stairs then down the second story open-air walkway to unit 217. He knocked twice. Larry answered and looked just like Jimmy Dale remembered him - except for the new corn rows.

"'Sup man?" Larry extended his right hand and they shook 'bro style. Larry pulled Jimmy Dale forward and embraced by touching him at the shoulder with his shoulder and patting the back.

"Hey man, how you doing?" Jimmy Dale inquired politely.

Jimmy Dale entered the room. There were two black guys on the couch. The larger man on the right looked familiar and gave Jimmy Dale a nod. The smaller man on the left had something hostile about him and didn't acknowledge Jimmy Dale at all. Both men were smoking cigarettes.

"How's your trip man?" Larry asked.

"It was alright. I'm glad it's over though."

"Sit down man. Have a seat right over here." Larry motioned to a dining room chair that had been pulled into the living room.

"Alright. Hey Larry you don't have any more of those do you?" Jimmy Dale made a motion with his chin toward the 40 ounce MGDs on the coffee table. He didn't want to try too hard to fit in but he did want to try a little bit. He had a shared a few 40s with Larry when he had worked in Chicago before and felt comfortable making the request. And it wasn't just a gesture. He really was thirsty for a beer.

"Yeah. Y'thirsty for one? I think I got a couple more." Larry strode into the kitchen accenting every other step. It reminded Jimmy Dale of Chavo. He wondered to himself why he never saw a white guy walk like that. Larry returned with the beer and Jimmy Dale took a big hit off the top. He hadn't had one in a couple of days and the taste of it calmed him down.

"Ya didn't have any problems did'ja?" Jimmy Dale knew that Larry was just making small talk and that he really wanted to talk about the coke.

"No. Everything made it in one piece if that's what you mean."

"'Das' good."

"You from Texas are ya?" The smaller hostile man on the left had decided it was time to chime in.

"Yeah. My name's Jimmy Dale." Jimmy Dale made a point of maintaining eye contact with what he sensed to be his newfound nemesis.

"Been there once. To Dallas. It was hotter'n shit down there."

"It get's pretty hot...especially in Dallas." Jimmy Dale made one of those awkward expressions where the lips are pushed together and the corners of the mouth are pulled wider and his eyebrows go up. He nodded his head up and down in agreement with his own meteorological assessment.

"What kind of car you drive?" The larger man on the right was now in the conversation.

"A GMC pickup. It's older but I maintain my vehicles pretty good. She's got some life left in her."

The man on the right nodded in agreement. Jimmy Dale decided that maybe he didn't know him after all.

"My name's Jarvis." The man on the right began to stand up and Jimmy Dale reciprocated. They shook hands across the coffee table white man style. Jarvis' grip was surprisingly weak. Almost like a woman's. Jimmy Dale decided that he probably wasn't used to shaking hands in that manner.

Jimmy Dale had glanced over toward the man on the left after finishing with Jarvis.

"Otis."

"Jimmy Dale." The hand shake was the same – weak.

Everyone sat back down and looked at one another.

****

Meetings around the globe have for centuries been characterized by posturing, awkwardness, strength of presence, and verbal and non-verbal communication. The meeting in which Jimmy Dale was currently engaged had all these elements and he was waiting for the next card to be played.

"So you got the stuff?" Larry again took the lead.

"I don't got it with me but I got it."

"Where is it?" Larry asked. He was fishing now.

"I got a buddy from when I was here before. It's at his place," Jimmy Dale lied.

"Does he know it's there?"

"No."

"How long you plan on stayin'?"

"Not long."

"How much stuff you got that you're keepin' over at your friend's place that he don't know is there?" Otis asked. Jimmy Dale had been wondering when Otis would join the conversation again.

"One key."

"How much you want for it?" Otis asked.

"I think 15 grand is fair...don't you?" Jimmy Dale looked around the room at his newfound business associates. All three of them were nodding their heads.

After pretty much agreeing to the price and contemplating the situation for a few seconds Otis continued the negotiation, "You realize we ain't buyin' no 15 grand worth of dope from you at one time."

Jimmy Dale's heart sank a bit. But it was short-lived, he knew going in that it was not going to be easy and he took the statement in stride. "Well...what ARE you doing to do?"

"We'll give you five right now and then ten after we sell it. We could do that," Larry said.

"I can't do that Larry."

"We got what we got man."

Jimmy Dale glanced at his adversaries. He thought about his grandfather - 15 years dead now - and the advice he had given Jimmy Dale one day when his grandpa was selling a bull. Jimmy Dale's grandpa's name was Eugene and he was asking $1,000 for the bull when a man named Sonny from two counties over had driven in to take a look and possibly take possession. He'd even shown up with his trailer. When he got there Sonny proceeded to disparage the bull something awful.

Jimmy Dale remembered Sonny saying to his grandpa, "Eugene, my neighbor is Smithy Tschirhart. And Smithy's herd bull and this here bull share the same grand-daddy. I've seen the calves out of that bull and I can tell you they're destined for chili meat. There's not a decent one in the lot. I have serious reservations about the quality of this line. I'm offering you $500 for this bull and I can tell you that even that is probably too high."

"Ok," Eugene came back, "I am not selling you this bull for $500."

"Well, that's what I'm offering."

Eugene knew better than to drop. The offer was under the radar and he knew the right move was a straight decline.

"I'm afraid I can't help you. But I wish you luck in your endeavors," Eugene said,

And with that, ol' Eugene walked back into the house. Jimmy Dale knew that his grandpa needed the money. He had heard his grandmother crying and he'd heard the arguments. He also knew what they ate for supper every night and he could not imagine that his grandpa would walk away from a sum as substantial as $500. But that's what he did. The man from two counties over got back in his truck and pretended to do some figuring. And within a couple of minutes he knocked on the kitchen door.

"Would you take $900? I got cash money."

"I will. And me and my grandson here will help you load him."

After the bull had departed for his new pasture, Jimmy Dale sat with his grandfather at the kitchen table with the windows open and the breeze on their faces. Jimmy Dale was drinking a Big Red. Grandpa Eugene was enjoying a Pearl beer. It was that day 25 years ago, that Jimmy Dale received the single best piece of advice he would ever receive.

"Jimmy Dale," Eugene had said to his grandson, "the man that wins is the man that cares the least."

That episode, all those years ago, flashed through Jimmy Dale's mind – condensed as a single thought to be pondered in a single instant and applied to the situation at hand.

"I'm afraid I can't do the deal. Thanks for having me out though and I'll wish you the best of luck." Jimmy Dale rose and was nearly to the door when Jarvis spoke.

"Hol' on man. We can probably work somethin' out. Sit back down and let's talk some more."

"We just don't have the money now so we need to work out some pay as you go plan," Otis said.

Jimmy Dale had the feeling all along that of the three men he was dealing with, Otis was the dominant personality.

"I'm listening," Jimmy Dale said.

"We got five grand so give us a third. We cut it and sell it. That frees up the cash flow and maybe we have enough to buy the rest. You get your money, we get our stuff and everybody makes out."

"I really don't mind that kind of arrangement Otis, but I can't be hanging around Chicago for six weeks."

"It won't take no six weeks. Let's just get started and see how we do," Otis said.

"So a one third key delivery tomorrow then," Jimmy Dale said by way of confirmation.

"Yeah. You bring that tomorrow and we'll give you five grand for that. We'll work from there," Otis answered.

"I'll call you tomorrow," Jimmy Dale promised.

Jimmy Dale finished his MGD and sealed the deal with handshakes and 'awright''s all around.

Now was when the real work started. Getting the dope to Chicago was easy. Getting it sold and paid for was going to be harder. Jimmy Dale needed a plan to maximize his chances for receiving payment and for survival – not necessarily in that order. The exchange with Larry and his buddies would be critical. Jimmy Dale placed the call to Larry that next morning at 10:30 and arranged to meet the day after that. Jimmy Dale assured Larry that the stuff was ready and that he would bring it. And Larry promised Jimmy Dale that he'd have the money.

After leaving Larry's apartment Jimmy Dale gave Rosalie a call and gave her a progress report. He also let her know that there was nothing to worry about concerning the text he was about to send her – that it was being sent as an insurance policy only.

I'm meeting Larry and Jarvis and Otis at the Marathon
Convenience Store on 47th and Michigan at noon
tomorrow. If you don't hear from me by 1:00, I'm
probably dead and you can call the police."

****

Jimmy Dale got to 47th and Michigan at 11:30. He saw Larry and his two buddies parked on the side street leaning against a green Monte Carlo. All three of them were smoking. Jimmy Dale decided to leave the .45 in the truck and got out and approached the men. Larry used his right hand to shake hands with Jimmy Dale while sliding his left around Jimmy Dale's back thinly disguising his search for a weapon as a hug. Jimmy Dale didn't bother - he knew Larry was armed.

"Hey man, I'm a little nervous, you mind if I grab some smokes?" Jimmy Dale asked.

"We're smokin'. Don't see why you can't smoke too," Otis said from the back passenger seat.

Jimmy Dale had the 1/3 kilo of cocaine taped to his lower leg. He had hoped that he would not be subject to a full body search and he had gotten lucky. Jimmy Dale paid the clerk for the Luckys and went to the restroom and taped half of the coke that he had with him behind the toilet. As he was hiding the product Jimmy Dale wondered casually if the guys that he was dealing with had the mental capacity to accurately describe the amounts they were dealing with. Specifically he wondered if they knew that half of 1/3 was 1/6. He decided that they probably didn't and that when he needed to describe the amount he would refer to it as a half of a third. He lit his cigarette as he crossed the parking lot back to where the car was parked. Larry was in the driver's seat now with the car running. Jarvis was in the back seat with Otis and the front passenger door was open. Jimmy Dale went up to Larry's door and leaned in.

"Can't we just do this right here?"

"Jus' get in man. It's safer," Otis said from the back seat.

"Safer for you maybe," Jimmy Dale said pointing out the obvious.

"Just get in the car," Otis said.

Jimmy Dale stared at Otis for a moment and decided to relent. He took possession of the front passenger's seat and Larry pulled out into traffic.   As usual Otis took control of the conversation.

"Let me see the stuff," Otis ordered.

Jimmy Dale took the package and showed it to him. He also showed Otis the text that he had sent Rosalie the day before.

"You think this message makes a difference to me you piece of shit. You tryin' to intimidate me?" Otis said angrily.

"I'm just trying to stay alive." Jimmy Dale answered.

Otis shot a glance at Jarvis. Jarvis was sitting behind Jimmy Dale and reached around the seat and stuck a 9mm in Jimmy Dale's ribs.

"Shut up," Jarvis barked.

"Man, this don't look like no third of a key," Otis fairly exploded.

"It's half of a third Otis. Take it easy." Jimmy Dale tried to exude some confidence even though he felt anything but confident.

"Don't tell me to take it easy. Where's the rest of the damn dope?"

"It's close. It's real close. I just didn't want to get ripped off."

"How close?"

"Head back to the Marathon and I'll show it to you."

Otis gave Larry the go ahead and Larry swung the car back in that direction.

"Can I see the money?" Jimmy Dale decided it was time for him to ask some questions.

On Otis' command Jarvis got the money out and showed it to Jimmy Dale. It was a role of hundreds wrapped with a thick rubber band.

"Can I hold it?" Jimmy Dale asked.

Jarvis pitched the roll into the front seat as they were pulling into the parking lot. Jimmy Dale didn't have time to count the money so he just did a quick estimate. He pulled off the rubber band and held the money flat in his hand. There would need to be 50 hundreds to make $5k. The stack seemed about right.

"Hey Larry, pull over by the mail box and I'll get the rest of the stuff," Jimmy Dale said.

Larry followed Jimmy Dale's request. As they rolled to a stop, Jimmy Dale pulled a pre-addressed, pre-stamped manila envelope from his pocket and slid the money in. He opened the car door as if nothing was happening and sealed the envelope as he walked around the hood of the car. The back seat erupted with threats but Jimmy Dale quickened his pace and dropped the package through the slot just as Otis caught up to him and pinned him violently to the mail box.

"You have half and I'll get the rest right now. It's 30 seconds away," Jimmy said in defense.

Jimmy Dale tried to remain calm but the tension in his voice gave him away. He had pushed these thugs a lot farther than they were willing to be pushed. He knew he had reached his limit.

"You ass hole!" Otis yelled, spitting out the words.

Jimmy Dale could smell the cigarettes on Otis' breath adding to the sinister aura of the man.

"You ass hole!" Otis said again menacingly.

"Let me go Otis!. I'll get your merchandise!" Jimmy Dale was hoping against hope that Otis would indeed release his grasp.

"You ain't going anywhere! Tell me where it is!"

"Check behind the toilet."

"What toilet?" Otis queried. He didn't understand.

"The toilet in the store."

Otis looked over at the store. He motioned for Jarvis to go inside and check. Otis loosened his grip on Jimmy Dale and allowed him to stand up straight. All parties stood nervously watching as Jarvis made his way across the parking lot and through the aisles of the store to the bathroom. Then they waited for him to reappear. It seemed like he was gone a long time.

"Someone was usin' it. I got the stuff though," Jarvis said when he got back to the car a few minutes later.

"I don't want any more bullshit out of you," Otis said as he slid back into the car pointing a finger at Jimmy Dale.

"How long will it take to get rid of it?" Jimmy Dale inquired.

"Three or four days," Otis said.

That was Otis' estimate but Jimmy Dale didn't have a lot of confidence that it was accurate.

"I'll call you on Tuesday." Jimmy Dale said.

****

Jimmy Dale got a call from Otis on Monday. It was one day before Jimmy Dale was supposed to call Otis.

"That's some good shit. It went fast." Otis said with some enthusiasm.

"Good. You ready for the rest of it?" Jimmy Dale asked optimistically. He was ready to head back to Seguin.

"Yeah. We're ready."

"Meet me at the same store tomorrow at 10:00 am. Bring the ten grand."

Otis hung up the phone without verbally accepting the meeting. It was implied.

Jimmy Dale was not willing to show up with his entire stash so Otis could kill him and get off without paying. He figured he would organize a couple of drops to keep things safe. Jimmy Dale found a crumbling brick wall near 50th Street and Langley and hid half the dope in a pile of cinder blocks. The other half he hid under a brush pile at 53rd and S. Prairie. He spent the next couple of hours driving around and getting familiar with streets, businesses and landmarks. By late that afternoon Jimmy Dale had a good working knowledge of what was roughly a 50 square block area.

Otis and his goons showed up the next morning at 10:00 sharp. Jimmy Dale was waiting and he got out of the GMC to approach the car. The seating arrangement in the Monte Carlo was the same as before except that Larry and Jarvis had switched positions and this time Jarvis was driving. Jarvis got out quickly and met Jimmy Dale halfway.

"You got the stuff with you?"

"I got some. The rest is nearby. You guys know how I operate."

Jimmy Dale looked past Jarvis to make eye contact with Otis but Otis was stone-faced with the knuckle of his left index finger to his chin. He was staring straight ahead.

"We ain't doin it that way bitch! Get it all and bring it to us!" Jarvis pulled a gun from his waist band, pointed it at Jimmy Dale's foot and pulled the trigger.

Jimmy Dale felt the pressure on his left little toe as a precursor to the actual pain. The moment was surreal, short-lived, and filled with dread. His knees buckled but he didn't go down. He skipped to the GMC, managed to open the door and climb in. Then he doubled over in pain. He was breathing heavily and could feel his blood pressure plummeting. He knew that he couldn't faint. Despite the white hot pain, he pulled off his left shoe and the sock. His little toe was gone. He balled the sock and applied pressure to the stub. He was bleeding but not as profusely as what he would have expected. The real danger, for now, was fainting and having the cops investigate. He bobbed back and forth as an involuntary response to the pain because there was nothing else to do. He wasn't all there but he did notice that Otis and the boys had vacated the area. He was surprised that there didn't seem to be any attention being paid to him. He knew that this situation was not tenable and that he had to move. To stay meant risking everything.   After six or eight minutes fighting back unconsciousness he started the truck and headed in the direction of his hotel.

Somehow he managed to make it back to his room and collapsed on the floor. Luckily the duct tape that he had used to package his product was within reach. He ripped a t-shirt and wrapped the wound using the strips and the tape. His head was in the carpeted area of the floor and his feet were on the hard surface of the bathroom under the sink counter. He pulled towels from the bathroom and used them to prop up his foot. He pulled the bed spread from the bed to prop up his head. Later, when he thought about it, he wasn't sure how long he had lain there. The pain was maddening. Eventually he passed out. He woke up later to someone pounding on the door. He had no idea how long he had been out. His foot was in agony.

"Who is it?" Jimmy Dale hollered towards the door.

"Open the damn door." Jimmy Dale recognized Jarvis' voice.

"Just a minute." Jimmy Dale cursed the Texas license plates and pulled himself across the floor to the door. He propped himself up and opened it. Jarvis squeezed through the opening and Larry followed.

"How's the foot?" Jarvis did a good job at feigning concern; it almost seemed sincere.

"It hurts. That's how it is."

"I brought you this." Jarvis dropped a bottle of rubbing alcohol on the floor. "We need the rest of that dope."

While Jarvis spoke, Larry was casually going through luggage, drawers, pockets, anywhere that something of value – like 2/3s of a kilo of cocaine – might be hidden.

"I don't got it with me. You guys don't seem to be able to pick up on that."

"How we gonna work this out. Otis is pissed. And I don't like it when Otis gets pissed. When Otis gets pissed people start dying, you know what I mean?"

"You got the money?" Jimmy Dale asked.

"I ain't got it with me," Jarvis smirked.

"Maybe we understand each other then. Bring the money tomorrow and we'll go get it. And bring some crutches with you," Jimmy Dale said.

"You need anything else?" Larry offered.

"Just the crutches." Jimmy Dale paused. "And the money."

Larry shook his head in acknowledgement and they left.

CHAPTER 16

The next morning Jimmy Dale knew that he needed to change the make-shift bandage on his toe. He knew it would hurt so he put it off but finally resigned himself to the task because he knew that Larry and Jarvis would be showing up soon and he wanted to be clearheaded for the meeting. He pulled the cloth off in one motion and poured the alcohol on the stub. It burned like a furnace. He put on a fresh bandage and taped it. He put some towels underneath the foot once again to prevent stains although the bleeding had pretty much stopped. He thought that it was probably completely futile but he took three more aspirin anyway. Then he tried to relax.

Larry and Jarvis showed up two hours later with some crutches. Jimmy Dale let them in and sized up their demeanor. It seemed somewhere between neutral and accommodating. Jimmy Dale noticed that everything seemed to go a lot easier when Otis wasn't around.

"You boys ok? Ya'll ready to go get your product?" Jimmy Dale asked.

"We're alright. But Otis wants to wrap this up today," Larry said.

"I'd like to go ahead and get this thing done here pretty quick too if that's ok with you guys," Jimmy Dale told them. "I have the feeling it might go a little bit better if Otis isn't here anyway."

"That's alright with us," Larry said with a sense of relief.

Jimmy Dale liked Larry. He'd gotten along great with Larry when he worked in Chicago last summer. That's why he had called him. But Jarvis was a different deal. It was hard to like someone who had just blown off your little toe. Jimmy Dale tried not to look at him.

"Let's go then. You two got the money right?"

Larry pulled out the ten grand and handed it Jimmy Dale. "I don't think you're going to be haulin' ass on me in your condition."

"We're going to 50th Street and Langley," Jimmy Dale said. "Don't walk too fast."

On the way to the intersection by the crumbling wall, Jimmy Dale stopped at a convenience store and bought several money orders in smaller denominations and then mailed them to back to Polar Bear Drive at the first mail box they came to. He held back $1,000 in cash for incidentals on the way home. When they got to 50th and Langley Jimmy Dale pointed out the crumbling wall and Jarvis retrieved the package. They went through the same routine at 53rd and S. Prairie.

"How's your toe?" Jarvis asked when Jimmy Dale opened the car door back at the hotel.

It was hard to say if Jarvis actually gave a shit but he was asking anyway. It was the first thing he had said all morning.

"I wouldn't know. I'm not in possession of it anymore," Jimmy Dale replied.

****

The next day Jimmy Dale just wasn't up to getting in the truck and driving 1,200 miles. He figured he would hang around the hotel a couple of days and let his toe feel a little bit better. He had held back $1,000 for personal expenses from the last envelope and over the next 48 hours he treated himself to delivery a half dozen times. He gave the kid from Dominoes an extra $50 to bring back a 12 pack. It was a pretty expensive tip but it was worth it. He needed the beer. At least he thought he did. It was a welcome relief to have the edge taken off the pain from the toe. The flip side was that Jimmy Dale felt like the toe hurt even worse the next morning after he'd had a lot to drink. He changed the bandage once a day and poured the alcohol over the wound each time.

After a couple of days holed up, Jimmy Dale decided that he felt well enough to head home. The endeavor had definitely had some challenges but the final exchange with Larry and Jarvis had gone well and Jimmy Dale felt like overall the enterprise had been a success. He was glad to be heading home for the Memorial Day weekend and to check his mailbox. He felt satisfaction in a job well done, illicit though it may be, and glowed in a way that only money in one's pocket could make one glow.

****

Rosalie collected Jimmy Dale's mail during his absence paying close attention to those items bearing a Chicago postmark. She had them in her lap and was sitting on the front porch of the trailer on Polar Bear Drive when he pulled up. She hadn't opened them. Jimmy Dale had told her to be on the lookout for some mail from Chicago and she pretty much knew what was inside. She was proud of Jimmy Dale for pulling off this business transaction and wanted him to know it so she thought it might be nice if they opened up the mail together.

Rosalie didn't say anything when she saw him on the crutches. She didn't feel concern but rather a sense of relief knowing that he had suffered through some unpleasant encounter and had still managed to make it home alive. She helped him up the porch steps and opened the front door for him. When Jimmy Dale collapsed on the couch she stood over him and looked at him. His left foot was up on the couch and she could see the blood stain on the bandage.

"Did it hurt worse than Mexico?" she asked him.

"I wouldn't say it hurt worse," Jimmy Dale answered. "More like it hurt different."

"How does it feel now?" she asked him.

"It still hurts…but I'll be ok"

"Is it worth it?" she asked him already knowing how he would answer.

"Let's open up the mail that you have there and decide," he told her with a wry smile.

Jimmy Dale had talked to Rosalie while he was in Chicago but it had been more of a courtesy. He just wanted her to know that he was ok and hadn't given her any of the details. He hadn't wanted her to worry. Now that he had made it home safe and the fruits of his labor were on the table in front of them he proceeded to give her the blow by blow of everything that had gone down with Larry and his friends. Rosalie's mind took in every word and every syllable immersing herself in the process. Jimmy Dale told a good story and Rosalie was a good listener and when it had all been revealed to her she felt as if she had been there.

"Can I go and help you next time?" Rosalie asked.

Jimmy Dale was surprised at Rosalie's question. He had expected her to be proud of his achievement and to be glad to have the money. But he had also expected a mild reprimand. He had expected her to ask him to give it up. But instead the opposite had taken place. He was glad that she was supportive but didn't feel like it was an appropriate environment for a woman.

"I don't know baby. It's a little dangerous," Jimmy Dale answered.

Jimmy Dale was unsure and he paused while he thought a little bit more about what she was asking of him.

"Have you been listening to me," Jimmy Dale said finally stating the obvious.

"Yeah I've been listening. And I think I can help."

******

Three weeks later - on the third leg of his second Acuña / Seguin / Chicago / Seguin round trip - Jimmy Dale approached Larry's welfare domicile with some apprehension. Jimmy Dale had decided against bringing Rosalie. He felt like he still had some rough edges that needed to be smoothed out. And she needed to work so he used that as his excuse to leave her in Seguin.

Jimmy Dale was not looking forward to seeing Otis and he knew Otis would be at the meeting. It occurred to Jimmy Dale that it was June Teenth but he dismissed the thought almost as soon as it entered his head knowing that it probably wouldn't have a positive effect on Otis' attitude. He knocked on the door and Larry answered. He saw Otis and Jarvis on the couch in pretty much the same position as he first saw them one month prior. Otis and Jarvis both got up from their seats and greeted Jimmy Dale with a handshake and a bro hug. Jimmy Dale was trying to put the tension between him and these two men behind him.

"How you been doin' man?" Otis asked. It looked to Jimmy Dale like Otis might be making the same attempt.

"I been alright. How ya'll been?"

"We've been doin' ok. Actually we been doin' a little too good."

"What do you mean?" Jimmy Dale noticed a precursor to a problem in the way that Otis had answered him. It worried him a little bit. He had hoped that most of the challenges were behind them.

"That stuff you sold us. It's some good shit. Like I say, maybe a little too good."

"How can it be too good? I thought you wanted good. Even if it is too good, then just cut it. I don't understand."

Otis continued, "Well we coulda done that, but we didn't. I mean we cut it, just not enough I guess. We just ain't used to dealin' with this level of purity. Know what I mean? Anyway, we've attracted some attention and it's the kind of attention we'd rather not have."

"Cops?" Jimmy Dale asked.

"I wish it was jus' the cops. But it ain't the cops. There's this fella up here. He's kinda got his thumb on the whole drug trade and everything. His name's Rennozo and he found out there's some really good new shit out there. He knows it's small time, so normally he'd just let us slide. But somebody turned him on to the quality and so now he's interested. He wants to know who's got it, where it's comin' from and all the particulars."

"Did you tell him?"

"I ain't told him anything. I never seen the man. Probably never will. But he knows how to get the word out and it's made it back to me. And once this guy gets his hooks in you - you're done. He owns you. I think he owns me already anyway. So you can understand my predicament. I can give you up or I can sit around here and wait for the firin' squad. See what I mean?"

"What do you mean, 'Give me up?' I don't really want to get killed either," Jimmy Dale said.

"I don't mean hand you over so he can clip you. He probably just wants to partner up with you. Who knows?"

"I'm not sure that Rennozo takes on partners." Jarvis jumped in and said exactly what Jimmy Dale was thinking.

"Jarvis is right. If this guy is who I think he is, he doesn't partner up...he takes over. And there usually aren't any witnesses." Jimmy Dale was speaking of the stereotypical mob boss. Jimmy Dale wasn't sure if he believed that Rennozo was a man of that position, or that he even necessarily existed, but he allowed for the possibility.

"What do you want me to do? I can't act stupid. He knows that I know. Ya know?" Otis pretended to care.

"Can I unload my shipment and be gone like we arranged?"

"No," Otis said with finality.

"Then I need to take a day and think about this." Jimmy Dale decided he needed to buy some time. If Otis wasn't willing to take his product, perhaps someone else was. He wasn't going to simply run back to Texas with his tail between his legs just because some person, who may or may not exist, has dictated an order to some lowlife, who may or may not have made the whole thing up.

"It's your life," Otis said and then, "And I mean that literally."

Jimmy Dale just looked at Otis waiting for an explanation.

"I had a buddy a couple of years ago get on Renozzo's bad side and he wound up at the dump."

"I'll talk to you later." Jimmy Dale said taking the statement in stride. He backed up toward the door and left. Nobody said anything else to him or tried to hinder his departure in any way. He walked across the lawn to his truck. He felt disappointed but he wasn't fearful. He was wondering to himself if he should be scared when he noticed a Cadillac parked behind the GMC with two men inside. As he neared the truck the two men got out of the car. Jimmy Dale had a premonition that maybe he was in over his head. The first man approached him.

"Hey how you doing? You Jimmy Dale?" the man asked. He was friendly but the friendliness was tinged with condescension.

"Yeah that's me."

"You got time for a little ride?"

He was a white man in his late 30s and appeared to be of Italian descent. He was dressed in a white shirt with a fly away collar with the first two buttons unbuttoned. His slacks were gray and his loafers were cheap. He was of average height and build. His partner - the second man - was a couple of inches taller and 100 pounds heavier. He pursed his lips just a bit and barely nodded his head when Jimmy Dale looked at him. He was letting Jimmy Dale know that he was in agreement with his partner's request. Jimmy Dale looked back toward the first man.

"Where we going?" Jimmy Dale asked.

"We're going to have a talk. We need you to get in the car," the first man said.

"What if I don't go?"

"I don't think you want that to happen." It was the second man now, the heavier one. He shook his head side to side as he delivered his advice to Jimmy Dale.

Jimmy Dale considered his options. He could run. And if he wasn't barely off crutches he could probably outrun these two guys as long as they didn't shoot him, which they probably wouldn't. The other problem besides his inability to run swiftly, would be the truck. They knew his truck and they'd either steal it or let it sit and pick him up when he came back to get it. Of course he could just abandon it but it would be a fairly simple task to figure out the address of the registered owner. Add to this that the vehicle would eventually be towed putting him on the authorities' radar and it just seemed like a bad idea to try to escape on foot. But of course it really didn't matter that he had decided against running anyway because he was, at least for the next couple of months or so, severely limited in his ability as a pedestrian. With his left foot still on the mend he wasn't going to be outrunning any Italian anywhere – not even the fat ones. Jimmy Dale looked back toward Larry's porch. Larry, Otis, and Jarvis were all out front watching. He realized he was not getting out of this. He decided his best bet was to go along with the abduction. He thought to himself, *what is it with these guys in Chicago that they always want to take rides?* The second larger man opened the front passenger side door and stood waiting for Jimmy Dale to get in. Once Jimmy Dale was inside the second man walked around the car and got in the back. Once they were on their way the driver joined the conversation.

"So you're from Texas?" the first man asked.

"I am."

"Never been there," he said and then paused before asking, "You like Chicago?"

"I do like it."

"You know your way around up here?"

Jimmy Dale noticed that the first man was doing most of the talking. The second guy – the fat one in the back – said very little.

"Can't say that I do," Jimmy Dale replied.

Nobody said anything for a couple of minutes. Jimmy Dale wondered why they wouldn't ask about his foot and why he was limping. If they were going to engage in small talk, it seemed like a likely point of conversation. He guessed though that they probably already knew how he had gotten hurt.

"We're just going to take a little ride today. Have a little meeting," the first man said.

"Good thing I like taking rides," Jimmy Dale said. "What's the meeting about?"

"You got some guys interested in how you put this whole operation together. We just want to talk to you about it."

The first man was leaning over with his right elbow on the center console. His left arm rested on the steering wheel at the wrist with his hand hanging down loosely. They drove around the south side but Jimmy Dale really didn't have any idea where they were and after about ten minutes they arrived at a warehouse. There was a door in the front of the building that looked like it might lead to an office. Jimmy Dale got out with the two men and went inside.

It was dusty with papers and binders and stuff stacked everywhere. The office chairs were thread bare and Jimmy Dale was told to sit so he did. The fat man that had ridden in the back sat down too. The first man left the room through a back door that looked like it led into the warehouse. Jimmy Dale looked around the office. There was a map of Chicago on the wall, a transistor radio, a calendar from 1992 that was frozen on the month of November, and an oscillating fan sitting on the desk. Jimmy Dale noticed that there was not a computer. Save the calendar, he could have been sitting in an office from the 1960s. The fat man sat contentedly and looked at Jimmy Dale. Jimmy Dale guessed that it was his job to keep him company. The man's arms were folded across his chest in an authoritative fashion. Jimmy Dale noticed that he didn't seem to blink much. Twenty minutes later the first man – the one that had done most of the talking and all of the driving – returned. A older man in his mid 50's, balding with a moustache and no beard, followed them into the room.

"Hello Jimmy Dale," the older man said. "My name is Marco Renozzo. It has come to my attention that you have been supplying cocaine to some associates of ours. The product that you are supplying is of a very high quality and I would be interested to know where you got it, how you got it here, and if you can get some more. We would like to be involved with your business as a partner. I think we can provide some services that could enhance the profitability of this venture."

"Do I have a choice?" Jimmy Dale asked.

"No," Renozzo responded.

"That's what I thought." Jimmy Dale paused. And then, "Suppose I just quit. Suppose I just close up shop and disappear. What happens then?"

"If that's what you would like to do, then you are welcome to do so. We can arrange to help you with that disappearance if you like."

Jimmy Dale looked at Renozzo. *Was this actually happening?* Jimmy Dale thought to himself. Jimmy Dale had been threatened before but it had been mostly small time hoods - scumbags with something to prove so they blustered and blew and let Jimmy Dale know that they were not someone to be messed with. But the rule was this: if you had to tell someone you were not to be messed with, then it was ok to mess with you. It was the ones that didn't have to say it - those were the guys that you needed to be worried about. Jimmy Dale noticed that Renozzo never said anything about not messing with him.

"Can I think about it?" Jimmy Dale asked finally.

"Certainly. Donny will accompany you back to your hotel room. Will one day be enough time to make up your mind?" Renozzo motioned toward the fat man seated on the other side of the room as he talked, identifying him as Donny.

"How do I let you know what I've decided to do?" Jimmy Dale knew the answer to that question but asked it anyway.

"You can just tell Donny. He'll be there with you and he will let me know. Is there anything else I can do for you? Is there anything I can get for you to make your stay more comfortable? You appear to have suffered an injury to your foot. Do you have adequate medical care?"

"I'll be alright," Jimmy Dale responded.

"Good. Then I will see you tomorrow at about this time. Donny will act as your chauffer. Have a nice day."

Renozzo got up and left without shaking hands. The first man from the car that had entered the room with Renozzo followed him back out the same door that they had entered. Jimmy Dale could hear Renozzo talking to him after they had shut the door but he couldn't make out what they were saying.

The fat man that had ridden in the back of the Cadillac on the ride over to the warehouse, the man Jimmy Dale now knew as Donny, got up and spoke for the first time since they arrived at the warehouse saying, "Stand up. I need to frisk you."

Jimmy Dale stood and spread his arms like a scarecrow. Donny worked his way from Jimmy Dale's shoulder down to his ankles. He confiscated the .45. He also took Jimmy Dale's wallet.

"I don't think you'll be needing these," Donny said. He put the wallet and the .45 in the top drawer of the desk. "You can have these back tomorrow. Let's go."

Jimmy Dale hobbled out the door to the Cadillac and got in the front passenger's seat. The car rocked significantly when Donny squeezed behind the wheel. The keys had been left in the ignition and Donny started the car and drove back the way they had come. Jimmy Dale recognized some of the businesses as they passed by them for the second time in 45 minutes. Donny didn't say much. Actually he didn't say anything at all. Jimmy Dale expected to go back to the hotel and thought Donny might ask about that but he didn't. Instead they went to the GMC.

"Give me your keys," Donny ordered.

Jimmy Dale gave Donny his keys.

"Don't move. If you move I'll shoot you."

Donny pulled out the nine millimeter and showed it to Jimmy Dale. He made a point of making eye contact so Jimmy Dale would be sure to get the message. Then he got out, pistol in hand, and opened the GMC. He pretty much tore it apart. He didn't find anything because there was nothing to find.

"Get out of the car and come with me."

Donny motioned to Jimmy Dale with the gun to add emphasis to his instructions. They walked to Larry's unit and Donny knocked on the door.

"What's goin' on?" Larry answered. The chain was still on the door and Larry spoke through the crack.

"Open the damn door," Donny said.

CHAPTER 17

Larry pondered the ribald man that had given him the command. He decided it was in his best interest to follow it so he opened the door. It was becoming obvious to Jimmy Dale that whatever this organization was that Donny belonged to; the mob, the mafia, whatever, they ran things. The scum around town – like Larry – were intimidated enough to follow orders and not ask any questions. Donny and the guys that Donny worked for, they asked the questions.

"Where does he keep the dope?" Donny asked.

"I don't know man. He played hell with us last time. Keepin' us jumpin' and shit. We never saw more than a few ounces at a time and he had us drivin' all over the south side."

"Where do you keep it?" Donny asked Jimmy Dale loudly and forcefully, his spittle making the point ever so much more salient.

When Jimmy Dale didn't respond Donny backhanded him with the butt of the gun. The gun struck Jimmy Dale in the lower front teeth and he felt his teeth grind together and break. He spit out pieces of his teeth mixed with blood from his lower lip. For the first time Jimmy Dale wondered exactly what the final toll would be – in terms of body parts – for this endeavor.

"It's at the hotel," Jimmy Dale said leaning over with a mixture of blood and saliva oozing from this mouth.

"We already looked there. There was nothing in the hotel room," Donny said.

"Your boys didn't look in the right place. It's in the cooler. Just quit hitting me." Jimmy Dale's voice was laced with anger, not fear. His instinct was to lash out at his fat tormentor but fought back the temptation.

"We looked in the cooler. It wasn't there."

"It's in the cooler. We'll go. I'll show you." Jimmy Dale said.

Donny got his head around the situation and barked an order. "I want you to drive his car to the hotel and leave it there. I don't want no cops looking at a car with out of state plates and asking any questions around here," Donny said as he tossed Larry the keys.

"Are you gonna bring me back?" Larry asked.

"Not my problem. Get one of your lowlife drug peddling friends to help you out."

Larry did as he was told and followed Donny and Jimmy Dale back to the hotel. When they got there Larry got out and wandered off.

"Show it to me," Donny commanded once they were in the hotel room.

Jimmy Dale dumped the entire contents of the cooler: cans of soda and beer, water and ice, into the bath tub and set the cooler, upside down, in the main room. The hammer had been kept nearby for just such a moment. Jimmy Dale took the hammer and with the claw, gently scraped away the mortar that had been set around the piece of the cooler on the bottom that had been cut away and then replaced. Then he tapped around the edges and the piece broke free. He pulled the cut out piece away and there the drugs were right in front of them. He was kneeling as he did all this and he now turned his head to the side and looked upward at Donny. Donny was pulling out his cell phone.

"I got it," he said to some unknown party and then hung up.

"Put everything in here," he said to Jimmy Dale and threw down a small blue gym bag. Jimmy Dale placed the drugs in the bag and then walked into the bathroom and wrapped some ice in a hand towel and applied it to his lip.

"Lay down on the bed."

"Why do I have to lay down?" Jimmy Dale asked.

"Lay down. You ain't moving around where I have to watch you."

"How long do we have to do this?"

"You asked for one day and Renozzo gave you a day. I guess we have to do this for one day."

"What if I'm ready to make a deal right now?"

"Renozzo wants to talk to you tomorrow. We'll go back then. Now lay down."

Jimmy Dale lay down on the bed near the back of the room and Donny handcuffed him to the bed post on the far side. The handcuffs had a long chain, maybe two feet, so Jimmy Dale had some latitude, but not enough to get his hands on anything important. Donny took off his shoes and shirt and sat down at the table by the window near the front door. He sat there in his wife beater t-shirt and looked out the crack in the curtains every couple of minutes. Twenty minutes later Donny got up and opened the door, the man who had driven the Cadillac earlier in the day was standing there and Donny handed him the gym bag with the drugs. He also gave him the keys to Jimmy Dale's truck.

"Take the truck and park it in the warehouse. I don't want anybody asking any questions," Donny told his accomplice.

Donny and Jimmy Dale spent the afternoon watching TV. Around 6:00 Donny got up to leave.

"I'm going to the café across the street. I can see the door to this motel room so don't try anything. It ain't worth it," Donny said. The arms of the recliner creaked under the strain of man's weight as he lifted himself up.

Donny put on his shirt and shoes and left. Jimmy Dale tried to come up with something but the prospects for escape were limited. Short of having the keys or a hacksaw, he wasn't going anywhere. Donny was back in an hour smelling like meatloaf. He threw a takeout bag on the bed. Jimmy Dale was hungry, but the open wound on his mouth slowed the process. It hurt - especially when he ate. Besides the sandwich from the café, Donny brought with him a fifth of Wild Turkey. He took two of the plastic wrapped cups from the counter in the bathroom, unwrapped one and filled it ¼ full while he stood.

Donny lifted the cup towards Jimmy Dale and asked, "You want?"

"Yeah. It's ok?"

Donny unwrapped the other cup also filling it ¼ of the way full and handed it to Jimmy Dale. Jimmy Dale sipped it. The burn was good. It hurt the wound on his mouth but felt good at the same time.

"It'll help against infection," Donny said offering up some free medical advice.

He took off his shirt again, sat on the bed and put the bottle on the night stand next to him. He drank two more drinks then lit a cigar. He didn't offer Jimmy Dale anything more. After the cigar he had two more drinks and then sat quietly. Around 10:00 the phone rang and he stepped outside and talked for ten minutes. Then he came back in and laid down not saying anything to Jimmy Dale. Within ten minutes he was snoring. Loudly. Jimmy Dale had hoped that Donny might get sloppy with the liquor and provide an opening but he hadn't. Donny didn't do anything that would put himself in harm's way or imperil his mission. Jimmy Dale took note of how Donny's physical appearance really wasn't an indicator of how he handled the task that had been put to him by Renozzo. He was all business.

Both men woke up about the same time the next morning. Donny showered and shaved and then left for the café. He returned with a croissant for Jimmy Dale. They spent the day in pretty much the same way that they spent the day before.

At 3:00 Donny returned from a late lunch and said, "Renozzo wants to see you."

Donny threw the keys to the handcuffs at Jimmy Dale, instructing him without saying anything to unlock himself.

They were, in short order, sitting in the dank, outdated office space they had been in the day before when they talked to Renozzo. After a few minutes Jimmy Dale and Donny were joined by the man who had driven the Cadillac the day before.

"You ready to make a deal Jimmy Dale? the driver asked. He emphasized Jimmy Dale's name and station by invoking a fake, over-the-top southern accent.

"What sort of a deal am I being offered?"

"The boss man will talk to you about that," he said. "You drink coffee?"

"Yeah, I'll take a cup of coffee."

"Here's a cup. There's the coffee maker. Renozzo will be here in a minute."

The driver walked out. Donny stayed and drank coffee with Jimmy Dale. Three minutes later Renozzo entered the room.

"Good morning Jimmy Dale," Renozzo said.

Renozzo had no condescension in his voice. He sat in the chair behind the main desk and looked at him. Donny sat behind Jimmy Dale.

"Good morning," Jimmy Dale said returning the greeting.

"Jimmy Dale, we would like to begin work immediately. And we want you to help us. There will be some risk involved, but the rewards will be high."

"How high?"

"We are aware of your present activity level with Otis and Jarvis. It's small time. We're offering you the opportunity to pick it up a little bit. How long does it take you now to move one kilo of cocaine?"

Jimmy Dale stared at Renozzo for a moment then answered, "Couple months maybe."

"We would like one kilo per week - to start with. I know that Otis and Jarvis paid you $15,000 and we're prepared to honor that agreement on all future deliveries."

"What exactly do I have to do? Do I deliver it to Chicago? Do I bring it to this warehouse? What?"

"You will deliver one kilo of cocaine to this warehouse every Friday at noon. Today is Thursday. Your first delivery is due one week from tomorrow. You will be paid in cash, in full, upon confirmation that the quantity and the quality are consistent with our agreement. That's it. And you don't have to work with the niggers on the south side any more. We'll take care of them."

Jimmy Dale took a deep breath and exhaled so that those around him could hear it. He was leaning forward with his elbows on his knees and his hands folded in front of him. He let his head droop as he exhaled. His mind was in high gear. After expenses he could make $8,000 to $10,000 per week. In two years he could have that ranch that he wanted. He could realize his dream. And Renozzo's point about Otis and Jarvis was a good one. It wasn't clear whether Renozzo's goons were any less dangerous, but he was dealing with undesirables no matter how you cut it.

"This offer is being presented as a choice. But yesterday you said I really didn't have one. Do I have a choice or not?" Jimmy Dale asked.

"There are always choices to be made," Renozzo began. "The choice that you have is to a) work for us under the terms that I have laid out for you and to get rich or to b) disappear."

Renozzo took out a piece of paper from a folder that he had brought in with him. He laid that paper on the desk in front of Jimmy Dale. The paper was a picture of Jimmy Dale's trailer in Seguin.

"You do want to get rich, don't you?" Renozzo asked rhetorically. "Maybe move out of this trailer? Maybe move into something a little more comfortable and respectable? Of course there is always option b."

Renozzo laid a second piece of paper in front of Jimmy Dale. It was a picture of Otis. His head was bloody and mangled. His body was laying among refuse in an alley somewhere. Somewhere that Jimmy Dale did not want to be.

Renozzo continued, "Otis knew better than to go out on his own. But he did it anyway. Jarvis is still alive. He pled ignorance and we chose to let him live. It doesn't really matter. You'll never see either one of them again."

Jimmy Dale noticed that Renozzo didn't say anything about Larry.

"One key a week is a lot. I'm not sure that my supplier can handle it."

"Perhaps you could reason with him."

"Perhaps," Jimmy Dale answered.

"We understand each other then. You seem very level headed Jimmy Dale. Do not disappoint me."

"When do I get my truck back?" Jimmy Dale asked implicitly agreeing to the terms of their arrangement.

"It's available now. We will see you a week from tomorrow at 12:00. Here's a number to call. Use it sparingly. For emergency use only," Renozzo said as he tossed Jimmy Dale his keys. "Your truck is in the back."

Renozzo walked out the back. Donny stayed in the office and looked at Jimmy Dale.

"Otis mentioned a buddy of his that ended up at the dump after getting crosswise with Renozzo. You know anything about that?" Jimmy Dale asked.

"That nigger was so dumb he had a hard time telling the difference between an egg and the number 4. I wouldn't pay any attention to anything he said. Look where he ended up. You just take care of Jimmy Dale," Donny said.

"Ok. I guess I'll see you next week." Jimmy Dale replied realizing the answer to his question was buried in Donny's statement.

******

Neal checked the location of the GPS unit regularly…Chicago, Seguin, Chicago again, Seguin again. *What's this guy doing?* he thought to himself. Neal surmised that it was probably drugs but he didn't know for sure. And to squeeze him Neal had to know for certain what James Dale was doing. Neal decided that the only way to find out would be to follow him around. The more he thought about it the more he liked the idea. He had some vacation time coming anyway. Why not head to Chicago, figure out what this James Dale guy was up to, and maybe enjoy the Windy City?

So Neal told Frank that he had a business deal working – the details of which he was not able to disclose - and that he might have to leave on a moment's notice. Neal had failings as a person, not the least of which was his dishonesty, but as an employee he was on the straight and narrow. He didn't take that trait from his upbringing but rather from his tenure as a bondsman. Joe at AAAA bail bonds had somehow managed to instill in Neal what his mother had failed to do. From 9:00 to 5:00 he played it straight and that meant letting Frank know in advance that he would be needing some time off instead of just going AWOL.

"Just let me know as soon as you can when you're taking off and try not to be gone more than a week. I can't handle any more time than that stuck here with Paulina." Frank pointed nonchalantly with his right thumb at Paul, the recently hired associate that had some decidedly feminine characteristics. "Can you handle that?" Frank asked.

"You got it boss," Neal said.

Eighteen hours later Neal checked the location of the GPS unit. It was in Uvalde, Texas and heading west. *Doesn't look like a Cubs game is in the making this week*, Neal said to himself. And just as Jimmy Dale had tracked Neal's landlord Jack Johnson six weeks earlier, Neal now tracked Jimmy Dale in the same fashion; following the unit in his vehicle and stopping every 30 minutes to take a reading on his quarry to make sure he was still on track. When Neal got to Del Rio he found that James Dale was already in Mexico. He thought long and hard about crossing the bridge but decided against it – he was just too self conscious about being white bread. So he found a park bench in a green space on West Garfield near downtown and continued his virtual vigil from there, glancing towards Mexico every now and then and wondering exactly what James Dale was doing.

****

"One key per week is a lot of cocaine. What has happened that you are so successful?" Chavo asked Jimmy Dale.

The two were sitting in the square in Acuña. Jimmy Dale had left Chicago three days earlier and was now attempting to put together the drug deal that had been mandated by his new partners in Chicago.

"I've got everything in place and I'm ready to start making some real money. You told me more volume wasn't a problem. Is it?"

"I don't think that it's a problem."

"Well I'm going to share with you what my problem is," Jimmy Dale said. "I don't want to get caught. Especially by the Mexican police. That's my problem."

Chavo looked at Jimmy Dale. His face was expressionless.

"Those cops…" Jimmy Dale continued, "…that day we made the exchange a couple of weeks ago…they shook me down. They were looking for the cocaine."

"You were stopped by the police?" Chavo asked with false incredulity.

"Yeah."

"Why?" Chavo continued with the ruse.

"I think that they thought I was carrying drugs."

"How do you know that?"

"Because you told them," Jimmy Dale answered directly.

"I didn't tell them anything. Police in Mexico are always looking for bribes. I would not be concerned."

Jimmy Dale looked to the ground and rubbed his brow with his left thumb and index finger. He looked back up at Chavo on the verge of exasperation.

"Chavo. Stop. I know that you have connections with the cops. I saw you sitting at the table with them at the café."

"I know many people in Acuña. Some of them are policemen."

"This is the way we are going to proceed," Jimmy Dale said cutting to the chase. "I need at least one kilo of cocaine. If I can get two I would like to get two. I have up to $6,000 to give you for two kilos if you can do that. And the next exchange will be safe. I will not risk imprisonment in a Mexican jail on drug charges. I'll call you tomorrow morning and I'll give you the instructions then. But I need to know now. Can you provide me with two kilos?"

Chavo pulled out his mobile phone and punched a two digit speed dial code. Jimmy Dale could hear a man pick up on the other end. Chavo stood and walked away from the bench where they were seated as he started the conversation. He paced in a wide circle around the bench as he talked – just outside of earshot. On his third revolution Chavo broke off from his orbit and returned to the bench.

"You are not running this operation here in Mexico Jimmy. We run the operations here. The Mexicans. Do you understand this?"

"I do."

"For someone that is dependent upon us here in this country you are making many demands. Many of these demands are not acceptable to us. The original agreement called for one kilo every couple of months. Now you want to change this. You want one kilo every week. You are also very demanding about the details of the exchange. We do not like being told when or where. We do the telling. Not you. Do you understand this?"

"I understand what you are saying to me. But what does it mean?"

"It means that you will have your two kilos. But the exchange will take place according to my terms. Not yours."

"Then I won't do it," Jimmy Dale said.

Jimmy Dale was not able to yield on this point and left the bench in a hurry. If Chavo was insistent on dictating the terms of the exchange he would be unprotected and almost certain to be picked up or killed - or both. He had been lucky after the last exchange. His precautions against just such an occurrence had been enough. But next time – there would not be a next time. He would rather take his chances with the Chicago mob then walk knowingly into a trap in Mexico. He was two blocks away when he heard the familiar rumble.

"Get in Jimmy." Chavo said as he pulled up alongside Jimmy Dale in his El Camino.

"Where we going?"

"To see my boss." Chavo moved the vehicle along at three mph.

"Is this the same boss that ordered the beating on me?"

"It's the same. But his temperament has improved."

They came to an intersection with a stop sign and Jimmy Dale got in the car.

"He was upset with me last time that I didn't have the money. You remember that don't you? 'Cause I don't have the money with me today either," Jimmy Dale said.

"It's ok. He just wants to talk to you."

"He asked for me?"

"Yes."

"Let's go see him then."

CHAPTER 18

The house looked the same as when Jimmy Dale had visited before. The gate was still held in place by baling wire and the same boy ran out to open the gate when Chavo touched off the horn. The same dogs were chained in the front yard but they seemed to have calmed down considerably. Gone were the snarls and snapping teeth replaced by inquisitiveness. Chavo parked the car near the front steps and Jimmy Dale got out and went the long way around the front of the car, squeezing between the front driver side fender and the house. Walking behind the bed of the El Camino would have taken him through the dirt circle worn down by the dogs and despite their improved temperament Jimmy Dale didn't trust Mexican dogs any more than he trusted Mexican people.

They climbed the steps and entered the main room of the house like before. The room was unchanged from their earlier visit except that the card table and chairs had been moved to sit directly in front of the TV. There was an old lady sitting at the table watching a novella. Chavo sat down on the couch and Jimmy Dale followed suit. The old lady never looked up. The Patrón came in through the back door and picked up one of the metal chairs from around the card table and set it in front of the couch. An associate followed him in – Jimmy Dale did not recognize him – and picked up a second chair, setting it just a little bit behind the Patrón's chair. The associate sat backwards in his chair in contrast to the Patrón's more dignified forward style of sitting.

"You want to make a deal with me?" the Patrón said to Jimmy Dale. The last time Jimmy Dale was barely noticed. He had been persona non grata and was spoken of more than he was spoken to. This time he was spoken to first.

"I want to keep the same deal that I had with Chavo…except I need more."

"One kilo per week," the Patrón said by way of confirmation.

"That's right. I need one kilo of cocaine per week."

"Why do you need so much?"

"I have contacts in America that want it," Jimmy Dale replied.

"Why do they need so much?"

"Americans want drugs. My contact is in a major American city and he controls the supply of drugs in a large portion of that city. I think he needs much more than one kilo per week. But this is what he has asked of me and I promised him that I would approach you on his behalf and ask if you would be willing to supply that amount."

"What city?"

"Chicago."

"That is a large city."

There was a pause. Chavo sat and listened.

"Could I ask your name sir?" Jimmy Dale asked. He had decided to press his new found status.

"My name is Miguel Arredondo."

There was a long pause as the parties attempted to grasp where the conversation was heading.

"How do you get the drugs across?" Arredondo asked breaking the silence.

Jimmy Dale had prepared for the possibility that Arredondo would probably ask him this question. He had decided in advance that he would be forthright. He was in deep now and playing over his head. As he prepared to answer the thought came to him that he could recruit Chavo or someone else in Arredondo's organization to take care of the business on the Mexican side.

"I shoot the drugs across with an air gun. I wrap it up in small packages." Jimmy Dale used his hands to describe the size and shape of the packages of cocaine.

"Then I load it into an air gun and shoot it over," Jimmy Dale continued. "I go to the other side and pretend to fish and I pick up my product."

Arredondo smiled and shook his head in approval. He looked at Chavo. Chavo was smiling too.

"All I need is to be able to buy the coke and be able to move about safely in Acuña until I am able to get the product across the river. I have the money and I am able to pay today if you're ok with it."

"I cannot promise your safety. That is up to you. I can promise that we will supply the cocaine."

"Can I get the coke today? I can be back in two hours with the money. Is that ok? Jimmy Dale was in a bit of a hurry. It was Tuesday and he needed to be back in Chicago by Friday noon.

"If you pay, you can have the cocaine today. Work with Chavo."

"Chavo tried to have me arrested last time," Jimmy Dale said although he realized it probably really didn't matter.

Chavo laughed loudly and Arrendondo and the bodyguard sitting backwards in his chair joined in.

"Everyone in Mexico gets arrested," Chavo said.

And somehow it all rang true with Jimmy Dale. He was tempted to laugh with them but managed to hold back.

"I already told Chavo that I won't buy under his terms. I'd rather walk away," Jimmy Dale said to Arredondo.

"My friend. We will work this out. It is ok. Everything will be fine." Chavo said to Jimmy Dale in an attempt to reassure him.

Jimmy Dale looked to Arredondo again hoping he would offer his assurance that Jimmy Dale would not be harassed.

"You will work with Chavo. It will be fine," Arredondo said with finality.

Arredondo got up and left. His bodyguard followed close behind. The old lady remained engrossed in the novella on the TV. Jimmy Dale and Chavo stood up to leave.

"I don't like this," Jimmy Dale said. "If you want my money then you and I will have to reach an agreement where I feel safe. I cannot continue to sidestep your spies. I'm not that good. Sooner or later I will be caught and it will probably be sooner rather than later."

"Let's go. We will talk in the car," Chavo said.

When they stepped on the porch, Chavo ordered the house boy to open the gate. They pulled out quickly, kicking up dust and loose gravel. Jimmy Dale spoke first.

"Chavo, I just don't see how we can make this work. I'm not going to make an exchange out in the open where I can get picked up. I'm not going to do it."

"What if I handle everything from Mexico?"

"I'm listening," Jimmy Dale replied. He had hope that Chavo would offer to handle everything from the Mexican side.

"What if you come to Mexico to pay me and then retrieve the packages on the other side just like you are doing now," Chavo said.

"Ok. How much is this going to cost me?"

"$1,000."

"Ok. So my cost has gone from $3,000 to $4,000," Jimmy Dale confirmed.

"Yes. But if you buy two keys at a time I will still only charge you $1,000. So that's only an extra $500 per key. And your risk is much less. You never have to touch anything on this side."

"That's not less risk, it's just transferring the risk from me getting caught to you taking my money and skipping out. Here's what I will do. I will pay you the $1,000 but you handle the product and I never touch anything. I don't even get in the car with you. I just follow you and watch. When everything is complete then I will head back over the river and pick up the packages. That sounds fair Chavo. It's $1,000 for two or three hours."

"Ok," the Mexican agreed.

"Ok then. Can we make the exchange tonight?"

Chavo nodded his head in agreement.

"Then how much are we doing this time? One key or two?" Jimmy Dale asked.

"We'll do one this time. We'll talk about more next time."

"I'll get the money and the air gun and I'll meet you at the café at sundown."

"I will meet you there," Chavo answered.

****

The human mind will create a version of reality when actual reality is not available. Neal had not yet seen James Dale Klein's face so his mind created a version of the man. And he didn't know exactly what James Dale was doing or what his surroundings were like some four miles to the southwest, so his mind filled in the blanks for him. He inserted James Dale into a scene from the movie *Zorro* with Antonio Banderas because that was Neal's version of what it was like on the other side of the river. Neal stuck to his post at the bench until after dark. He was about to start making arrangements for his overnight stay when he saw that James Dale was on the move heading southeast and hugging the river. At 8:42 the unit stopped and remained idle for a little over an hour. At 9:58 the unit began to retrace its path along the river this time moving northwest and arriving at the bridge a few minutes later. The unit proceeded more slowly now, presumably in line at the international bridge, and finally crossed back into the U.S. at 10:16.

Once in the U.S. the unit moved predictably quicker. So quickly in fact that Neal could see that a very close encounter with James Dale Klein of Seguin, Texas was imminent. Neal glanced up from tracking the unit to see a GMC single cab pickup truck rolling past him heading north. Neal remembered the vehicle from that night at the Adobe Palms. The driver was only within Neal's field of vision for a brief second, barely enough time to get an impression of the man, but enough for Neal to notice that James Dale looked completely different from how he had imagined him. The GMC passed by and made a right on 277. Neal skipped quickly to his Grand Cherokee and then settled in as a tail on the pickup.

Neal kept one eye on the road and one eye on the GPS. When Neal came to the point where the GPS unit had veered off the road and moved down a gravel two-track toward the river, Neal stayed with the main road. It was too conspicuous to follow him down the path. The pathway to the river was too lightly travelled and if Neal were to encounter James Dale his cover would be blown. So he stuck with the main road driving on for a mile or so and then made a u-turn. He passed the gravel road a second time, this time with the path on his left, then pulled into a convenience store ¼ mile farther on. He took up his vigil from there.

It didn't take long to get interesting. A green and white border patrol SUV drove past the convenience store in the direction of the gravel road that James Dale had taken a few minutes earlier. Neal saw the blinker indicating a right turn and caught intermittent glimpses of the vehicle's brake lights through the brush as it descended the alluvial plain to the river. Then Neal saw that the agent hit the light bar. The brush was illuminated with pulses of light a few hundred yards from where Neal was sitting. His curiosity concerning the events just down the slope was nearly overwhelming. He sat in the driver's seat with his back off the back rest of the seat and leaning slightly forward from 90 degrees. His head was tilted back a little and he looked down his nose like an old lady looking through her bifocals. It was as if he was trying to direct his line of sight over the top of the brush and then down on to the scene with the border patrol agent. *What was going on?* he thought to himself.

Two minutes after they started, the patrol lights from the border patrol truck went dark. And a minute after that James Dale's truck emerged from the brush and came back northwest on 277 toward downtown Del Rio. Almost immediately James Dale had his blinker on indicating an impending right hand turn into the convenience store. *HE WAS COMING INTO THE STORE!* Neal didn't do anything. He just watched as James Dale drove within 20 feet of him, parked, and went inside. James Dale made a quick purchase – Neal couldn't tell what it was that he bought – and then got back in the truck. James Dale unexpectedly made a left out the store parking lot and then the quick right back onto the gravel road. He was going back to where he had come from. Neal quit trying to figure out what was happening. He just watched.

At about midnight James Dale's GMC came out of the brush again and pulled into the parking lot of the convenience store. He got out, and getting something from the bed of his truck, threw it in the dumpster. It looked like a fish. Then James Dale got back in the truck and left, driving toward Del Rio. Neal observed Jimmy Dale's movements on the GPS map and recognized the spot where he came to rest at a motel on the main drag. *Good*, Neal thought to himself, *maybe I can take a little break.* Neal drove back to the parking lot at the green space on West Garfield and lay down in the front seat.

There's nothing like an uncomfortable sleeping situation to motivate you to get up and get going. So despite a propensity toward sleeping in, combined with an eventful day that ended after midnight, Neal was up when the sun came up at 7:00. After a quick reading he saw that the GPS unit had not moved.

Neal had purposefully waited until he was out of the San Antonio area to make a withdrawal from his prepaid credit card. If anyone ever scrutinized the paper trail from the card that he was using as a clearing house, Neal wanted that trail to be inconsistent and without any kind of discernible pattern. So now that he was well away from his base of operations, it seemed like it might be safe to make a withdrawal. Neal fired up the Grand Cherokee and drove east along East Gibbs Street stopping at the Fiesta El Mercado grocery store. It was a large establishment in a relatively new retail strip mall on the south side of the street. By describing it as relatively new, it could be said that it was merely not old and dusty. There was an ATM in the parking lot. Neal parked the jeep about 50 feet from the ATM on the backside facing away from the cameras that recorded the participants in the transactions making their withdrawals. He changed his t-shirt from the blue one he had on with the Dallas Cowboys Star on the front to a plain white one. He wrapped his red handkerchief around his head bandana style and put on his sunglasses. Then he got out of the car and walked to the ATM. When he came around from the side of the ATM toward the front, but was still outside of the field of view of the cameras, he tied a second handkerchief – this time a blue one – across his face and then walked up to the front of the machine. He inserted the card, typed in the PIN and then chose ACCOUNT

SUMMARY. The readout on the screen showed $1,000. *Thanks Billy*, he thought to himself. He then made the maximum withdrawal for that day - $400. Twenty 20s flipped from the dispensing mechanism and pushed forward slightly for the taking. Neal grabbed the cash. He pulled the blue handkerchief from his face as soon as he was away from the prying eyes of the camera. He half ran and half walked back to the Grand Cherokee. When he got back in the jeep, he counted the cash confirming the amount dispensed from the ATM was correct and checked the GPS unit again.

****

Chavo was already at the café when Jimmy Dale showed up at 8:00. He was sitting at what had become their table. Jimmy Dale sat down and ordered a lemonade.

"Are you ready?" Jimmy Dale asked.

"I am ready. You have the money with you?" Chavo inquired.

"It's in the truck. But let's take your car."

Jimmy Dale grabbed the duffel bag from the truck and a few minutes later Jimmy Dale and Chavo were travelling down Libramiento. Jimmy Dale directed Chavo to the barrio near the river. Jimmy Dale scanned their surroundings, taking special care to survey the remote area across the river. Chavo was impatient.

"I need to prepare the merchandise to be shot across the river. Is it safer to sit in the car or we should we do it down by the river?" Jimmy Dale asked.

"It's ok here in the car. The police - they never come here."

Jimmy Dale explained to Chavo how the gun worked and what it was for. He then showed Chavo how to prepare the drugs so that the package would not explode when shot out of the gun and then land safely on the other side. Jimmy Dale was surprised that Chavo never asked to see the money.

"And this little gadget should help us avoid any undesirables," Jimmy Dale said as he pulled out the night vision goggles.

Jimmy Dale had bought them at the army supply store for $700. They worked surprisingly well. Jimmy Dale had considered a cheaper pair for $200 but the clarity of vision was dramatically reduced so he had opted for the higher quality despite the extra nickel. They stumbled and slid down the embankment to the same spot that Jimmy Dale had launched the drugs from before. The dry heat of the Chihuahuan desert summer had withered the vegetation along the banks of the river but there was still adequate cover. They sat, concealed by the moonless night and the dry brush. Jimmy Dale donned the night vision glasses and scanned the other side for several hundred yards in either direction. 200 yards to the southeast sat a border patrol agent in his Yukon.

"Better wait," Jimmy Dale said. "Border patrol a couple hundred yards downstream."

"How long?"

"'Til he leaves. That's how long. I think I can see him from the café anyway. Let's wait up there." They scuffled back up the embankment.

They ate gorditas and drank lemonade in the open air seating area along the street. Jimmy Dale was glad that he could make out the vehicle without the benefit of the night vision goggles. He looked out of place already and the goggles would have been a bit much. Forty-five minutes later the vehicle with the distinctive green and white markings pulled away from its vantage point and crawled over the rocks upstream and back to the main road on the Texas side. Two minutes later, Jimmy Dale and Chavo were at their post by the river. Jimmy Dale handed Chavo the gun.

"Give it a try," Jimmy Dale said to Chavo.

Chavo loaded the package. He checked the CO_2 cartridge and took aim. Jimmy Dale tapped the under-side of the barrel indicating the need for a slightly higher trajectory. Chavo made the adjustment and looked at Jimmy Dale for approval to fire. Jimmy Dale nodded and Chavo squeezed off the trigger. The package was blown from the end of the barrel with a pop and landed delicately in the grass just beyond the bank on the opposite side. Chavo nodded and smiled.

"You gringos," Chavo said under his breath.

Chavo repeated the process of loading the gun and firing four more times.

"Here's the money," Jimmy Dale said as they drove north on Libramiento. He held up the duffel bag and showed Chavo the contents. Then he dropped it back to the floor board. "It's all there. You keep the gun over here. I don't want even the slightest whiff of what we are doing to leak out in case I'm searched. I'll take the CO_2 cartridge with me and have it refilled for you. I'll bring back the cartridge next time and the money for the next key. I'll see you one week from today."

"Be careful my friend," Chavo said.

"Igualmente."

The line at the bridge was short and Jimmy Dale was over in ten minutes and taking the turn on to the dirt road that led to the dropped cocaine in another ten. When he reached his destination he surveyed the surrounding terrain with the night vision goggles and found the area to be free of law enforcement. He got out and strolled down the path to the river, carrying his fishing pole and his tackle box, and retrieving his inventory. He walked the rest of the distance to the river and surveyed the area again. He was looking for law enforcement but also wanted to appear to be interested in the river – and the fishing – just in case law enforcement should be looking at him. He glanced up the opposite side to the top of the trail that he and Chavo had climbed a half hour before. Jimmy Dale could see Chavo standing there with the lights from the street and the café behind him. His lean silhouette had a menacing appearance. He stood and looked back at Jimmy Dale. Chavo touched the brim of his hat and disappeared.

Jimmy Dale felt a little spooked. He mostly resisted the temptation to hurry but still moved a little more quickly than he should have. He threw the fishing equipment in the bed of the truck and started up the gravel road. He met the border patrol agent almost immediately. The agent hit the light bar on top of his vehicle and pulled to a stop. He got out and approached Jimmy Dale's GMC with flashlight in hand. Jimmy Dale rolled down the window. He recognized the agent as the same one he had talked to about fishing a few weeks earlier.

"How you doin' tonight?" the agent asked. He shined the light first on Jimmy Dale's face then on the front seat and then swung the light to the bed of the truck.

"I'm doin' ok." Jimmy Dale's heart was pounding. He knew that fear did not have to leak out and become obvious. It could be controlled. He saw the name on the badge. Roberts.

"Whatcha doin' down here?" Roberts asked.

"Trying to catch a fish. Didn't have much luck."

"Didn't put forth much of an effort. I saw you drive in. Couldn't have been here more than ten minutes."

"I bet I wasn't here that long." Jimmy Dale was thinking quickly. "I realized I forgot my live bait, so I tried it with just my lure and got discouraged. I'm heading back to get some worms and some stink bait. I'm not giving up just yet." Jimmy Dale felt like this was a pretty reasonable explanation. He wanted desperately to leave but knew that any anxiety would be a red flag. He remained calm.

"Alright." Agent Roberts checked out the truck again quickly. Front and back. "I guess I'll see you back down here in a bit then."

"We'll see ya."

Jimmy Dale felt the aggravation well up inside as he pulled into the convenience store parking lot. He had dodged the bullet. That much was true. But now he was on Robert's radar screen. If Roberts was to catch him driving down to the river again he would be sure to watch him more closely. He would likely be searched next time and not be let off with a perfunctory examination. Jimmy Dale tried to put it behind him but his mind kept coming back to it. Jimmy Dale waved at Roberts when he got back to his fishing spot a few minutes later. He caught a 20" channel catfish on a worm and was glad to have it. It helped complete the charade. When he left 90 minutes later Roberts was gone. He threw the cat in the dumpster back at the convenience store where he had bought the bait.

CHAPTER 19

Neal was relieved when he saw that the GPS unit travelled straight back to the hotel and stopped. It was well after midnight and he was tired. He followed the path that the unit had taken and checked into a room on the other side of the hotel so James Dale would be less likely to see the Grand Cherokee again – if he had even seen it at all – and then he crashed. The next morning Neal followed James Dale around as best he could and tried to get a handle on how James Dale's United States operations operated. He watched James Dale fire up the welder, put something in a small metal tube and then weld it shut. *That works?* Neal thought to himself.

Then Neal followed James Dale to the Kountry Kitchen. Neal parked at the Subway Sandwich place across the highway and watched James Dale watch the parking lot at the restaurant. 45 minutes later he saw James Dale approach a fifth wheel, crawl under it and then back out from underneath within the space of 30 seconds.

"Is he doing what I think he's doing?" Neal asked aloud to himself.

Thirty minutes later all three vehicles: the truck pulling the fifth wheel, the GMC that was following the truck, and the Grand Cherokee that was following the GMC that was following the truck were on their way east out of Del Rio headed toward San Antonio with Jimmy Dale and Neal both electronically watching the fifth wheel. With the GPS unit now affixed to the RV, Neal was not able to ascertain Jimmy Dale's exact whereabouts, but he knew pretty much where he was located - he was some reasonable distance behind the truck that was unknowingly carrying the drugs. When the wagon train reached San Antonio the fifth wheel stopped and then continued eastward.

"To hell with this", Neal said to himself and peeled off in the direction of the Adobe Palms. "This is James Dale's responsibility. If you want to set up a drug smuggling ring, then sometimes you have to drive out of your way. Blackmailers get to go home and watch TV." And that's exactly what Neal did.

****

Jimmy Dale knew that every mark couldn't just head back to San Antonio and pull over. And tonight he felt like he was more than likely heading for Houston so he decided to give Rosalie a call and let her know what was going on.

"You're coming through Seguin anyway and I want to go with you. Jimmy Dale, I've hitched my wagon to your wagon; and technically speaking I'm already guilty anyway. So I ain't asking, I'm tellin'. I'm going with you," Rosalie said.

She told him to meet her at the Bill Miller BBQ place on the south side of 1-10. When he got there she had on a sundress with a matching hair band that pushed her hair straight back and then down in the back 60s style. She wore small hoop earrings and sandals that attached with a single band across the widest part of the foot. The outfit pleased Jimmy Dale because it accented Rosalie's femininity. Rosalie liked it because it was easy to travel in. She had two giant sweet teas ready to go. When Jimmy Dale pulled up she handed the drinks to him and threw the bags in the back.

They followed the GPS unit and entered the greater Houston area about 4:00 Wednesday afternoon. Jimmy Dale had only been to Houston a couple of times so he didn't recognize the area where the fifth wheel came to rest but could see that it was upper-middle class. Jimmy Dale and Rosalie gave the owners of the RV 20 minutes to get settled and then circled the block that popped up on the GPS tracking software. It was pretty easy to spot the RV. There was a fence around the property but it didn't appear to have a lock and the RV was parked under a large structure separate from the house that served as a carport. They circled again and didn't spot any activity at the house or at any of the neighboring houses. The light was on at the house but the curtains were closed and Jimmy Dale decided to pull up and get it over with.

"Wait a minute," Rosalie said.

"What do you mean?"

"I mean wait a minute, that's what I mean. You're not going to park and leave me sittin' here while you jump that fence and crawl up under the RV are you?"

"Not any more, I'm not. You have a better idea?" Jimmy Dale asked.

"Westheimer is two blocks from here. Let's park there and I'll wait with the truck while you walk in. That way if anything happens out of the ordinary, nobody will have seen the truck or anything – you'll just be some guy walking down the street. I noticed a Shell station in the strip mall over there. I'll buy a car wash and get the code. Then I'll park at the entrance to the car wash and keep my eye on the spot where you walked into the neighborhood. If I see you coming back out at a fast clip, I'll know you need to disappear and I'll punch in the code. Then you just jump in the back of the truck. You'll get a little wet but anybody that's in hot pursuit would never think to check a truck coming out the car wash. It's the perfect get away for you."

"That's why I love you baby." Jimmy Dale said.

He had started to say, *That's why I married you baby*, but caught himself. He'd do right by her and Zack pretty soon. He leaned in and gave her a quick peck on the cheek then drove the GMC around the corner to the Shell station and waited on her while she went in to buy the car wash. When she got back he took a stroll into the adjacent residential neighborhood.

It was easy at the house. Not even a dog this time. He walked through the unlocked gate, approached the fifth wheel, dropped to the ground and retrieved the metal tube with the cocaine and the GPS. He was back in about two minutes. The truck was idling at the entrance to the car wash with Rosalie at the wheel. Jimmy Dale slid into the passenger seat.

"Ready to get your truck cleaned up baby?" Rosalie said wryly. Her lips pursed, eyebrows raised in an exaggerated questioning look, and the right corner of her mouth turned up a tiny bit.

"It's been needin' it. That border country is pretty dusty," Jimmy Dale said. But Jimmy Dale wasn't thinking about the truck. He was thinking how smart and tough and pretty she was.

****

From his apartment at the Adobe Palms, Neal monitored the GPS unit's trek to Houston that afternoon. He felt like he pretty much had James Dale's operation figured out. He wasn't sure why the GPS unit was heading north out of Houston that next morning. And he didn't understand how James Dale was getting the drugs across the river but these were minor points. The primary piece of information that he did have was that James Dale was attaching the drugs to the vehicles of law abiding citizens and allowing them to carry his illicit cargo unawares. That was all he needed to know for now.

Just as he had done when he had crafted the blackmail letter to Billy, Neal typed the letter, printed it, then closed the document without saving it.

James,

I know that you are involved in trafficking drugs. And I know how you are doing it. I know about Del Rio and Acuña and the clever way you are using unsuspecting mules to get through the U.S. checkpoint. I will not turn you in to the authorities if you pay me. Send an email to gohorse314@gmail.com and I will email you back with instructions.   Don't wait too long.   I like to watch procrastinators go to prison.

A Friend

Neal folded the letter and put it inside the envelope without ever touching it with his exposed fingers. Since he was on the computer anyway he logged into the gohorse account and fired off another email to Billy.

Hi Billy,

The cost of your continued operation is $1,000 per month. Payable to the same account. It needs to be in by the 15th of every month. As long as the deposits are made you won't have to worry about any emails demanding payment; or worse, getting turned in.

Your Friend

Then Neal drove to the South Side and dropped in a mailbox the letter addressed to JD Klein, 2046 Polar Bear Drive, Seguin, Texas.

****

Rosalie and Jimmy Dale were in Chicago by 3:00 Thursday afternoon – 21 hours before the scheduled meeting time at the warehouse with Donny and Renozzo. They checked in to a midrange hotel and showered. Rosalie went first and took 30 minutes. Jimmy Dale went second and took three. Rosalie took another 20 minutes applying her makeup and he waited on her flipping through the cable and attempting to memorize his favorite channels. That evening they went to a pizza place that Jimmy Dale had seen once on the Discovery Channel. They took a cab partly because they didn't know where the pizza place was located but also because Jimmy Dale wanted to drink his fill and didn't want to take chances with traffic cops in downtown Chicago. It would be a bad night to wind up in the clink. So they split a large one-topping. Jimmy Dale had a pitcher of Heineken and Rosalie had two glasses of red wine. They checked out and left the hotel at 10:30 the next morning leaving plenty of time for wrong turns and missed exits. They had neither and drove past the warehouse at 11:00. Jimmy Dale wasted the next 45 minutes showing Rosalie some of the drop sights from his previous encounter with Otis and the gang a few weeks earlier. She listened to him but her mind was on the warehouse meeting.

They pulled around to the back door of the warehouse at 11:55. Jimmy Dale got out and knocked on the door. The door opened but all Rosalie could see was an arm and Jimmy Dale went inside. Three minutes later a fat man with a carefully trimmed moustache and pressed suit crossed in front of her and entered the same door. As he passed by the truck he looked at her without acknowledging her. Rosalie just stared right back at him.

"Hey Jimmy Dale, who's the piece of ass in the front seat?" Donny asked as he came into the room.

"My girlfriend," Jimmy Dale answered with a bit of impatience. He didn't like Donny talking about Rosalie that way.

"What's her name?"

"Does it matter?" Jimmy Dale answered with a bit more impatience.

"Not yet it doesn't," Donny replied. They stared at each other.

Jimmy Dale threw that week's delivery on the table. Donny cut into it and tested it informally. He nodded his approval – more to himself than to anyone else. Then he took a manila envelope out of his left inside coat pocket and pushed it across the table. Jimmy peeked inside, folding back a couple of the bills, and in doing so, tested the entire package for reasonableness in a similar way to how Donny had tested the package containing the dope.

"We done here?" Jimmy Dale asked.

"Yeah…" Donny confirmed with a nod and slight pause, "…we're done."

"I hope that guy never shows up at your trailer," Rosalie said as they were pulling out of the parking lot, "'cause if he does you're going to have to reinforce the deck."

Jimmy Dale was happy to be out of the warehouse and grinned at Rosalie's comment. He really liked her dry delivery.

"What's that guy's name?" she asked.

"Donny."

"Donny what?"

"Donny Osmond."

"I thought he was Italian."

"Donny Osmondoni then…how the hell should I know?" Jimmy Dale said with fake exasperation."

"I don't know. You just made ten grand or more off this guy in the space of a week. I thought you might know his last name."

"This is a no receipt, no last name kind of business." Jimmy Dale responded. At the conclusion of the sentence he peered over at her with his head cocked forward so he could make direct eye contact and not have the sunglasses that gripped the end of his nose obscure his line of sight.

"Ya' savvy?" he asked her rhetorically.

****

Things were going well for Terry and Raul. They had three car salesmen on three separate lots all providing 5-10 IDs per day. Billy in San Antonio, one in Dallas, and one in Houston. Billy had been their first supplier, and the only one that Terry knew personally. Billy had served as the guinea pig and it had gone nicely. But now that they had a program in place they went in and recruited incognito then stayed that way even after Raul went trolling on the lot. The plan was to stick with one salesman on one car lot for a month or six weeks and then move on to another lot or to another city entirely. Terry found that this was actually a selling point for the salesmen that they recruited. *Make 10 or 20 grand in a few weeks and then we're gone.* And it made sense. If the authorities were able to identify that anything suspicious was going on at a particular lot – and that's a big if – they'd be long gone and there'd be no way to associate any particular person with the scheme. So Billy was due to be cut off. They'd been working Kuykendall motors too long. In fact it was probably time to pull out of San Antonio entirely and move down the highway for a while.

Terry dialed Billy's number and after the briefest of introductions let Billy know that the ID scheme at Kuykendall Motors would be coming to an end.

"Well Billy, the thing is this, we're probably going to have to move on."

"What do you mean move on?"

"I mean we probably need to put the ID scam on hiatus for a while. I think we might be pushing it and sooner or later someone is gonna figure it out."

"So that's it?"

"That's it."

"What about the IDs I have right now. I was planning on making a delivery tomorrow."

"We'll take that delivery but that will have to be the end of it."

Billy sat on the other end of the line not saying anything and eventually the line went dead. He didn't know how to respond. He hadn't known how to respond to anything in quite a while. He was now making $1,000 per month payments to his blackmailer, ostensibly to allow himself to continue operating. And now the operation was being shut down. Billy didn't think that his blackmailer would be very understanding about his criminal unemployment. But he had just made his second payment and had nearly a month until the next payment was due. Perhaps he could figure something out.

****

Chavo's room was an after the fact lean-to attached to an already decrepit adobe home in a crime ridden area of Acuña. The home belonged to a widow whose husband had passed away a few years ago. Chavo had come across the house three years ago when he had ducked into the narrow side yard attempting to evade local law enforcement. He had been glad that day that there was not a dog to announce his arrival, instead inciting only a minor ruckus among the chickens. The pursuing cops, not exactly paragons of tenacity, quickly lost interest and wandered off to wherever it is that lacksadaisical Mexican cops go when lukewarm pursuits chill still further.

The widow that was to be Chavo's landlady was sitting on the back patio that day. Chavo quickly engaged the old lady in conversation hoping she wouldn't squeal out. She didn't. While the cops strolled by along the narrow street that ran in front of her house, Chavo struck a deal to rent the room lazily attached to the back of her house based at least partly on the unsubstantiated promise that he would provide protection. Although in actuality his presence would subject her to an increased level of danger. Chavo negotiated a rental rate equivalent to about 20 American dollars per month. In the three years since the verbal lease agreement took effect, Chavo had made rent maybe ten times.

There was no running water - only a bucket that Chavo used when he couldn't make it to the corner grocery. There was one light bulb, exposed and naked hanging by a single wire from the ceiling. A black and white TV sat on a board stretched between two cinder blocks in the corner. There was a cot along the back wall and a threadbare Indian rug covered a small portion of a wooden slat floor. It was in this room that Chavo smoked his dope and schemed against his business associates.

It had been a sometimes spoken and sometimes unspoken agreement between Chavo and his three friends on the Acuña police force that he would provide a semi-steady stream of marks for their malevolent bribery enterprise. But as is frequently the case with the seedy underbelly of Mexican society, the hunter was becoming the hunted. This had happened with Chavo once before, when an identified mark was a little smarter and a little more ambitious than average. By tipping off the corrupt peace officers, Chavo had inadvertently brought a future partner to the law's attention. There was no way of knowing it at the time of course, but he wished now that the cops had no idea who Jimmy Dale was. If they began to suspect that Chavo and Jimmy Dale were making money together then they would expect their share from Chavo and it would probably be pretty high. The advantage that Chavo had though, and he knew it, was that the cops were lazy and stupid. With a modest effort, they could be avoided and it was unlikely that they would catch on to what Chavo and Jimmy Dale were doing in Mexico.

Chavo was beset to one degree or another with a tendency toward all seven of the deadly sins but on this day, the dual temptations of greed and envy welled up within him.

CHAPTER 20

Jimmy Dale and Rosalie got back to the trailer on Polar Bear Drive at 10:30 pm on Saturday. It was a little late but Rosalie drove on home to see Zack. Jimmy Dale just crashed. The next morning he slept late and planned on enjoying a day off before heading back to Mexico on Monday. He checked the mail at 11:30. It was not pleasant.

James,

I know that you are involved in trafficking drugs. And I know how you are doing it. I know about Del Rio and Acuña and the clever way you are using unsuspecting mules to get through the U.S. checkpoint. I will not turn you in to the authorities if you pay me. Send an email to gohorse314@gmail.com and I will email you back with instructions. Don't wait too long. I like to watch procrastinators go to prison.

A Friend

"SHIT!" Jimmy Dale hollered, "HOW IN THE HELL DID THIS HAPPEN? WHY CAN'T ANYTHING, AND I MEAN ANYTHING, JUST GO THE WAY IT'S SUPPOSED TO GO?" Jimmy Dale was in a panic. He paced around the trailer looking up into the sky and then down at the ground, holding the letter flush against his face and then flush against his chest. He was moving around because he didn't know what else to do. The situation kept sweeping over his mind like a tsunami. He couldn't accept the reality of what was happening to him. It crashed against the sea wall of his brain again and again. This went on for an hour and Jimmy Dale found himself on the couch staring at the ceiling muttering to himself, "No…no….no." He was shaking his head back and forth in sync with his mutterings. The letter lay face down on his chest. He dialed Rosalie's number.

"We're in trouble," he said calmly but with resignation.

"What's the matter?"

"Somebody knows what I'm doing and he's squeezing me."

"What do you mean he's squeezing you? Who's squeezing you?"

"I don't know, but he knows what I'm doing and how I'm doing it and he wants money or he'll turn me in."

"How could anybody know what you're doing? How is that possible? Did he call you? What happened?" Rosalie was struggling to get her brain around the situation.

"There was a letter in the mail today. It was postmarked two days ago in San Antonio. He knows my name and where I live. It was addressed to me at my address here on Polar Bear and has my name on the envelope. The letter says, 'James, I know that you are involved in trafficking drugs…'" Jimmy Dale went on to read the demand letter to Rosalie over the phone. "I'm screwed. It's all over. I finally have something good happen to me and it crashes down around me before it even gets started going good."

"It doesn't have to come crashing down. At least it's not the cops."

"It may as well be. At least with the cops you know what you're dealing with. With this guy it's impossible."

"It's not impossible. Jimmy Dale I can't talk anymore right now. I'm dealing with Zack and my mother right now. Let's just talk about it later. We can handle it."

The other end of the line was mute.

"Jimmy Dale?" Silence. "Jimmy Dale!?"

"Yes."

"I'll talk to you later. Jimmy Dale, I'll talk to you later. We'll work through this."

"Ok. I'm sorry I bothered you with this."

"It's ok. I'll see you tonight."

****

"This is really weird," Rosalie said as she scanned the letter later that evening. "How could anybody possibly even know what you are doing? I mean the cops don't even have an idea. How could some guy out there in the world figure this out? How would he even know to look at you?"

"I don't know." Jimmy Dale had calmed considerably over the afternoon and was at least able to speak in a rational fashion.

"This just doesn't make any sense." She stared at him from the other end of the couch. He was horizontal on the couch with head resting on the armrest. His arms were folded across his chest. It was a position of surrender. He was going with the flow. She was sitting at the other end of the couch with her feet on the ground, leaning forward and angled toward him. Her elbows were on her knees and she grasped the letter with both hands. Hers was a position of action. She was searching for the answer. It was there. She could sense it. It was right there just outside her grasp. She searched Jimmy Dale's eyes. She searched them not for the answer so much but instead for a clue as to where the answer might be. This whole thing was an enigma and she intuitively knew that finding the answer would not be a straight forward path. It was something outside of the paradigm. It would have to be sought out.

"Jimmy Dale, this is not adding up and you need to help me figure it out. Now somebody must have seen you do

something somewhere." Jimmy Dale stared past her into space and
shook his head *no*.

****

Neal's operation was beginning to flourish. He had one steady
payer and things were looking good to add a second. It was a
Wednesday afternoon. He got off at 4:00 on Wednesdays so he
drove to the Brookhollow Library and logged on to the gohorse
account. He had sent the letter out a few days ago letting James
Dale know that he needed to contact him and he was curious how
his latest mark would respond.

> Inbox (2)   monkeybiz_911@yahoo.com
>   culebra837@gmail.com

He recognized the second message as being from Billy.
The first message, from monkeybiz_911, was an account that he
had not seen before. The subject line read: Making Contact.

> *Gohorse,*
>
> *What do you want me to do?*
>
> *JD*

Good. Looks like we have a player, Neal thought to himself.
He typed back his response:

> *James,*
>
> *I have a prepaid credit card. You need to dial customer service and
> put $1,000 on the card.   (888) 676-8000. The account # is
> 7472-8203-5545-1191. It's Wednesday afternoon. I'll expect to
> see the $1,000 in the account by noon on Monday.*
>
> *Gohorse*

Neal hit send and then opened the email from culebra837.

Gohorse,

My situation has changed. I am no longer involved in the business.

Billy

"That's too bad," Neal muttered to himself. He typed out his reply.

Billy,

You are not paying me as a commission on your take. You are paying me to not turn you in. If you want me to continue not turning you in then you must continue to pay. You have three weeks until your next payment is due.

Gohorse.

Neal logged out and went out front for a smoke. He didn't smoke often. Maybe only a cigarette or two every week or so but every now and then he had the urge. And he wanted one now. So he sat on the concrete bench and smoked. He basked in the late afternoon sun and the anonymity of his endeavor.

****

Billy's problems were just beginning. As the cash began to roll in over the last two or three months he had begun to spend it. At first the satisfaction of being able to pay the bills was enough. The removal of that pressure from his everyday life felt as if a size 12 boot had just been lifted from his throat. It was a really big relief. And that lowering of the financial barometer was felt throughout his household. Denise didn't think about it. All she knew was that Billy was having a couple of good months at the dealership and that it looked like they were finally about to turn the corner. But Billy's old friend had begun to tug at him. On the ride home from work at night, when his mind was empty and groping for topics to embrace, he found himself thinking about the prospect of the easy dollar through gambling. The Thursday before last, on his usual day off, he told Denise that he was going into the dealership to try pick up an extra sale for the month. Instead he went to the horse track and indulged his appetite without limitation.

He walked through the gates with $5,000 and by the time the horses crossed the wire after the 4th race he was up to $11,000. The 5th race was a disaster. He put a $3,000 wheel on horses 2 and 5. The number 5 horse, Conquistador, was bumped out of the gates and never recovered finishing 7th. The number 2 horse, Shiney Lady, finished 4th and Billy was down to $8,000. Billy decided to double down to get his money back. The #4 horse in the next race, Parallel Parking, was a three year old stallion with an impressive bloodline and recent top finishes in Oklahoma and Arkansas. He seemed like a lock and was the pre-race favorite at 3 to 1.

As the horses paraded past the grandstand on their way to the starting gate, Parallel Parking seemed skittish and reared twice. Billy watched the horse closely trying to pick up on some imperceptible clue that would reveal to him how the horse's energy would manifest itself. He decided that Parallel Parking was a sound wager and placed $6,000 on the horse to win. Parallel Parking reared again as he was led into the starting gate and the sound of metal clanging against metal after being struck by 1,100 pounds of horse flesh was plainly audible in Billy's seat 400 yards away. The crowd responded with a buzz as they watched Parallel Parking being brought under control and then reloaded. The final five horses were loaded without incident. When the bell sounded Parallel Parking bolted wildly to his right bumping the horse on his immediate right, who nearly fell, and pushing that horse into the next horse over. When they disentangled, Parallel Parking was on the outside six lengths back and disoriented. As they passed the grandstand for the first time and headed into the first turn, Parallel Parking was last, trailing the leader by eight lengths. Billy was concerned but not panicked. Parallel Parking hugged the rail and then began to make a move in the middle of the back stretch moving past three horses to take possession of fifth place as the horses entered the far turn. Billy stood and began to feel a rush as his payday began to take shape. Coming out of the far turn and entering the home stretch the jockey swung Parallel Parking wide to free him from the pack. The track announcer's voice went up a notch in pitch and in volume announcing, "AND IT'S PARALLEL PARKING WITH A MOVE ON THE OUTSIDE…". The rest of the grandstand was now on their feet cheering and feeding off the energy of the mob and the horses. After a horrendous start and a mediocre effort through the first half of the race, Parallel Parking was now making a strong challenge for the lead. With a furlong to go, Parallel Parking was ¾ of a length back and charging hard. Billy no longer attempted any restraint, "Go Parking Go! Go Boy! Go Parking! You Can Do It! Go!" The word *GO* was emphasized each time by a fist that was thrust into the air with such force that it caused Billy to come slightly off the ground. Billy's stomach muscles were tightened. Every nerve in his body was on high alert. As the horses moved to the wire, Billy's exhilaration began to fade. Parallel Parking was no longer closing the gap! The final 75 yards of the race were spent in slow motion with Billy coming to grips with the fact that he was going to lose. The other horse had answered Parking's challenge! Parallel Parking paid $2.80 to place and $2.30 to show.

Down to $2,000 Billy placed conservative $1,000 bets on the 7th and 8th races losing both. Now broke, Billy sat and watched the final two races of the day as a spectator only. He stared blankly at the track and the horses quietly despising himself.

****

Rosalie set her mind to work on the pressing problem of eliminating the blackmailer from the equation. That Wednesday evening, while Jimmy Dale was somewhere driving in the heartland of America, Rosalie checked the email account that Jimmy Dale was using to respond to Gohorse and saw the demand for money and the instructions. Her initial instinct was to not pay. But was it the right move? The stakes might be too high for such a bold move. Perhaps a partial payment? Maybe just deposit $500 or $250? Gohorse might be hesitant to turn in a paying mark. But was that the goal? To merely minimize the financial damage? Or should the goal be to eliminate him entirely? Rosalie decided that it was best to pay. At least for now. Jimmy Dale was making $40,000 to $50,000 a month, so $1,000 was easy to swallow. And it would buy them time. One or two payments, maybe three, and maybe then they could figure out a way to get to him. But she had to start working on getting to gohorse now.

She needed to be away from Zack and her mother to think so she drove to Polar Bear Drive and sat on Jimmy Dale's back deck. It was the end of June, just past the summer solstice, and she watched the sun go down neither knowing nor caring that the sun was near its most northerly point in the sky. Her body was at rest but her mind was in high gear, working and churning, searching for the answer that she knew was there. As she sat, rocking back and forth, Rosalie allowed her eyes to drift from the traffic on the highway a mile in the distance to the cloth rags at the edge of the deck just a few feet away. Then to the cars and the trucks on the highway again. She thought about Jimmy Dale out there on the highway and wondered if there was a girl on a back porch up there on the plains and if that girl was sitting and watching the traffic right now just like Rosalie was doing; and Rosalie wondered if that girl might be watching Jimmy Dale roll by in his GMC on his way to Chicago. Then Rosalie looked at the cloth rags again. They were wrapped in duct tape and Rosalie knew what they were for. Jimmy Dale had told her about how he had used them to practice and how he had wrapped small bags of flour in them to simulate the weight of cocaine so he could gain the accuracy that he needed to shoot the dope across the river. Rosalie admired the plan. It was creative. And to use unsuspecting retirees as mules…man that was smart. The whole plan moved around in her head and the solution to the problem at hand began to come into focus.

There were only three points in the process that Jimmy Dale was exposed to being seen in connection with the drugs. Someone could have seen him at the river, at the Kountry Kitchen Kafe in Del Rio, or at the mule's house when Jimmy Dale retrieved the metal tube with the coke. Rosalie decided that any of the three were very real possibilities. But what did it matter? Even if someone saw Jimmy Dale compromise himself in any of these three places how could they possibly put the whole thing together so perfectly? How could they know the entire operation? Then she had it. The contact in Mexico! Jimmy Dale had mentioned his name. What was it? Charro? She dialed Jimmy Dale's number.

"Hello."

The second she heard Jimmy Dale's voice she realized her reasoning was flawed. Why would this Charro guy jeopardize the entire operation? He was making money off the system too. Hadn't he actually approached Jimmy Dale in Mexico? It was possible that he would take on the gohorse persona with the idea that if Jimmy Dale paid then great, but if he didn't, then Charro would do nothing. There was no down side. Unless of course, the attempt at blackmail scared Jimmy Dale into hiding and everything stopped. What made perfect sense ten seconds ago somehow right now didn't seem quite so plausible.

"I thought I had the problem solved but I just realized it was a bad idea," Rosalie said.

"What was your idea?"

"I thought that this Charro guy that you're dealing with in Mexico was our blackmailer."

"You mean Chavo?"

"Chavo. That's right. Anyway I thought it might be him but I changed my mind."

"Why would Chavo blackmail me? He wants this thing to keep going as bad as I do."

"I know that. That's why I changed my mind. Where are you at right now?"

"Springfield Missouri. I decided that going this way is a little shorter than going through Little Rock. Would you mind checking my exact location? There's a feature on the service that allows you to plug in a destination and it will give you an exact distance from where you are to where you're going."

Rosalie followed Jimmy Dale's directions, pulling up the website and logging on. As she waited for the website to load she said, "You know that they make cars now that have GPS units built in. Then you wouldn't have to ask me to do this for you."

Jimmy Dale accepted the good natured chiding. He wanted a vehicle to drive that was a little older. One that fit his style better. And the GMC fit the bill. Jimmy Dale felt like it helped him remain incognito.

"Looks like you're about 512 miles out. Got a ways to go yet," Rosalie reported.

"I figured there was about 500 miles ahead of me." Jimmy Dale said by way of confirmation.

Rosalie fiddled with the software, impressed with the accuracy and robust quality of the product. "209 to St. Louis."

"I'll probably stop in St. Louis then. So if it's not Chavo," Jimmy Dale said switching the subject, "then who is it?"

"I don't know baby. I'm working on it. You stop when you get tired. 'kay?"

"Okay."

Rosalie bumped around in the module for a while, watching Jimmy Dale's progress. The tab toward the right hand side of the tool bar caught her eye and the faintest glimmer of an idea took root. She wasn't even consciously aware of it. The tab read SET UP. She moved the mouse and held the pointer over the icons along the right side of the page. The fourth icon down read NEW MONITORING ACCOUNT. She clicked on the option and was prompted to create an account. The warning message informed her that a total of five accounts came with the purchase of the unit. Apparently two were currently active: JD123TX and JD124TX. The idea that had begun to form a few moments ago flourished now into a full-fledged inkling. She dialed Jimmy Dale again.

"Yeeuuss," Jimmy Dale answered in a drawn out fashion similar to the way Ed McMahon would draw out the *HERE* in *HERE'S JOHNNY*. It was his way of making light of the fact that he had just spoken with her only moments before and here she was calling again.

"When did you set up the account on the internet so the GPS unit could be tracked?" she asked.

"Right after I bought the unit. Probably couple of months ago."

"Did you know that you can have up to five accounts?"

"Yeah I think I remember reading something about that. Didn't see any need for it though."

"So you never set up an account after that first one?"

"That's right."

"What's the name of the account?"

"JD123TX."

"Did you know that there are two accounts set up? There's a second account called JD124TX."

"I didn't do that."

"Well it's there. I'm looking at it right now."

To confirm her suspicions Rosalie attempted to login to the 124 account using Jimmy Dale's password and access code that came with 123. Maybe Jimmy Dale had forgotten that he had set it up.

"I can't log in."

"I told you I didn't do it. I forget things but I don't think I would forget that."

Rosalie called Jimmy Dale back three or four times over the next three hours and by the time he hit the outskirts of St. Louis they had worked out the plan to nail their adversary.

CHAPTER 21

Rosalie called her friend Marcus around 10:00 Thursday morning. Marcus worked from home as a freelance computer programmer and web site designer. He recognized her number and picked up on the first ring.

"Hello there," he said with a tone that indicated he was grateful she was calling.

Marcus was originally from Florida but had moved to Seguin four years ago with his future ex-wife. She was from the area and had talked him into moving from the Sunshine State so she could take a job as a sales rep for a local manufacturer of Ziploc baggies. Two years later she decided she didn't love Marcus anymore and moved out. Darrel at the Sage law firm had used Marcus on a very complicated, very technical lawsuit pretty soon after Marcus had moved to town and then helped him out with the divorce too. So Marcus had been by the law office a number of times and had struck up a friendship with Rosalie. Rosalie sensed that Marcus would like to be a little more than friends but she knew that would never happen. She actually felt a little guilty about it. Marcus was good looking, nice, and smart. But as a black man she knew it would be difficult with folks around town. She felt bad that this was the case but not bad enough to do anything about it. And she knew that if she really liked him enough she would go for it anyway. It just wasn't quite there for her.

"Hi Marcus. How are you doing?"

"I'm ok. You must need something. I'm not usually granted an audience with the queen unless she needs something." On the surface Marcus was kidding around but underneath there was an element of truth and Rosalie knew it.

"I'd like to ask a favor. It's kind of involved. Is there any way I could stop by later this evening and talk about it?"

Rosalie knocked on the door at 6:27. Marcus was dressed sharply but still casual. He smelled good. Rosalie didn't recognize the fragrance but decided to ask him about it later when she felt as if it wouldn't appear that she was coming on to him. Rosalie had been to Marcus' place before. It was picked up and neat. It looked like the kind of place a guy like him would live in. She stood for a moment while they got used to being around each other again.

"You want something to drink? I got margarita mix."

"You have any sweet tea?"

"Yeah. I think I have some of that." Marcus strolled the few feet into the kitchen and put a glass under the ice dispenser. The mechanism was so loud that Rosalie didn't feel awkward about the conversational hiatus and took the opportunity to take a seat at the end of the sofa facing away from Marcus and towards the living area. Marcus brought her a tall glass of sweet tea with crushed ice. In his other hand he had a Michelob. He sat at the other end of the couch and smiled at her.

"So I guess you're needing something," he said half questioning and half telling.

She smiled back and said, "I could use your help."

"Whatever I can do. Just let me know."

"I don't know all the terms…" Rosalie crossed her legs under her skirt in a full cross and then leaned forward with her elbows tucked in between her torso and her thighs and hands facing forward so they could move and help her talk, "…but I need some kind of application that will allow me to get a password for someone's email account. I need it kind of bad."

"Is this email account someone you know or someone you don't know?"

"Someone I don't know. That's why I need it. This person is causing me a problem and I need to figure out who he is."

"Is he harassing you?"

"Sort of." Rosalie made an expression with her face like she had bitten into a lemon and then accented it with her hands. The concept that she wanted to convey to him was that this was a delicate issue to be handled with some discretion and she didn't want to get into every last detail.

"You realize that this is illegal." He placed a heavy accent on the word *realize* and then trailed off the last two syllables of *illegal*. It had the same effect as his earlier query – half question and half statement.

"I thought it might be," she said.

Marcus stared at her. He wanted to help her but this request had some hair on it. Rosalie stared back. She could tell that he was teetering and could go either way.

"Three grand?" Rosalie threw the figure out there in the open without warning hoping it would tip Marcus over in the right direction.

Marcus had not intended to ask for money but now that it was offered it swayed him. $3,000 off the books would really help out.

"Rosalie you know it's not about the money."

"I know it's not about the money. But this whole thing is related to something my friend is involved in that is a little unsavory. It's also fairly profitable. So there's a little something there to help you out." She paused and then said, "And I'm not the one paying you. It's coming from my friend. He's the one with the problem so he's the one who'll pony up."

"What kind of email account is it?"

"It's a gmail account," she said, relieved that he was going to help her out.

"I can do this on a laptop you know. In fact I think it might be best if we buy a cheapie, do all the work at places with public WIFI and then pitch the thing in the river when we're done."

"I'll go buy one right now. So we can get started tomorrow?"

"I get off work tomorrow at 5:00. I can meet you at IHOP at 6:00."

"Thanks Marcus. I'll bring $1,500. I'll get the rest to you when we finish up." Rosalie got up and then leaned over to give him a peck on the check before walking out the door.

Marcus sat and stared at the wall. His eyes never wavered as she got up from her seat, approached him, kissed him, and then walked out.

"You're welcome," Marcus said quietly as the door shut and the sound of her footsteps declined to inaudibility.

****

Rosalie slid a plain white envelope across the table. Marcus did not move his head but she did notice his eyes dart to his right and downward slightly locking onto the envelope for a half second and then returning to the computer screen. Ten seconds later, unable to fight down the urge to smile he chose to give in and glanced across the top of the screen. Rosalie was waiting for him to look at her. She was leaning forward resting her weight on the table with her left forearm flat on the surface. Her right elbow was on the table with that same hand cupping her chin. Her head was cocked to her right at a slight angle and she smiled back at him waiting for him to say something but was ok too with him not saying anything.

"I think this will work," Marcus said.

"Good. Now tell me *how* it will work."

"Do you really want to know?"

"I'm interested. Just give me the 20,000 foot view and we'll take it from there."

"I'm going to create an application that will duplicate his inbox. We'll send it via the email account that you use to send him messages. When he opens the email that you send him, the app will launch. It will look like the email account was logged out and it will appear as if the email account is asking him to reenter his password so he can log back in. But in reality he will be typing a reply to your email. When he hits enter, the email will be sent and the app will shut down returning him to his inbox. For the sake of perfection I'll add a function that will delete the message from his sent folder and a message letting him know that he has been successfully logged back in, even though, in actuality, he was never logged out. All you have to do is check your email. His password will be in a reply from his account."

"You're good." Rosalie said with a slight raise of her eyebrows and a gentle nod of the head three times.

"I'm starting to think you'll never know just how good I really am."

She just smiled back at him ignoring the innuendo. "So how long will this take?"

"Three or four days. Can you wait that long?"

"I'm actually surprised that you can do it that fast."

"I'm good, remember?" Marcus said smiling.

****

Jimmy Dale got home Sunday afternoon. He had the rest of the day Sunday and then all day Monday before heading back out for Del Rio Tuesday morning.

"Baby I'm going to need you to go ahead and buy a new GPS unit for your tracking. I'm going to need the one that you're using right now," Rosalie said.

"Why would you need that?" Jimmy Dale asked.

****

"I have a password for you," Marcus said as soon as Rosalie picked up the phone.

"Are you going to share that with me or am I going to have to weasel it out of you?" Rosalie flirted with Marcus. She knew that he liked it and he had earned a little praise so she gave it to him with a sexual subtext. She even enjoyed it a little bit herself.

"What if I choose to have you weasel it out of me? What would that entail?" Marcus asked wanting to draw out the exchange.

"I guess it would entail a little weasling."

"I'm up for a little weasling this evening."

"I get off at 5:00," Rosalie said. "I got a couple of things I need to do with Zack but I could be there about 6:30." Rosalie was fine with picking up the password in person. She needed to give Marcus the rest of the money anyway. When she got to the house Marcus was sitting on the front porch swing. His eyes stayed fixed on her from the moment she pulled into the drive to the time until she sat down next to him on the porch swing.

"Here's your money. Thanks for helping me out," Rosalie said as she handed him the envelope. She never liked delaying payment. She felt it relieved anxiety if the money part of the transaction was out of the way.

Marcus accepted the envelope graciously. "You're welcome. You wanna take a look at some emails? There's two or three in there that might be of interest."

Rosalie nodded her acceptance of the invitation and Marcus continued, "Let's take a ride. I don't want this traced to me if I can help it. I've played this completely clean so far and I'd rather not expose myself."

"Let's go," Rosalie responded.

The thump from the speakers started with the turn of the key in Marcus' Maxima. It was the kind of thump that rattled windows on houses near the street when the offending vehicle rolled by and Rosalie found it annoying. To her it accented the cultural differences that existed between her and Marcus. Rosalie hit the power button on the stereo system dropping the decibel level from obnoxious to zero.

"On top of the three grand I'm going to give a small bonus in the form of advice. You're not 20 years old anymore. Women like men that act like men. And men don't listen to music like that." Rosalie tuned the receiver to KWED 1580 AM and reset the volume to an acceptable and pleasant level. Classic country flowed from the speakers.

"You don't have to listen to this, but you can't listen to that other trash. It's just stupid," she said.

Marcus smiled at her. "I didn't know the system was even capable of playing music like this. YEE HAW!" It didn't matter to him what kind of music was playing. He just liked being around her.

"The Dairy Queen ok? They got WIFI."

"How about the library…it's quieter." Rosalie felt like there was less chance of them being seen together at the library.

"The password is mustang123," Marcus said as he pulled up the account. "And it looks like your boy Jimmy Dale isn't the only guy out there getting squeezed."

"Really?" Rosalie was instantly drawn in and switched chairs from across the table to the one right next to Marcus. She leaned in to look at the screen so close that her left shoulder was applying pressure to Marcus' right.

Marcus pulled up a few emails and gave the verbal summary as he did. "Looks like the guy's name is Billy and he works at Kuykendall Motors in San Antonio."

"What's he doing?"

"Stealing IDs as near as I can tell."

Rosalie cut to the chase. "Is there anything in here that identifies our guy?"

"I couldn't find his name anywhere. He sticks to this gohorse pseudonym all the way through. But…"

"Oh Marcus, we have got to get this guy," she said to him implying with her words and her body language that she wanted him to continue.

"I think I might have an address." She looked at him waiting for him to end the suspense. "Looks like he's involved with some KKK type shit. Kinda makes me want to start helping you out ya' know?" Rosalie felt a little twinge of guilt that she had been rejecting his polite but obvious advances mostly because he was black.

"Where does he live?" she asked.

"I don't think he lives there but the address is on Blanco Road in San Antonio. I looked it up and it's a place called the Wild Snail pawn shop."

Rosalie looked at him. She was processing everything she was hearing.

"He's had some tickets sent to that address for some kind of white supremacy meeting or something. So I guess there might be a good chance that he works there."

"But no name?"

"No. I guess he doesn't want anyone at the Wild Snail to know who he is either. I don't know what that says about a guy when everything you do is hidden from everybody you know. Know what I mean?"

"I know what you mean." Rosalie paused again. Her mind was working. "The Wild Snail," she said to Marcus but thinking about what this place must look like.

"The Wild Snail," he said back.

Rosalie gazed a while longer into the stacks of books and then turned to Marcus, "Could I get you to do me another favor?"

The plot was thickening for Marcus. Helping Rosalie was reward enough. But nailing a blackmailing bigot on top of everything else? He knew the answer to her request before she had completed the sentence.

"We might be able to work something out," he said to her implying that the answer was undoubtedly yes.

****

Rosalie called the pawn shop and pretended to be a former customer trying to speak with someone that had helped her two months ago. She had the guy that answered the phone run through the names of everybody that had worked there for the last two months and what they looked like. There were four full time employees: Neal, Paul, Trace, and Jeremy. There were four part time employees: Justin, Jim, Peter, and Lyndon. Frank owned the place and worked there too. The blackmailer could be any one of them. Then she called back the next day and asked the guy that picked up, Trace, if he knew anything about GPS units. He told her that he did not. She repeated the application of this systematic elimination process several times over the next two days, always calling from a different number or from a blocked number. If someone picked up that she had already talked to she hung up. If the guy that answered said that he did know something about GPS units she then asked him what brand he would recommend. At the end of this exercise she decided that their guy was either Neal, Paul, or Frank.

The next step was to arm Marcus for the final assault. It was a Friday and she wanted to invade the Wild Snail on Saturday figuring that would afford him the greatest chance of having all three in the store. She got on Craig's List and found a GPS tracking unit similar to the one that Jimmy Dale had been using and made arrangements to stop by the seller's house the next morning to pick it up. She paid the asking price for the unit at the door while Marcus sat in the car. Then Marcus took over. They drove to the Wild Snail and Marcus walked through the front door. Rosalie sat in the car and watched through the rear view mirror. Marcus was greeted by a clean cut young man who called Frank over when Marcus told him that he had a GPS tracker that he was thinking about pawning or selling. Marcus and Frank discussed the transaction and Marcus did his best to read the facial expressions and body language of the man he was talking to but wasn't able to pick up on anything. He couldn't say for sure but Frank didn't seem like the guy. Marcus thanked him and asked permission to browse a bit before leaving. He wandered through the hand tools and pulled out his cell phone. He texted to Rosalie, *call and ask for paul.*

The store phone rang and Frank picked up and listened to the voice on the other end for a few seconds. Then hollered, "Paul, you gotta customer on the line." He handed the phone to the same young man that had greeted Marcus when he came through the door. Marcus heard Paul say, "No I don't think we have any depth finders in our inventory."

Marcus texted, *call neal now.*

The store phone rang again and Paul answered but hung up the receiver immediately. Three minutes later Marcus heard the phone ring again and a dark haired man that had been behind the counter the whole time picked up.

"Wild Snail...yeah this is Neal...no we don't close 'til 6:00...thanks for calling."

Marcus wandered around the shelving for a minute or two until he was near enough to Neal to ask a question. "You don't ever get any confederate flags in here do you?"

Neal looked at the black man standing across the counter from him and said, "No."

"Thanks," Marcus said. He feigned interest in the flat screen TVs that were on display between him and the front door and then left 90 seconds later.

He took his seat on the passenger's side of the car and said to Rosalie, "I think Neal's our guy."

CHAPTER 22

Rosalie was preparing to win the war with Neal on all fronts. The physical and financial victories would come later. But today she would win the psychological war. She turned off Jimmy Dale's GPS tracking unit, put it on the passenger seat and drove to San Antonio. When she got to the intersection of Loop 410 and I-10 on the northwest side of town, she turned the unit on and drove south about a mile to where 1-10 veered east and intersected Vance Jackson. She turned left onto Vance Jackson and drove a couple of miles north until she was back at 410. Then she made a u turn on Vance Jackson and drove back to I-10 and made a left, then another left on West Avenue and north to 410 where she made another u turn and drove straight back south to I-10. Then she turned the unit off. She made her way east to Blanco, turned the GPS unit on and drove north two miles and then turned the unit off.

She worked her way east across the northern half of the city in a series of carefully planned maneuvers that involved turning the unit on and off so that only certain segments of the trip could be viewed. When she made it to the corner of Broadway and

Austin Highway, she turned the unit off again and turned on the laptop to view the results of her disjointed sojourn. And there, superimposed on the map of San Antonio, were the crude but undeniable letters W–I–L–D. It had taken 45 minutes. In another hour she would have the letters S-N-A-I-L scripted across a map of the south side. Rosalie knew that her actions served only to establish her superiority in Neal's mind and to reinforce that same concept in her own. She was hoping to have Neal think of his adversary as someone who was so smart, so far above his pay grade, that there could be no hope. She was firing a warning shot across his bow that was so big that the message was unavoidable. The message was that this scum bag Neal was going to lose.

When she made it back to the trailer on Polar Bear Drive, Jimmy Dale was asleep on the couch. She set the laptop on the table and pulled up the visual for Jimmy Dale when he woke up. She hadn't told him where she was going or what she was doing and thought the surprise would help his spirits. She poured herself a drink. She heard Jimmy Dale stir as she started straightening up the kitchen.

"Where you been?" Jimmy Dale asked her, not yet fully awake.

"Been out laying down some rules for our friend Gohorse."

"What do you mean?"

"Take a look at the laptop."

"What does this mean? Why does it say Wild Snail on the map?" Jimmy Dale asked.

Rosalie had purposefully kept quiet about all the investigative work she had done over the last week or so. As she went through the explanation about the fake password and the reconnaissance mission to the pawn shop Jimmy Dale shook his head in disbelief. He couldn't believe how smart she was.

"Sweetheart there is something about you. You're smart. You're beautiful. You have style." While he was speaking to her he grabbed her around the waist and pulled her body close to his own. He put additional emphasis on the words with pulses from his arms that tightened his grip when he verbalized the adjective at the end of each sentence. He put special emphasis on the last sentence in its entirety. Rosalie smiled broadly as she basked in his approval and allowed him to support her body as she leaned backwards and he dipped her like in a dance move from the 1930s.

She grabbed his face with both hands and told him, "I'm just glad I can make you happy, baby."

And he was indeed very happy.

Neal, on the other hand, was not happy. He had received the email from monkeybiz_911 instructing him to check the GPS unit for more information and he was now staring at the screen and the crude letters superimposed on a map of San Antonio. What kind of a guy was this James Dale Klein that he was able to send a message like this? It was James Bond-esque. *Doesn't this guy live in a trailer?* Neal thought to himself. *How is this happening?*

The tables had been turned on him and he knew subconsciously that he was not man enough to turn them back. He just hadn't completely accepted it yet.

****

"Hello Neal. This is monkeybiz." Rosalie's voice was low and calm when Neal answered the phone at the Wild Snail. Even sultry. The undercurrent of sensuality added to the insult. It said that *I'm a woman and I'm going to beat you. I know you're a man and it doesn't matter because I'm better than you.*

Neal was a little surprised to hear a woman's voice. And a little insulted.

"Neal, do you realize that blackmail is a felony offense?" Rosalie didn't know for sure if what Neal was doing was a crime at all but that was irrelevant.

"No." Neal wanted to talk and defend himself but could not talk out loud in the middle of the store.

"Well it is. And here's the problem – you pissed me off," Rosalie said placidly. "And I'm guessing that since you're blackmailing my friend and that guy down at Kuykendall Motors that you're guilty of two offenses. I'm also guessing that this isn't exactly your debut at this sort of thing. I'm sure if I poked around in your background I could find a whole slew of other indiscretions. Are you listening to me Neal?"

"I'm listening. I just don't know what you want me to do about it." Neal – like most of the population on the planet – was noticeably less able to remain in the flow of the conversation once the conversation went somewhere that he did not like. He was getting defensive.

"I'm going to tell you what you are going to do. You're going to start making deliveries for me. You're going to go to Del Rio on Tuesday and coordinate the purchase."

"I have to work on Tuesday. I…"

"If you need for me to call Frank and get you the day off I'd be happy to do it." Rosalie said in a calm but sinister fashion.

"But I'm not the one who's smuggling drugs…"

"Listen asshole. You don't seem to be picking up on what's happening here. What you have is an accusation only. You think you know something about somebody that might be involved in something down on the border. You can't prove anything and neither can anybody else. You don't have shit. What I have is direct proof that you are extorting money from a good friend of mine that lives on Polar Bear Drive."

Rosalie was not comfortable using Jimmy Dale's name even though they both knew who she was talking about.

"I have a letter sent to that address with your fingerprints on it," Rosalie continued.

Once again she was guessing at the underlying facts of her accusation - she didn't know for sure that there were fingerprints on the letter but she figured it was a safe assumption.

"And I wonder if Billy down at Kuykendall Motors would be willing to testify against you? So I want you to take off on Tuesday and be ready to head to Del Rio. Do you understand?"

"I understand," Neal answered.

****

Jimmy Dale spied the Gateway Arch in the distance as he dialed Chavo's number.

"Hey Chavo," Jimmy Dale said when he heard his partner pick up.

"Hello my friend." The connection was crackly and distant.

"Chavo I need you to help me out." Jimmy Dale rarely called his Mexican contact outside of his weekly visits to Acuña but he had a special request. There was a long pause filled with static. "Chavo are you there?"

"Yes. I am here. What is it that you need?"

Jimmy Dale tried to make it quick. He was afraid the call might drop. "I need you to help me out," he repeated. "I have a little trouble with a guy here in the US. He's involved in my operation and he's becoming a problem."

"What do you want me to do?"

"I'm bringing him to Acuña on Tuesday. He needs to disappear."

"You want him to disappear?"

"Yes. Disappear." Jimmy Dale repeated the request. He thought that Chavo understood his meaning but he wasn't sure.

"Disappear for good?" Chavo asked in an attempt to confirm his suspicions as to the meaning of Jimmy Dale's request.

Jimmy Dale knew now that Chavo understood what it was that he wanted him to do. "Yes…" he answered. "…for good."

"That is an expensive request."

"How expensive?"

"Your friend will be in Acuña?"

"Yes. I'll bring him to you."

"Five thousand," Chavo said to Jimmy Dale. He was testing the waters. He was willing to make Jimmy Dale's problem go away for much less but it never hurt to run something up a flag pole to see if Jimmy Dale might salute. And salute he did.

"Agreed. You will make the arrangements?"

"Bring him to me and I will have him disappear into the desert."

"I don't need to know where or how. I just need him gone."

"I can handle this for you," Jimmy Dale heard Chavo reply as the call to Acuña Mexico dropped.

****

Neal was told to be at the HEB parking lot in Del Rio on Tuesday
at noon. He followed the orders and arrived at 11:47. He decided
to smoke a cigarette and was leaning against the Grand Cherokee
when Jimmy Dale pulled up. Jimmy Dale's GMC slowed to a halt
facing in the opposite direction as the Jeep so that the driver's side
windows faced each other like descending crossing guard arms at a
railroad intersection at the approach of a train. The window slid
down.

"How you doin'?" Neal asked in that false way that people
will sometimes talk when they know they've been caught but think
that perhaps bogus confidence exhibited boldly and without regard
to station will reverse the facts of the situation.

Jimmy Dale responded in the same way that people
generally do when faced with posers like Neal…by ignoring the
greeting.

"Cross the international bridge. I'll meet you at the Café
de Los Toros on the square in an hour and a half," Jimmy Dale
ordered contemptuously.

Neal kept up the charade and asked for directions as if
they were equals. He had exited the Grand Cherokee and was
leaning in on the driver's side of Jimmy Dale's truck as he spoke,
"So when I cross the bridge, I need to…"

Jimmy Dale drove off as Neal was speaking to him. Neal
stumbled slightly as the support for the weight of his body was
taken from underneath him and watched Jimmy Dale disappear,
making a gradual left turn several blocks down the street. He
finished his cigarette and then proceeded to do as he was told.
Neal still harbored some fantasies about how he might best his
adversary on the Mexican side. Maybe show Jimmy Dale what
kind of man he was. Make him realize that he wasn't to be messed
with. The fact that he had no history of strength wasn't a concept
that even entered into his thinking. It was contrary to his version
of reality, and as such was filtered out prior to ever being formed as
an actual thought in Neal's mind. So Neal proceeded toward the
bridge and then across. The busyness of the place struck him. The
city was busier than its counterpart north of the border. Busier and
dustier. Neal was unsure of himself but managed to gain a
foothold in terms of where he was and where he needed to go and

found the town square and the café after a little while. He walked the two blocks from the parking spot back to the café and took a seat. He was 15 minutes early. Jimmy Dale showed up ten minutes later and didn't bother to sit.

"We're going for a ride," Jimmy Dale said.

"Where are we going"? Neal inquired.

"You're driving. Let's go." Jimmy Dale commanded again ignoring Neal's question and reaffirming his superior position.

Neal shook his head expressing his exasperation that he wasn't being informed of the destination. But he followed orders. If he wasn't nervous before he was now.

Chavo was waiting outside the café. He made eye contact with Jimmy Dale and then fell in behind them six or eight strides back. When they got to the Jeep, Chavo approached Neal from the rear and stood at the rear driver's side door. Neal had sensed someone was behind him and turned to glance at Chavo standing three feet away. Neal fumbled with his keys before unlocking the Jeep.

"I'm Neal." Neal stuck out his hand toward Chavo in greeting but was ignored. Chavo stared into space.

"Don't worry about him. He's just a friend of mine," Jimmy Dale told Neal. "He's going on this ride with us today."

Neal looked at Jimmy Dale and then back at Chavo who was still staring into space. Then back at Jimmy Dale. He had a questioning look on his face.

"Let's go," Jimmy Dale said.

Neal got into the Jeep, hit the unlock button and started the engine. He was feeling really uneasy now. The unknown was beginning to weigh on him, pressing on him in a way that it hadn't before. He fought down the panic. Jimmy Dale got into the driver's side and Chavo slid into the seat behind Neal.

"You mind tellin' me where we're going?" Neal's false confidence was beginning to fail him.

"Just drive. We want to talk to you about our situation," Jimmy Dale said.

****

"What is the Kamchatka Penninsula?" Billy said out loud to no one in particular.

And then from the TV, as if it were an echo, "What is the Kamchatka Penninsula?"

"Correct, the board is yours," Alex Tribec said directing the actions of the participants.

"I'll stick with World Geography for $800 Alex." It was the heavily bearded and slightly rotund security guard from Tulsa, Oklahoma that provided the correct response. He was in the charge of the board.

"Emptying into the world's largest inland delta, this river never reaches the sea."

"What is the Okavango?" Billy said, again providing the information to anyone within earshot as a preface to the response from the Jeopardy participants.

"What is the Okavango?" repeated the security guard. "Revolution for $600."

"During the early 20th century he was commander of El Division del Norte," Alex said, providing the answer to the anticipated question with perfect Spanish pronunciation.

"Who is Pancho Villa?" Billy yelled out quietly.

Billy's phone rang before the security guard from Tulsa or either of the other two contestants could answer. Billy glanced at the number - unavailable. He considered letting it go to voice mail and continue his winning ways on Jeopardy but picked up on a whim after the fourth ring.

"Hello?" Billy said with a questioning tone.

"Hello Billy. You don't know me," a woman's voice began. "But I think we might be able to help each other out."

"I could use some help," Billy said matter of factly. He was grasping at a life line. And even a stranger calling on a blocked line offered hope. He didn't care that he didn't know her. He was in such deep shit that he'd talk to anyone.

"I know. I'm aware of your problem and I think I'm in a position to help you out," she said.

The stranger's words caused Billy some concern. Was this another tormentor? Another vulture looking to take her pound of flesh? On the other hand how could it get any worse? He needed help and he needed it desperately.

"I am in a bit of a pickle. Would it be possible to ask who this is?"

"You can ask Billy but I'm not going to say. At least not truthfully. You can call me Norma."

"Ok…Norma. What are we talking about?"

"We're talking about getting you out of this mess with gohorse."

"You know about gohorse?" Billy asked incredulously.

"I know about him. I know what he's doing to you. And I know who he is."

Billy's hopes soared. "Can you do something about him?" Billy phrased the question vaguely in the hopes that his supposed benefactor would reveal her intent.

"I am in a position to make this little problem go away."

Billy didn't say anything.

"That's what you want. Isn't it Billy?" Rosalie asked, still in the persona of Norma.

"Yes Norma…it is."

"Then here is what I'll need you to do…"

####### *******

Neal Maresty had arrived in Mexico that afternoon around 1:00. By 5:00 his body was in a shallow grave 13 miles from the Rio Grande. By 7:30 that evening, the vultures on the fringes of Mexican society had taken possession of his abandoned Grand Cherokee. By noon the next day the vehicle had been completely stripped and sat in a field with the skeletal remains of other vehicles that had met the same fate. At the Wild Snail, Frank noticed his absence and was disappointed, but he was used to dealing with people and he knew that people sometimes disappeared, so he allowed a grace period to expire and then hired a new assistant manager.

Neal's mother was more concerned but not by much. When he hadn't called by the end of July she called him and left a message. When he didn't return the call after a week she called the Wild Snail and then drove by the apartment. She called Terry Amman but he hadn't heard anything either. She talked to Jack the landlord but he hadn't seen him either so she waited another day or two and finally called the police. The cops came out and talked to her and then to Frank and then to Jack letting everyone know they would pass along anything that they found out. Neal's mother took a business card from the detective in charge and put it on the coffee table.

CHAPTER 23

Charlie Manor's cellmate was Jesse Dethamuke. Jesse was serving three to five for kidnapping. Jesse never really saw what he did as a crime. All he did was take his own son and camp out for two or three months in the Gila National Wilderness in New Mexico. He never told his ex-wife what he was doing or where he was going and that was pretty much where he got into trouble. But despite the longevity of the trip and the lack of communication with the managing conservator, he described it as camping. Charlie told Jesse that if you don't tell anybody and you are actively evading the authorities, then it becomes kidnapping.

"That's what my wife's attorney said," Jesse responded when faced with his cellmate's legal analysis - the statement at once exhibiting an understanding of the letter of the law but also showing a failure to grasp the reasoning behind it, or at least how it applied to this situation. Charlie liked Jesse quite a bit. Jesse liked to talk about former girlfriends or about movies he liked. And he liked to tell stories in general. The other good thing about Jesse was that he was a good source of information.

"Hey Jesse, you ever hear of something called gohorse?"

"Gohorse?"

"Yeah…gohorse. One of the Mexican ninjas in the yard walked up to me a couple of days ago and told me he knew about gohorse," Charlie explained.

"What is it?" Jesse asked

"I don't know. That's why I'm asking you."

"Is it one word or two?" Jesse probed further.

"I don't know. He just said 'gohorse'."

Jesse was working on a pen drawing of his next tattoo. It was a voluptuous sword wielding warrior princess. All of Jesse's tattoo images were voluptuous warrior princesses. Not all of them wielded swords but a good many of them did. Jesse liked the sound of the phrase: *Gohorse*. He thought that maybe his next voluptuous warrior princess could be mounted astride a mighty steed and the steed's name could be Gohorse. Jesse wrote down the name under his sketch. He wrote the word in an elaborate script and kept going over it – darkening it or expanding it where it needed to be darkened or expanded and it became part of the drawing. It looked good in writing.

"What was his tone when he said that to you?" Jesse asked.

"Who?" Charlie asked back.

"The Mexican Ninja. Was he kidding around or what?"

"Those guys don't really have much of a sense of humor Jesse."

"So what was he acting like?"

"Accusatory." Charlie paused. He thought about the Mexican that had approached him. "Defiant maybe," he added. "I really don't think they can act any other way. At least in terms of how they act to the whites, any body language is pretty much some form of aggression."

"I don't know," Jesse responded half-heartedly to the original question posed to him by his cellmate, "can't say that I ever heard of it." Jesse's mind was on the voluptuous warrior princess…the one astride Gohorse, the mighty steed."

****

"Hey Mike." Billy addressed Mike Josper at the sales desk. Mike was leaning back in the roll around chair and was clicking his

$40 pen against his teeth. And the way he wore the suspenders. Ugh. There was just something about him. Billy despised him.

"I was taking a look at the employee handbook the other day," Billy said. "And the way I read it salesmen get one week of paid vacation every year and I think I'm due. You wouldn't have a problem with me taking off next week would you?"

Mike's eyes diverted from Billy's to staring directly out the large front window. He leaned forward in the chair and put his elbows on the sales desk bringing his clasped hands upward with index fingers extended and touching his lips. It was an introspective look. It was meant to divert attention away from himself. Billy doubted if Mike was striking this position on purpose. It was probably done out of weakness; an inability to look an adversary in the face.

"I usually require about three or four months lead time with regards to time off. I need to make sure I have coverage on the lot." Mike was lying. He wanted every salesman to be on the lot selling. And if there was paid vacation coming to one of the salesmen, then Mike would deny the salesman's request based on this bogus reasoning. Mike had no honor whatsoever.

Mike continued staring straight forward out the window. His weakness prevented him from making eye contact so he stared straight ahead. Billy just looked at him. The assistant sales manager – Billy didn't even bother to learn his name because they came and went so frequently - was seated farther down the sales desk and opposite from where Billy was leaning on the counter top. Billy looked at the assistant sales manager who stared back nodding his head and pursing his lips slightly in expression of awareness. The assistant sales manager knew what was happening. Billy looked back down at the moron occupying the chair just three feet in front of him.

"You're an idiot. You know that?" Billy was going to quit anyway. His new boss, Norma, paid well and despite the criminal nature of his responsibilities, it allowed Billy some freedom. Billy wanted to get an extra week's pay out of the dealership before he took off so he'd made the vacation request. Billy's accusation of idiocy brought Mike back to life.

"You can clean your desk out now Billy if you like. If not, I can have everything boxed up for you and we can send it to your house. Either way it might be best if you're off the lot in five minutes."

"I'll be out in two. I don't want to have to hang around this cesspool any longer than I absolutely have to."

"Two minutes sounds good to me Billy."

Billy turned toward the main open area of the showroom and said in a normal tone, "This guy is so dumb he buys popcorn and soda on the way out of a theatre so he has something for the ride home."

Billy caught the look of approval on the assistant sales manager's face as he spun on his heels and headed toward his desk.

****

Jimmy Dale had been locked up at county two or three times but had never been to an actual prison and the size of the facility at Huntsville is what struck him most. The parking lot, situated as it was in the middle of a heavily forested stretch of nowhere deep in East Texas gave the impression of being even bigger than it actually was. Jimmy Dale thought to himself that it appeared adequate to handle parking for a good sized high school football game. It was Saturday at 9 a.m., the most popular day and time for visitors, and the lot was at least 3/4 full. He entered the building, passed through a metal detector, and then into a central processing room. After a six or seven minute wait in line he found himself at a window with ID in hand.

The correctional facility employee was behind a plexiglass window with the half oval cut into the counter below so that items could be passed back and forth. Jimmy Dale slid his driver's license forward and into the depression. He wondered if the woman in front of him had ever been in a difficult situation here at the prison. She appeared to be about 75 pounds overweight and probably incapable of handling an inmate of even average physical means. Was she a guard? A clerk? She was wearing a uniform with a badge and a gun. Not many clerks wear guns, Jimmy Dale thought to himself. He was curious as to what her job was here at the prison and considered asking but decided not to. Like most prison employees she didn't give the impression of having a sense of humor. Not that she needed one to answer a simple question about her job title but having a sense of humor helped in terms of communication in general. Jimmy Dale assumed that the fact she was lacking in this area was probably why she was working at the prison to begin with. It really doesn't require much in the way of people skills. Jimmy Dale decided to think of her as a guard/clerk.

The guard/clerk swiped his driver's license and Jimmy Dale's personal information was immediately loaded into the system.

"Who are you visiting today?" the guard/clerk asked.

"Charles Manor."

The guard/clerk tapped on the keyboard, her nails clicking like someone tapping out morse code. Jimmy Dale noticed that her nails were immaculately done. The right pinkie nail even had some sort of charm on it.

"What is the nature of your visit?" The guard/clerk looked up but still somehow managed to avoid making eye contact.

"He's my girlfriend's ex-husband. We got some family issues to work out," Jimmy Dale said. And then after a quick thought added, "But there's no hard feelings between us or anything. It should be friendly."

The guard/clerk tapped the keyboard again in a flurry and two seconds later a small printer the size of a pencil sharpener spit out a name tag complete with first and last name of both the visitor and the visited. There was even a black and white version of Jimmy Dale's driver's license picture and a head shot of Charlie in his prison uniform. Neither picture was very complimentary. Jimmy Dale peeled the sticker off the back, slapped the name tag on his chest and passed through another metal detector into the general visitation room.

****

Billy was apprehensive as he sat in the pothole riddled parking lot of the abandoned vacant Southside warehouse. He felt anxious and noted curiously how he had become somewhat used to feeling this way. It seemed as if it was the only emotion he was capable of having anymore. Calmness and serenity were distant, foggy memories. But at least he seemed to be out of the unenviable position of being blackmailed. And Norma, whoever she was, despite pressuring him to make drug deliveries to Chicago, seemed to have some sense of humanity about her.

Billy had never been to Chicago. He noticed that for the middle of August, it was surprisingly cool – a lot cooler than San Antonio was at this time of year. He had never spoken to the man he was about to meet with. Billy didn't think that he had ever even met a person named Jarvis before. And he certainly had never engaged in felonious cocaine trafficking.

Billy kept up a good front as a beat up Astro van pulled alongside him on the driver's side facing in the same direction. From what he could see there were at least three or four black guys inside. He didn't expect Jarvis to show up alone but it was still disconcerting. He didn't have a chance against these guys if something went wrong. The van was close enough that Billy could have touched the finger of the van's passenger in the same way that Adam and God were touching fingers in Michelangelo's *The Creation of Adam*, which of course, he was not inclined to do. The driver's side window lowered and Billy was a little surprised that the motor for the window was even operational. The van's driver leaned forward so he could see Billy across the guy in the passenger seat.

"You Billy?" the driver inquired.

"Yeah I'm Billy." Billy thought about confirming that the driver's name was Jarvis but decided there wasn't really any point to it.

"You're supposed to have something for me. You got it?" Jarvis asked still leaning on the steering wheel. The man in the passenger seat kept his eyes front and center.

"I got it. I was supposed to get something from you when I deliver it. Is that right?" Billy said following Jarvis' lead of never using any specific nouns.

"Yeah I got it right here." Jarvis held up a roll of bills wrapped with a rubber band. Billy was close enough that he could see that the outside bill was a hundred.

"So hand the package over to my friend and let's get out of here," Jarvis said.

The passenger looked at Billy now and placed his arm on the window with the elbow hanging over the edge, implying that he was getting ready to receive something in case something was given to him. Billy reached under the seat, fumbled around for the package, then picked it up and handed it to the black man in the white t-shirt in the front passenger seat of the Astro van. Jarvis tossed the money roll through the window and into Billy's lap. He nodded at Billy indicating that their business transaction was complete. Billy nodded back and Jarvis pulled away. Billy scanned his surroundings for anything unusual and then decided it was best that he vacate the area. He was well south of Chicago before he felt calm enough to pull over and count the money. It was all there - all $15,000 of it.

****

Jimmy Dale took a seat in the middle of a long metal bench that ran nearly the length of the visitation room. The bench, and one just like it on the opposite side of the table, was connected structurally to the table itself. It looked like a very long picnic table. Charlie entered the room by way of a door in the far corner. He was 15 or 20 back in a long line of inmates streaming into the gymnasium-like space. He made his way through the mob of fat wives and skinny wore-out girlfriends and all their screaming kids. He sat down on the bench next to Jimmy Dale. The din was considerable and it was easier if they didn't have to talk across the table. Jimmy Dale spoke first.

"Hello Charlie. Everything going alright?" Jimmy Dale had only been around Charlie once before, and although that encounter had gone well, you just never knew how an ex-husband might react to a guy that's sleeping with his ex-wife so he tried to kick off the conversation innocuously and test the water a little bit.

"I'm alright. How's Rosalie?" Charlie responded without animus. His demeanor was friendly and conversational.

"Rosalie seems to be getting along ok."

"She's not getting fat is she?" Charlie asked.

"No. She's not getting fat."

"I ain't seen her in a while y'know."

"Yeah I know," Jimmy Dale responded.

Jimmy Dale wasn't quite sure where Charlie wanted to go with the conversation so he just nodded in agreement, allowing Charlie to take the lead.

"Is she wearing her hair long or short or what?" Charlie asked.

"It's medium length just past her shoulders."

"I was hoping she hadn't cut it short. I never liked it short," Charlie commented.

"I don't like it short either. As far as I'm concerned a woman should have long hair," Jimmy Dale replied. Now it was Charlie's time to nod.

Jimmy Dale was getting a feel for the man. He could tell by the way Charlie spoke and the way he presented himself that Charlie was intelligent. Jimmy Dale respected that. He respected it to the point that it almost didn't make sense and to the point where other serious character flaws were more easily forgiven just because the man was smart. It was at this point that Jimmy Dale realized that Charlie only wanted to talk about Rosalie. He had not mentioned his own son Zack.

"Hey Charlie I'm not sure if I really understand how life works here at Huntsville. So I don't really know how to ask this exactly…but…do you know most of the other guys?"

"You need a contact for something?" Charlie asked getting to the point.

Jimmy Dale went on to explain to Charlie how he needed a contact that could act as a middleman, buy IDs, and then resell them to the coyotes.

"Jimmy Dale, if you're willing to help me out a little bit I'm happy to ask around down here and come up with a contact for you. Are you willing to do that? Help me out I mean?"

"Yeah. I'll help you out if I can."

"Here's what I want you to do…" Charlie began.

CHAPTER 24

Rosalie sat on the back porch of her mother's house and watched the sun's rays cascade over the clouds. The only type of cloud that Rosalie could identify were cirrus clouds and she knew that the clouds that she was looking at now were not cirrus. Cirrus clouds were waif-like, formless, and independent of one another. These clouds were the opposite, mostly uniform in size and shape and bound to one another in a series of fairly uniform rows. The appearance of the clouds reminded Rosalie of weathered stones in a creek bed through a run where the drop in elevation was greater than normal and the stream was flowing quickly. The clouds acted as prisms and the light filtering through the formation yielded variations of pink and orange that didn't occur very often, maybe only once or twice a year. Rosalie couldn't scientifically explain the canvas laid out before her although she knew that there were people in the world that could. Jimmy Dale had tried a couple of times to lay out all the reasons why the sky was the color it was at certain times of the day but she was never quite able to grasp it. It didn't matter to her if science could explain it anyway. In her mind, God had created science so anything coming into existence by way of a scientifically explained process – cloud banks at sunset, stalagmites in a cave, a human baby at conception – all had God as their begetter. It was her trump card.

Her mind wondered through her various relationships and enterprises. She pondered the legality and morality of it all and she didn't like the unsettled state of her conscience. She had hoped her reflections might support her chosen path but she could never quite make it work. Despite the increased financial security for her and Zack there was always this background uneasiness. So as the last sliver of the now blood red sun dipped beneath the horizon, and the edge came off the brilliance of the cloud's palette, she knew she had simply exchanged one burden for another.

****

Jimmy Dale was not surprised by Charlie Manor's request. Five grand in cash delivered to Charlie's mother seemed a lot like something an inmate might ask for. Especially one like Charlie. Who knew what made these convicts make the choices that they made? Why Charlie would want to have money delivered to his mother instead of having it go to his only son was beyond Jimmy Dale. He simply took it in stride and promised to make the delivery. He accepted a lined, yellow piece of paper handwritten and torn from a tablet. It had Charlie's mother's address and phone number:

> *Esther Manor*
> *122 Lookout Ridge Road*
> *Hallettsville, Texas 77964*
>
> *(361) 555-8922*

Jimmy Dale agreed to make the delivery within the next couple of days and get back out to Huntsville on Thursday to get the contact information on the coyote directly from Charlie.

****

El Milagro received with serenity the news that the quality of the stolen IDs being delivered by Raul Barrientos was inferior. He was not surprised. He had heard rumors over the last few weeks of sloppiness. So when his underling reported to him that there were incorrect social security numbers and driver's license numbers among those being provided by Raul, El Milagro took it in stride. He was not angry. Like any truly mature businessman, El Milagro accepted bad news as part of doing business. It was human nature for underlings to get sloppy and a good leader would respond to correct the situation. But unlike a subordinate that worked as a data entry clerk in a local accounting firm, there would be no written warning, no second chance, and certainly no compassion. You only disappoint the Mexican Mafia once.

The news that El Milagro had received from his associate in Acuña though, required contemplation. El Milagro considered his next order. He balanced the benefits against the consequences. Raul would have to be killed. That was certain. You only disappoint the Mexican Mafia once

"Se mata," he ordered. And as a follow up, "Quiero a conocer el guero con el contacto." He was ready to meet the white boy with the contact. He was ready to meet Charlie Manor.

Raul's body was found two weeks later on the south side of San Antonio in a large abandoned lot behind a pile of trash that had started out as a discarded pop up camper, but had quickly grown into a reasonably sized pile of refuse once residents from the area ceased to view the camper as a camper and started to accept it as trash. Some effort had been made to conceal the body but the buzzards and the smell led one of the employees at the welding shop next door, to investigate. The body was beginning to decompose but even a welder with no training in forensics, could tell that the cause of death was a slashed throat. The wallet and the watch along with whatever jewelry he had happened to be wearing was still on the body. At least until the welder found him. It wasn't pleasant, but it was worth fighting back the gag reflex to relieve the body of several hundred dollars in cash and jewelry. The wallet, ID and credit cards intact, was returned to the back right pocket.

"Hey boss," the welder yelled back to the shop after relieving Raul of his final effects, "I think you might want to take a look at this."

****

"Did Charlie give you this piece of paper?" Rosalie had wanted to ask Jimmy Dale about his meeting with Charlie in Hunstville and the note lying on the coffee table, written in Charlie's hand provided a convenient segue into the topic.

"Yeah," Jimmy Dale hollered from the back bedroom.

"Why is Charlie's mother's name on it?" Rosalie had wanted to ease into the conversation but curiosity got the best of her and she dove in without any pretense of indifference.

"Because he wants me to give her some money," Jimmy Dale hollered back.

Rosalie stared at the note and ran through the implications of Charlie's request. She didn't like yelling from one end of the trailer to the other so she wandered down the hall still inspecting the paper that Charlie had given Jimmy Dale.

"How did he seem?" she asked.

"I don't know." Jimmy Dale did not like the subjective nature of the question. He made only a slight effort to conceal his aggravation. It wasn't something that he wanted to get into. "He's a convicted felon locked up at the state pen. Given his circumstances I guess I would say that he seemed fine."

Rosalie knew that she was annoying him and decided not make a big deal of it. It wasn't in her to fight with him tonight. She was feeling good about life and diffused the situation. She did it without even trying.

"Baby I'm just asking if he seemed open to the idea of helping us out is all. You couldn't come out here and scratch my itch could you?" Rosalie and Jimmy Dale used the phrase, *scratch my itch* to imply any form of affection from a nearly platonic hug to something more intimate. In this case Rosalie used the phrase in a conciliatory fashion and left the meaning open for interpretation. It made Jimmy Dale feel better and he followed Rosalie down the narrow hall to take a seat on the couch behind her. He pulled her hair back and up off her neck and shoulders. Rosalie sat in front of him and stared at Charlie's note. She noticed something on the paper.

"Do we have a pencil?" she asked.

"I don't know. Do we?" Jimmy Dale didn't feel like getting up and looking for a pencil. He felt like running his fingers through Rosalie's hair.

"Baby I think there's a pencil in the junk drawer by the sink," Rosalie said.

Jimmy Dale noticed she was staring intently at the piece of paper. He pulled himself from the couch and walked to the kitchen, opened the drawer, got the pencil and returned to his spot behind Rosalie almost in one motion. She leaned forward and placed the paper on top of the dated copy of Field and Stream that had been lying unread on the coffee table for the last two years. It had finally come in handy. She scratched the upper part of the note with the lead tip and the pencil turned sideways. Lettering began to appear. She was not prepared for the image that took shape.

****

"I speak fax," replied Charlie when questioned about his linguistic abilities. "That's what I meant when I said I was bilingual, I meant I speak English and my second language is fax."

Charlie then verbalized a remarkably accurate imitation of the tones, beeps, and clicks produced by a fax machine when it's trying to talk to another fax machine. So accurate was the representation that a casual bystander might not have questioned a resume materializing from thin air accompanied by a cover letter explaining why the sender of the fax is imminently qualified for the position of Accounting Clerk II.

The inquisitor – a go-between for El Milagro - grinned with genuine appreciation for the humor but followed it up with a warning, "My question, Charlie, is if you speak Spanish. El Milagro does not have the same sense of humor that I do. You understand that it might be best to stick to business. ¿Comprende?"

"Comprendo," Charlie answered.

"I will let El Milagro know that I have spoken to you and that you have serious business. He'll be available for you tomorrow in the yard. Make sure that you do not have any contraband on you. You will be searched before you are allowed to approach him."

As he approached the Mexican section of the bleachers the next day in the yard, Charlie saw that one of his adversaries from the laundry closet incident some months earlier was standing as a sentry. Charlie nodded his recognition. The guard nodded back and began to frisk Charlie. Charlie cooperated by raising his arms and was granted entry.

"Thanks for meeting with me," Charlie said as he sat down next to El Milagro on the upper bench.

El Milagro looked straight ahead. He didn't say anything. Charlie wondered if he even spoke English. It didn't look like he did. And even if he did it didn't appear that he was willing to use it. El Milagro gave the impression that we was above the English language. So Charlie waited. Charlie felt like he was being made to wait for no particular reason other than he was of lower status, which was exactly what was happening. After what El Milagro deemed an appropriate amount of time he reached into his shirt pocket, pulled out a piece of paper and handed it to Charlie. Charlie took it. Written in script that was barely legible was a phone number accompanied by the name *Lorenzo*. Charlie looked at El Milagro again but the Mexican's gaze continued to be fixed straight forward on the yard. El Milagro motioned with his left hand that the meeting was over and that Charlie should leave.

****

Rosalie stared at the resurrected illustration on the paper given to Jimmy Dale by Charlie at Huntsville earlier that day. Charlie's mother's information was written in blue ink. But beneath that script was the outline of something that had been written before, on the preceding page of the note pad. The person that had originally drawn the image had pressed hard on the paper, and appeared to have gone over the image with a pen again and again. The artist – the person who had created the image originally did indeed appear to have some ability – had left a very distinct impression on the page beneath the original drawing; and that image had now been brought to life by Rosalie.

The image was of a scantily clad, full-breasted woman. The woman had a very full head of hair and, other than the sword and the horse, gave the general impression of a Barbie doll. But it wasn't the image that struck Rosalie; it was the script that accompanied the illustration. The script was ornate and hugged the contours of the horse's body so that it seemed like it was part of the image and not just a title:

GOHORSE

Rosalie stared long and hard. She was leaning forward with her elbows on her knees and her knees pressed together. Her fingers extended straight out from her hands covering her lips. The position was common, especially to women, when anxious or surprised. The pit of her stomach lurched with anxiety at what the reappearance – for just seconds before the word had been gradually and peacefully fading into memory but had now been exhumed to once again wreak havoc on her life – of this word meant.

"Oh no," she muttered, the regret apparent in her tone. She dropped her head now into her hands and stared at the floor between the cracks in her fingers.

"What is it?" Jimmy Dale asked sensing something was very wrong. Rosalie passed the paper back to him with her right hand, not moving any other part of her body. Jimmy Dale took a couple of seconds to absorb what he was looking at. When it hit home he let his anger vent. He took one giant step across the coffee table with the Field and Stream magazine on it. He spun and lifted the table with his left hand sending it flipping several feet to the end of the living room and barely missing Rosalie.

"THAT PIECE OF SHIT! THAT NO GOOD..." Jimmy Dale didn't have the words. He had to do something but didn't know what to do so he paced and clinched his fists and clinched his teeth. He moved quickly from one end of the living room to the other. At every turn he would face Rosalie. "I CAN'T BELIEVE THAT HE WOULD DO THAT TO YOU AND TO HIS OWN SON...THE GALL...THE SELFISHNESS!" Jimmy

Dale paced for fifteen minutes with the verbal tirades gradually lessening in intensity.

Finally, the initial shock having worn off just a bit, Rosalie said something. "Baby I know this hurts. It's a blow and it's a setback but there has got to be a way to get through this. There is a single best way to respond. We just need to find it and then go out and do it. Now I need you to help me. I need you to focus."

Jimmy Dale stared at her, his jaws still clinched in rage. Right now, when things looked bad was when she shined the brightest. She was strikingly beautiful and so strong. He knew that as the man he was called to be the strength, but deep down he knew - he knew that the real strength of the relationship was with Rosalie.

"I'll help you sweetheart," he said.

"I love you baby," Rosalie said reaching out her hand toward Jimmy Dale from the couch inviting him to sit with her. Jimmy Dale took her hand and did what she had asked him to do. He focused.

****

Billy was sitting at the end of the bar when Cupcake walked through the door at Rod Dog's. Billy had a pitcher of beer on the table. One mug was sitting in front of Billy half full, the other mug was still crusted with ice but starting to sweat a little. It looked like it had been there only a minute or two.

"Before I say anything else," Cupcake was saying as he approached the table, "I have to tell that your performance this afternoon was awesome. Awesome. You really put that asshole in his place."

For the first time Billy saw the resemblance between Cupcake and Chris Farley. It was the similarity between Cupcake's emphatic overuse of the word *awesome* and the Chris Farley character when he interviewed Paul McCartney on Saturday Night Live that triggered the recognition. Cupcake was a little more muscular and not quite as flabby, but he was the same general size and build and had the same fair features. But the affable manner in which Cupcake's immaturity manifested itself was really the thing. You couldn't help but like him for it.

"Thanks Cup. I have to admit. It felt good."

Cupcake sat down and wrapped his huge right paw around the mug in front of him. He immediately feigned surprise and made a crackling sound with his mouth meant to indicate that his hand was freezing to the mug. It was very realistic. Cupcake was good at imitating people and imitating sounds that occur in nature. Cupcake giggled at the joke and Billy chuckled along with him.

"Hey Cup, you remember three or four months ago when you were selling those bootleg DVDs?"

"Yeah. I remember."

"Did you ever make any money off that little endeavor?"

"Couple hundred."

Billy was inclined to think that Cupcake was exaggerating the revenue generated off the illegal enterprise but let it go. It didn't really matter anyway. "How'd you like to make $500 a day?"

Cupcake looked at Billy and blinked. Finally he said, "I have the feeling this might involve some bending of the rules."

"There are a couple of rules here that might get bent...yes." And after a long pause, "Actually they'll be broken outright." Billy nodded slightly and smirked a bit to bring levity to the conversation. Then Billy laid it all out for him, promising Cupcake the same pay scale that he himself had received from Terry and Raul. Cupcake agreed to deliver 10 IDs the following evening.

CHAPTER 25

Why would this guy be wearing a kilt? Jimmy Dale thought to himself as he pulled into the parking lot at the convenience store to rendezvous with the coyote. Jimmy Dale had called the number that Charlie had provided as the point of contact after his meeting with El Milagro. The voice on the other line spoke curtly and in broken English but the message had been clear. Meet him at 2:00 on Wednesday in the parking lot at the corner of Thousand Oaks and Wetmore. Jimmy Dale checked his mobile phone. 2:01. He looked at the street signs more for the psychological benefit than as a confirmation of his actual physical location. He was merely going through the mental checklist. He was on time and he was in the right place. But the man in the kilt threw him off. Could this guy be his contact? He didn't look like a coyote. Yet there was something about him. So Jimmy Dale watched and waited. The would-be Scotsman walked into the store and dug something out of the beer bin filled with 24 ounce beers and ice. His angle of observation prevented Jimmy Dale from determining what brand of beer the Scotsman had purchased. When he left the store, the Scotsman was carrying the beer wrapped in what is commonly called a Texas koozie, that is, a beer-sized paper bag provided by the store clerk. In an act of defiance to the liquor laws in place as determined by the State of Texas and the City of San Antonio, or perhaps more likely he simply didn't give a shit, the Scot, while still on the premises, opened the beer and took a long draw. Jimmy Dale watched.

The Scotsman was of average height and a little chubby. About 30 years old, his hair was a scraggly dark brown and poked out from under a black beanie. The beard matched the hair on his head except that, if anything, it was even more scraggly. The kilt was checkered black and brown. His shoes were slip on tennis shoes and he wasn't wearing socks. He wore a t-shirt with an image of Che Guevara on the front. He walked across the parking lot and sat down on the curb by the dumpster and took another long draw off the big boy beer. Then he looked Jimmy Dale's way and made eye contact from across the parking lot for an instant only to look away and take another hit from the beer.

I think this is my guy, Jimmy Dale thought to himself incredulously. He pondered the situation for a few more ticks before he opened the door of the GMC and got out. The Scotsman didn't look Jimmy Dale's way again until he was real close.

"You don't know anybody over at Huntsville do you?" Jimmy Dale asked.

"You got something for me?" the Scotsman asked. His tone was sullen and abrasive. No trace of an actual Scottish accent. He gave the impression of someone that was fed up with society. It takes an effort to exist in society and interact with others. This man was unable or unwilling to put forth that effort. He didn't dress the way he did out of a sense of uniqueness or style, he did it out of laziness. He simply did not care what others thought of him and he refused to make even the slightest effort by way of his manner, appearance, or hygiene – the smell of him was offensive – to fit in with the rest of the world.

"I got a piece of paper with some information on it. Is that the kind of thing you're looking for?"

"Give it to me," the Scotsman said.

"I'm going to need the money..." Jimmy Dale paused waiting for confirmation that the smelly Scotsman was indeed his contact. "you have the money..." Jimmy Dale paused again and then, "Right?"

"I just need the paper man. Just give me the paper with the names and the numbers on it." The smelly Scotsman was terse and impatient. In keeping with the face that he put out to the world – an ugly one – his demeanor was best described with the same adjective. Jimmy Dale'd had enough encounters with lowlifes like the one in front of him now to know that the Scotsman was making an attempt at bullying him into handing over the information without making the payment. Jimmy Dale felt sure that some kind of assurance was forthcoming guaranteeing payment at some future date. A date that, if agreed to, would then morph into a promise of payment at some date still further out, which if agreed to would coincide with some other as of yet unforeseen event, perhaps a fire at the Scotsman's home, or some fatal illness befalling a member of the Scotsman's family that would necessitate postponing payment still further into the future, and so on.

"I'm supposed to get the paper and then bring the money to you next week when everything checks out." The Scotsman said, true to Jimmy Dale's instincts.

"Listen man, I can appreciate that you need some money. I'll even float you twenty bucks if you really need it. But if you think I'm handing over this list to you without the $500, you're crazy. And if you try to squeeze me again, I'll get word back to that Mexican in Huntsville about what the hell's going on. I really don't think that's a good idea. Do you?" Jimmy Dale laid it on the line.

The Scotsman looked at Jimmy Dale with a surly countenance. As if Jimmy Dale was the one that was being unreasonable. Jimmy Dale accepted the situation for what it was. The Scotsman, despite his accusatory manner, was the one being unreasonable, but at some level, he really couldn't help it. Jimmy Dale thought about an interesting stat that he had read once. Eighty-seven percent of all Americans think that they are of above average intelligence. *They* – presumably the twenty-three percent of Americans that by definition must fall below the 50% mark but still think they are smarter than average – are too dumb to know that they're dumb. This fact reconciles the inconsistency of the statistic. To recognize intelligence, or lack thereof, especially in one's self, requires a level of intelligence to begin with. And they don't have it. The same thing is true about unreasonable people. They're too unreasonable to know that they are being unreasonable. Jimmy Dale recognized this characteristic in the Scotsman and knew the correct manner in which to deal with him was then *not* to reason with him. Force was the only way.

"Well do you?" Jimmy Dale asked again.

"Man I thought you were cool," the Scotsman said making one last attempt at manipulating Jimmy Dale into walking away without the money.

"You're not getting the information that the Mexicans need without the money," Jimmy Dale affirmed.

The Scotsman reached into a pocket sewn into the front of his kilt and took out a ragged #10 envelope and handed it to Jimmy Dale. Jimmy Dale thumbed the five bills and, satisfied, handed the Scotsman the paper with the stolen IDs – the IDs that had been stolen by Cupcake and delivered to JD through Billy. The Scotsman grabbed the paper and stuffed it back into the same pocket that he had extracted the envelope from without even looking at it. He stood up and took another long pull off the beer giving Jimmy Dale a disdainful look. The transaction completed, he lumbered back across the parking lot to his 15 year old Toyota with the bad paint job and grill held in place by a bungee cord and drove off to God knows where.

****

The FBI showed up at Kuykendall Motors in a dramatic yet understated fashion that only trained federal law enforcement is capable of pulling off. Four very dark, very sleek sedans entered the two front gates with the two lead cars driving quickly through the gates and up to the main building. There were two cars bringing up the rear that stopped at the front gates and parked at an angle as a deterrent to fugitives. Lazy salesmen are disinclined to work the morning shift or much past 5:00 in the afternoon.

Maybe the FBI factored that into their decision to arrive at 2:00 on a Friday or maybe they didn't, but either way the time of the raid combined with the fact that it was payday came together to produce a very high percentage of on-duty salesmen.

Only God in heaven could have known that fully one-third of the salesmen on duty that afternoon – eight different men - became very nervous at the sight of the federal authorities. Of the eight that were suffering anxiety attacks, six were merely concerned about their assorted nefarious activities, unsure of whether the feds cared about their own small bookmaking operation or their scam on craigslist. Two of the eight though, mired in criminal activities that would justify hard time in prison were terrified and actively sought an escape route, praying that somehow, perhaps, it might be that the feds had arrived that day looking for someone else. The prayers of both these men were answered. The FBI agents were indeed looking for someone else. In fact the particular salesman that the FBI was coming to arrest that day wasn't worried at all. Cupcake was asleep in his glass walled cube.

Six FBI agents, dressed in dark suits with guns undrawn but plainly visible in the shoulder holsters beneath the jackets came through the doors of the dealership and asked for Stephen Gorman. Ironically Gatewood, the convicted murderer, was among the salesmen on the lot who wasn't concerned about the presence of law enforcement because he knew he'd done nothing wrong. He didn't scamper when the raid came down. He was standing near the front door and when queried about Cupcake, turned and pointed to the large man engaged in what was presumably blissful slumber toward the back of the showroom.

It was an unpleasant awakening from a very pleasant dream. Cupcake was dreaming about something only a gregarious man-child could dream about when the vaguest realization began to creep into his consciousness that something was wrong. About a half second later he was fully awake and in the throes of being arrested. The agent in charge asked him his name and upon confirmation that they had the right guy, asked Cupcake to stand. The agent read him his rights while he brought the handcuffs to bear on Cupcake's thick wrists. It was at this point that Mike emerged from the restroom and caught Cupcake's eye. Mike could see that Cupcake was about to cry and nodded slightly in an attempt to convey his sympathy. It was a rare display of human emotion from the man.

The agents made no attempt at discretion. It was not their job. So as the arresting agent read the warrant out loud pretty much everybody in the showroom became aware that Cupcake was being arrested for suspicion of violating Federal Statute 1028 (a) (7). The question that then buzzed through the dealership: *What exactly is Federal Statute 1028 (a) (7)?*, was answered as soon as one of the salesman had enough time to look it up on his iphone - Cupcake was going down for felony identity theft.

Later that night in his cell, Cupcake's memory of the arrest was blurry. It just seemed all so surreal. Cupcake didn't remember the name or the face of the arresting agent. He didn't remember being read his rights. He didn't remember what he was dreaming about when the agents woke him up at his desk. He didn't even remember what clothes he had been wearing. He did remember standing up and the sharp chill of the handcuffs. He remembered the sedans parked by the gates blocking entry and exit. And he remembered the stares of his co-workers as he was paraded through the showroom, their faces forlorn and empathetic, knowing it was but by a mere twist of fate that they themselves were not on their way to the clink.

****

"Ya' know Charlie, I'm not keeping score, but if I was I'd be ahead 11-9," Rosalie said to her ex. They were sitting in the middle of the visiting facility at Huntsville. It sounded like a junior high cafeteria at lunch time. The background noise could have been a distraction if the subject matter of the conversation wasn't so gripping.

Charlie still loved her, despite his unwarranted bitterness toward her. It seemed to him that there was an old country song that had said it somewhere before, but he loved her for all the wrong reasons. Looks and personality...mostly looks. In Charlie's mind she was at minimum very pretty and on occasion stunning. She was funny and charismatic so he liked the way he felt when he was around her. Most of all he just liked looking at her. In actuality, most men felt that way around Rosalie just maybe not to the extent that Charlie did. His anger at her would boil up from time to time but not now. Right now he just felt that old glow. Thus far in the conversation, Charlie had failed to realize that Rosalie was angry and he took the comment incorrectly as flirting, so he just smiled back at her. He even reached out his hand only to have her withdraw.

"I know what you did you piece of shit." What was at first undetectable in her manner was now apparent as the vitriol began to leak out.

"What?" Charlie didn't understand the hostility. He had hoped for a light and friendly exchange.

"You know damn good and well what I'm talking about," Rosalie didn't think she needed to answer the question but answered it anyway. Rosalie hadn't really calmed down but she had regained her composure. It was her style to not get rattled. She didn't let anyone or anything take her out of her game…at least not for long. Charlie stared back at her. She perceived his expression as feigned incredulity.

"You're the gohorse. You've caused me some problems Charlie and I can't just let it go."

"You know about gohorse?" Charlie was surprised that she knew and let it show.

Rosalie's fears were confirmed. *How could he do this?* she wondered. *How could Charlie hold so much against her?* Rosalie could feel herself losing control and she didn't want to do that. Not here. Not in this public place. Rosalie stood and looked down at Charlie one last time. The look that was returned to her was the same look that she had received so many times in the past, a look that was totally disconnected from the circumstances, a look of detached blissfulness.

****

"Katie Couric called. She wants her skirt back." Jimmy Dale couldn't help but laugh as he leveled the jab at the Scotsman.

"Why do you act like that?" the Scotsman asked. Jimmy Dale's life experiences had had taught him that socially deficient people were typically devoid of humor. A normal knock-knock joke or something they might get, but anything dry or simply witty would generally go right by them, especially if it required self-deprecation. Jimmy Dale knew this and it was, in fact, what caused him to deliver the cheap shot in the first place.

"Like what?" Jimmy Dale played dumb.

"Nobody thinks you're funny you know," the Scotsman argued.

"Who put a brick in your pantyhose?" Jimmy Dale asked taking another dig aimed at the femininity of the Scotsman wearing what Jimmy Dale perceived to be a skirt.

"Let's just get on with it," Jimmy Dale said. Jimmy Dale decided to drop the girlie jokes. He'd had his fun and didn't want to spend any more time with this jerk than he had to. The Scotsman handed him the envelope with the money and Jimmy Dale handed the Scotsman the latest batch of stolen IDs.

"There's something else," Jimmy Dale said. "I need your boss in Huntsville to have someone take care of this guy." Jimmy Dale handed the Scotsman a piece of paper with a name on it. The Scotsman read the paper and looked at Jimmy Dale.

"You askin' what I think you're askin'?"

"He spends a fair amount time right there in Huntsville. I don't think your boss will have much trouble finding the guy. Just find out what I need to do get him taken care of."

The Scotsman didn't say anything else. He crammed the paper without folding it into the pocket that was sewn into the kilt. Jimmy Dale stood and looked at the Scotsman. He continued to be puzzled about how this white scum could possibly be in with a Mexican Mafia warlord in Huntsville but decided it was something he would just never figure out. The Scotsman stood a minute letting the request soak in then got back into his piece of crap Toyota. He careened onto Thousand Oaks Drive, his back passenger tire jumping the curb as he cut the corner and the middle finger of his left hand lifted prominently through the open driver's side window.

"I hate that guy," Jimmy Dale said out loud to himself.

****

Rosalie was reluctant to make the trip to Huntsville. But the letter from Jesse Dethamuke was compelling. It had said that he had important information about Charlie's death. Rosalie didn't see how Jesse could know of her involvement, but figured it was worth the trip to make sure. And who knows, maybe Jesse would share something that might be of value to her. As she sat down in front of her ex-husband's former cellmate she was filled with calm. She was about to find out that this was the calm before the storm.

"Rosalie?" Jesse knew it was Rosalie sitting in front of him, but he lacked the social graces to open up a conversation with an attractive woman that he didn't know. He should have just assumed and said *hello*.

"Hello Jesse." She didn't want to be there and she didn't want to talk about Charlie so she was just friendly enough to come across as not being unfriendly.

"I appreciate you coming," Jesse said. He paused and looked at her for a moment. It was nice to have a female visitor and he nursed the moment.

"I was happy to come Jesse. I was glad to hear that you had some information on Charlie's death. It's hard enough as it is, but not knowing the circumstances is really hard. I know it was a brutal murder but nobody seems to know who or why. I just can't believe that it was a normal prison fight gone bad."

"I don't know if I can tell you why, but I do know the who part. I didn't tell the cops because it's Mexican Mafia and if I say anything it's pretty much a death sentence."

"Why would the Mexican Mafia go after Charlie?" Rosalie lied. She was glad that Jesse didn't appear to have any unpleasant information for her – anything that would indicate the trade that Rosalie and El Milagro had agreed to via the Scotsman. Now she just needed to complete the visit without raising any suspicions in Jesse that she was complicit in Charlie's murder.

"I don't know, but the guy that did him in was a little off," Jesse said.

"I'm not sure that you're going out on limb there when you say that he was *a little off*. Pretty much all of them are *a little off* aren't they?" Rosalie explained.

"You're dead-on there," Jesse said and leaned back in his chair. He laughed a little too loud as he responded to Rosalie's observation. It was a little awkward and Rosalie just looked at him.

"But what was weird about this Mexican dude," Jesse continued, "was that he was playing these word games with Charlie before he got him." Rosalie was still looking at him but now she had her arms crossed. She was ready to leave and her body language was beginning to betray her.

"He came up to Charlie in the yard a couple of days before they killed him and told Charlie that he knew about something called gohorse."

Panic swept through every molecule in Rosalie's body when she heard the word out loud. Her lips pursed and her eyes blinked. She bit the inside of her lip as a way to alleviate the psychological pressure. She could taste the fear in her mouth and was trying to not show it.

"So anyway I don't know what you can do with the information, but I thought it might help to know."

"Actually Jesse, it does help quite a bit." Rosalie allowed her emotion to show a little bit. She knew it would be interpreted as grief and provide cover for her to leave.

"I probably need to get going," Rosalie said as she rose from the bench.

"Ok. I hope I didn't upset you too much. I mean I just wanted to help you out."

"You have helped Jesse. I need to get going now." Rosalie said looking back over her shoulder as she rose and walked quickly to the exit.

CHAPTER 26

"Marcus I need to know how someone might hack into the gohorse account. I mean I know how you did it when you helped me out but that hasn't happened to me. I mean I think I would notice if a screen pops up and asks me to sign in again, ya' know? Is there another way to find someone's password?"

"There's tons of ways. The problem is that they get progressively more sophisticated and expensive."

"What I need to know is how every convict over at Huntsville knows about that damn email account. That's what I want to know."

"Let me take a look. You couldn't get me a beer could you?" Marcus was willing to help but he was going to get something out of it. Rosalie knew what he was doing and played along, like normal.

"Is your usual brand ok?" She touched his arm as a way to personalize the offer.

"If you have it," Marcus said.

"I try to keep one on hand for you Marcus."

"I hope you have more than one. This might take a while. I think we're looking at a six pack at least."

Rosalie pulled a Michelob from the fridge. Jimmy Dale looked at her with a questioning look. She knew what he was implying - *He's nice and I know that he's helping us but there's no need to act like that.*

"You don't have to hang on him." Jimmy Dale said to her when Marcus was out of ear shot.

"Jimmy Dale, we need his help here."

"My mind works better when it's doused with alcohol," Marcus yelled from the other room.

Jimmy Dale cringed. He didn't like Marcus or the way he looked at Rosalie. He stared at the TV for three hours while Marcus looked at the computer screen, tapped on the keyboard, and mumbled to himself. Rosalie sat beside her boyfriend and leaned on him. She was doing her best to mollify two male egos. Finally Marcus sat motionless at the screen for three or four minutes. Rosalie noticed it was a departure from his recent behavior pattern. He eventually appeared to reach some type of conclusion concerning the issue confronting him and spun on the office chair to face Jimmy Dale and Rosalie.   "Who do you know in Acuña Mexico?" he asked.

Jimmy Dale's opinion of Marcus changed on a dime. "I know someone in Acuña. Why would you ask that question? Why Acuña?" Jimmy Dale lifted his left arm from around Rosalie's shoulders and leaned forward toward Marcus.

"As near as I can tell, the account was set up sometime last spring. And all the logins took place from a San Antonio ISP. Then about three weeks ago someone started logging in with an ISP in Acuña." Marcus leaned back in the office chair and looked at Jimmy Dale. Then he looked at Rosalie. Then he looked at Jimmy Dale again. They appeared stunned. Finally Rosalie spoke.

"Marcus I think Jimmy Dale and me need to talk about this. This information comes as a bit of a shock to us."

Jimmy Dale swept the top of the coffee table clear with his right arm launching the objet d'art into the far wall, shattering it and barely missing the flat screen TV. Rosalie stood and squared off against Jimmy Dale leveraging her inferior body weight against his and pushing him back onto the couch. She knew he wouldn't resist her when she challenged him physically like this. She straddled him and grabbed his face with her hands. He averted his eyes to the left and then to the right. Each time he attempted to turn his head in that same direction and Rosalie would counter his efforts with her own trying to force him to look at her. Finally he acquiesced.

"Baby we need to think this thing through. We have a problem and we need to face it. Baby do you hear me?" Rosalie asked rhetorically. Finally Jimmy Dale made eye contact.

But the moment that Rosalie came to the realization that they'd had Charlie killed in error was a bad one. Rosalie had known for some time now that she had crossed a line and that her life was irrevocably changed for the worse. Before it was at more of a subconscious level - but not now - now it was there bloated and bleeding, a puss-filled, vomit-inducing, feeling of regret. She called out quietly to God to forgive her but it didn't feel like He was there. Her thoughts were locked in an endless loop, constantly running through her misdeeds and how she had exposed herself and Zack to this lifestyle.

****

Billy's arrival at Huntsville preceeded Cupcake's by about two months. Both were assigned to cells in C wing, the wing used for non-violent offenders. Which was appropriate; both men were distinctly non-violent. Cupcake was paraded down the main corridor to his cell with four other newly incarcerated men. The other men in the group were acting in a way that was typical of a man's first day in prison. Dour…dour and scared but trying valiantly to hide it. Inexplicably, Cupcake was glowing; it was almost like he was fulfilling his destiny. Billy's cell was two-thirds of the way down.

"Hey Cupcake," Billy said in a normal voice. Cupcake looked Billy's way, surprised to hear his own nickname. He had hoped to perhaps shed the label upon his arrival at Huntsville. He wasn't confident that the Cupcake moniker portrayed the right image. He was concerned that it might perhaps give the wrong impression. But sure enough, he'd only been a full-fledged inmate for 45 minutes and already every convict in C wing thought of him as Cupcake.

"Oh hey Billy," Cupcake answered raising his right hand just slightly at the wrist and extending his index and middle fingers toward his friend peering at him through the bars. Billy was immediately warmed by the private joke. It had been a long time since the thought of it had entered his mind at all. His existence at the Huntsville Correctional Facility was bleak and any glimpse of his former life was like manna from heaven.

"Didn't think I would bump into you today Cupcake. You got everything you need there?" Billy's smile was broad and bright.

"I didn't get my 30 weight ball bearings or my gauze pads. What kind of operation are ya'll running down here?"

"What do you need ball bearings for?" Billy asked with a grin.

"Everything's ball bearings these days," Cupcake answered, playing his part to a tee.

****

One month after his cattle buying trip to Old Mexico, Heironymus Donsbach was waiting on his friend and business partner Bruno Bartoskewitz. They had agreed earlier in the week to meet at the Guadalupe County Courthouse and finalize some documents on the cattle sale. The Oak Tavern was about a block from the Courthouse and the two men stopped in for a beer after conducting their business. The establishment happened to the have a copy of the Seguiner Zeitung and something drew Heironymus' eye to the picture on the front page. The photograph accompanied an article on the Mexican Revolution that had been taken on by the paper from the Associated Press. Heironymus looked at the photo first with curiosity and then with some recognition. After three or four seconds his mind was actively engaged in grasping for the nature of the familiarity. A few seconds more, with synapses in rapid fire, that afternoon in the cantina in Acuña came flooding back to him.

"Bruno, do you remember the two Mexicans in the bar that day in Mexico?"

"There were a lot of Mexicans in the bar that day in Mexico." Bruno replied. He knew what he'd said was obvious..

"Do you remember the two men in the corner? One had the big hat," Heironymus said while holding up the newspaper with a picture of Pancho Villa and Emiliano Zapata and their men in the Mexican Presidential Palace.

"I remember them," Bruno answered. "I remember they hated goldfish."

AUTHOR'S COMMENTS

My great-great grandfather's name was Heironymus Donsbach. I decided that a name like that had to be in a novel so I wrote one. I've always been fascinated by the ways that different cultures come together. The German culture and the Mexican culture of South Central Texas is my experience so I used it as a backdrop.

I know what it's like to struggle what it's like to succeed. I know what it's like to win and what it's like to lose...sometimes unfairly. But in the end we make our own bed. Thanks for reading the book.

Bryan Baese
San Marcos, Texas
March 2015